CW01501837

THE
LADIE
UPSTAIRS

THE
LADIE
UPSTAIRS

Jessie Elland

BASKERVILLE
An imprint of JOHN MURRAY

First published in Great Britain in 2025 by Baskerville
An imprint of John Murray (Publishers)

1

A CIP catalogue record for this title is available from the British Library

Hardback ISBN 9781399817769
Trade Paperback ISBN 9781399817776
ebook ISBN 9781399817790

Typeset in Adobe Garamond by Hewer Text UK Ltd, Edinburgh
Printed and bound by CPI Group (UK) Ltd, Croydon, CR0 4YY

John Murray policy is to use papers that are natural, renewable and
recyclable products and made from wood grown in sustainable forests.
The logging and manufacturing processes are expected to conform
to the environmental regulations of the country of origin.

Carmelite House
50 Victoria Embankment
London EC4Y 0DZ

www.johnmurraypress.co.uk

John Murray Press, part of Hodder & Stoughton Limited
An Hachette UK company

The authorised representative in the EEA is Hachette Ireland, 8 Castlecourt
Centre, Dublin 15, D15 XTP3, Ireland (email: info@hbgi.ie)

For Mum, who has always been my first reader.

We, Hermia, like two artificial gods,
Have with our needles created both one flower,
Both on one sampler, sitting on one cushion,
Both warbling of one song, both in one key;
As if our hands, our sides, voices, and minds,
Had been incorporate.
So we grew together,
Like to a double cherry, seeming parted;
But yet a union in partition,
Two lovely berries moulded on one stem:
So, with two seeming bodies, but one heart.

William Shakespeare, *A Midsummer Night's Dream*, III.2

Autumn

1

THE SKY WAS marmalade, and the many eyes of Ropner Hall splintered and reflected it back on itself in all its blazing glory. Ropner's grounds yawned and the river stretched around them like a noose. It was a squat beast. Stony and stern, immobile but immortal, important because it is the only constant. And the story begins here, with the sugared sky, in the depths of Ropner where Petra decided to let herself be fucked by the footman.

Ann always felt, always knew, that fucking was for pigs. It was dirty and involved too much skin and was coloured a screaming pink or an evil dripping brown. 'It feels good and it dun't hurt anyone,' Petra had said. 'Except for if he tried to ram it up where he shouldn't. But if you tell *her*, I'll come for you in the night. I'll cover your head with your blanket and stick pins where I know your eyes are and curse you to be a mute like Rachel.'

Petra was going to burn in hell.

That stupid bitch's skin would fissure into leather slices of pork crackling and even the tiny hairs on her arms would twist into burning orange worms. Petra would roast until there was nothing left but chalky ash that would draw itself back into her shape and burn all over again for all eternity. (God willing.)

Ann and Petra shared a room. It was cramped even by the standards of the servants, their thin beds abreast and almost touching. The peeling ceiling sloped sharply to kiss the headboards, and at night when the stub of their candle was snuffed and Mrs Hardy, the housekeeper, had locked them in, the room was pitch black.

Ann didn't know where Petra got it, or even when; none of the servants ever left the grounds. Still, she knew Petra had a second key made or stolen because that was how the footman got in.

The footman was Scarecrowfootman; tall and thin with yellow hair thatched over his head like straw. He had a crooked look, with gaps in his teeth that he whistled at the women through, and a slouch about him as well, as if he had been pecked in the field for too long and the frost had got to him and all his straw was spilling out. He was odious and lecherous and foul. All his badness had taken to his skin like a hatchet and disfigured his face with pockmarks. Ann hoped, very sourly, that it hurt him. That his skin itched so furiously that he would one day be overcome with the urge to scratch and scratch and scratch until he bled to death. That unpleasant beast tramped along the servants' garrets every night. The vile creature would steal out his secret second key and twist open the heavy door Mrs Hardy had only just locked to leak into Ann and Petra's room like gas and soil it all over with sin.

The first time it wasn't so much the sounds that woke Ann, but the air; clotted with clouds of condensation that pressed on her. The air that turned the room sticky with sweat and wet, heavy breaths. The tangled sheets on Petra's bed twisted around flesh that writhed in the shadows. Their words, sordid and sinful, were no louder than the brush of the sheets, but they seemed to drip and hiss and sizzle before settling like silt on her skin. Ann lay awake through it all. She held herself completely still so she could feel all the darkness around her and say to herself, *This is death. Here I am dead, I have died and I am dead and when they are finished, or in the morning when Mrs Hardy unlocks the door, they will find me perfectly cold and stiff and then they'll be sorry. They'll kneel by my corpse all clean and noble in death, and cry into pressed lace hankies, sobbing and clutching one another and lamenting about how careless they had been, how, oh, if only it was them instead. And then they will put me gently into a pristine white tomb that I can look down upon from heaven with all the other nice clean angels who all have clean fingernails and pearly teeth that you can count.*

That was a fancy, of course. She knew, in actuality, should she die, they would likely less than blink at her, before putting her corpse in a horrid hole in the woods where maggots and beetles would nibble away until the river water poured out from her dead eyes and mouth. That's the kind of dirty wicked people they all were. Why couldn't they fuck somewhere away from her, in amongst the scraping bark of the woods or the dank rat holes in the servants' stairway? Or just not at all. Because now every morning she had to scrub off their sin from her skin. With that lump of lard soap and the brush with bristles so unyielding they may as well have been iron nails.

Start with the shoulder because that's near the heart, where sin cobwebs most easily, and scrub with passion. Hate was bad unless justified, so her hate for Petra was allowed. Petra who slacked at her work, Petra who spoke ill of the house, Petra who made eyes at the men and accepted their returning looks and remarks with all the openness of a devout worshipper, Petra who was growing fat with sin, Petra who had eyes too close together, which perhaps was the most offensive thing of all.

Don't forget to catch the flakes of sin clinging to elbows, and bring the suds right under knuckles and nails. Their hands had been used for instruments of sin last night; it wouldn't do to have hers getting ideas – though Ann assured herself they never would. What want would she have to dig them into a man's flesh? She could not understand it. Those horrid men who trampled through the kitchen, shoving their dirty limbs through the air, pausing to scratch at stained trouser seats, shovelling food in so deliriously that globs of porridge dropped from their spoons and slapped the flagstone floor she would later have to scrub. (Bastards.) And yet she saw some of the women, not just Petra, eye them with that greedy look, like they were hungry for it.

Lift up the skirts and scrub at all those burning folds of flesh too. 'I'm doing us all a favour, Ann. If we didn't placate them they'd be driven mad with lust and kill us all, y'know.' She knew Petra was lying when she had said that. They all were, they had lost sight of what really mattered, what they were here for; for Ropner, and for the two ladies who lived upstairs.

Ann had never served the ladies directly, she had never seen them in the flesh, but she knew exactly how beautiful, how clean and good and proper they were, oh yes, she did. Because there was a painting, you see, on the second floor, a floor neither she nor any of the other lower servants were permitted to step foot on. A painting that could be seen from the servants' stairwell when the door flashed open and shut to admit Petra or Mrs Hardy, or if, on occasions when Ann was feeling particularly bold, the door was eked ever so slightly open, and a desirous eye was pressed to the shivering slither of space.

The big painting, as she had named it, was magnificent in size; it straddled the entirety of the corridor wall visible through the crack. It was dark, and its paint was layered on so thick and glutinous that from Ann's viewing point its contents were hard to make out at all. But when Ann stood at an angle just right, when the light from outside filtered through the corridor *just so*, Ann could see the triangular tableaux of the big painting's subjects.

The first woman was dead centre, seated in a dark red armchair, hands cupped delicately, oh so ladylike, in her lap. Her jewel-studded head was bowed slightly in what would have been a show of meek submission if her eyes were not staring up and out of the painting; at once numb and steeped with a furiously intense emotion that Ann could not quite place.

She was Lady Charlotte, the young lady of Ropner, niece to the Duchess, and she was the most beautiful thing Ann had ever seen. Elegant and regal too; painted into a lilac get-up so pale it could almost be white. A jacket tightly buttoned from that little hollow pool of her collarbone down to her navel, where it parted itself into wide pleats to accommodate the full skirts beneath. Only royalty, only someone godly, could wear something so beautiful and still manage to outshine it.

The second figure stood to the left of the first, slightly older, slightly larger, wholly more opulent (but still tastefully so); the jewels in her hair were not dainty little gems, but shaped as butterflies and flowers, her pink skirts were held in ostentatious positions by various bows and drooling lengths of lace. The Duchess was bent towards the first lady so that her face was partly concealed from view; showing only the round globe of her cheek and small tilt of her smile. Her eyes were closed as she bestowed a gentle kiss on her counterpart's forehead, or perhaps, Ann thought on some viewings, she was whispering something in her ear. It was hard to tell through so lean a crack, but she never dared open the door any further.

Perhaps, if she had, she would have found it easier to notice the third woman. Granted, the final figure could easily be missed. She may be standing slightly apart, observing rather than participating, her black dress may be painted so loosely it, and she, seemed to blend in perfectly with the wallpaper behind her; she may have her head tilted in such a way that her face was half obscured by shadows; but oh, she was there all right.

Behind her, in the artistically hazy background, hung another painting. The painting within the painting was an impression of a building. Even at a distance, even with its artistically vague brushstrokes, it was clear to see that the building was unmistakably Ropner itself.

She knew because of the glamour of the big painting, because of the regal nature of its women, that the two ladies of Ropner were surely good and clean and proper and wonderful, and she knew in her heart of hearts that she was theirs, and they were hers to dutifully serve and wait on, and how lucky she was to be in service to such people.

And there: with the thought of the ladies of Ropner, with the thought of their lives of order and cleanliness and purity, Ann was free from the sin of the night and could dress once more in her starched-to-stiffness apron.

2

EVERY MORNING BREAKFAST stared up at Ann from a brown bowl. The food was dark and evil; grey like dirty snow, like a wet stone. She imagined lifting it and seeing all the horrible things that squirmed underneath. If it wasn't this insipid gruel it was hunks of stale bread and cheese that were always the wrong shape so she could not possibly eat them. They looked at her obstinately and laughed with one another, shifting about the plate. She tried to concentrate on them very closely so that they would not sneak up into her mouth when she wasn't looking, so that she wouldn't be forced to chew and swallow them.

But it was hard: in the mornings the kitchen moved like it was a tin box being shaken. Endless hordes of servants came from all angles, moving fast and illogically. They streaked and smeared around her in a cacophony of ragged yells, battling time for their chores and each other for loose scraps of food, or for sly stares up skirts. They were likely all in on a plot against her. The brutes. They likely all put their lice-ridden heads together to see how they could best make her squirm and push her closer in proximity to sin. The barbarians.

Ann eyed them with disgust: the women and their wet mouths, the men with their sharp eyes that tried to snag her own. She didn't bother with learning their names. Knowing their names would mean getting too close to them, close enough for them to infect her with their slovenliness, their badness.

She knew Petra's name only because they shared a room. That information had infiltrated her brain unwarranted. And she knew Rachel's name only because it was impossible not to notice Rachel, not to know her. She was so . . . different.

The cook was opposite her, sat like a scar; with her too-long body hunched over her bowl. Her face was covered in boils and blisters. The old crone sat to Cook's right, positioned too closely, so that her shoulder kept knocking against her neighbour's, causing Cook to mutter darkly. Old Crone paid no heed, she was wholly focused on dripping porridge into her mouth by holding the spoon a few inches above her head and tilting it so that fat globules landed on her tongue. Her success rate was slim; grey sludge oozed down her ample breast and splattered the table, but she couldn't chew from her spoon like the others on account of the complete absence of even a single blackened tooth. Still, dental ailments did not deter her from talking. Her gummy mouth gnashed out loud streams of gossip, grating details of her every bowel movement, superstitious drivel, and the like.

'I can feels them,' she said. 'The spirits. Those naughty beggars are hungry, youse mark my words something is coming soon.'

Petra jeered at her from the corner. 'How would you even know they were hungry? They told you, did they?'

Petra liked sitting apart from them. Ann supposed it was to remind them that she acted as lady's maid when occasion called for it. (As if she were worthy of it. As if that would disguise all her wickedness.) The kitchen maid sat with her giggled. The maid was thin and very pale but when Ann glanced at her she blushed furiously. She looked like a matchstick.

'Theys don't need to tell me.' Old Crone missed her mouth again so a lump fell into her black woolly hair. 'I hears them. I hears their tummies rumbling.'

Petra and Matchstick laughed. 'What a load of rubbish. There's no such thing as spirits.'

'Of course there is,' Old Crone persisted. 'I should know, I've worked here a thousand hundred more hours than anyone else.'

At this, Cook snorted and picked at one of the pustules on her neck. 'Well, that's a crock of shite.' Her voice was flat and rumbled with a caustic accent. 'A thousand hundred hours, my arse. I've never known anyone slack so much at their work. My bunions could do a better job of washing the coppers than you.'

Old Crone sighed and shook her lumpy head. 'It's a terrible thing to be this old and be so surrounded by the insolence of bairns.'

Cook stood up sharply, so her chair scraped in the most unappealing way. 'You should watch your black tongue.' Ann rested her chin on her hands so she could block her ears without anyone noticing. 'You should watch your black tongue for the way you speak of spirits *and* the way you speak of work. I have seen how you drop the stitches, and miss spots, and spit on the silver instead of polishing it.'

It went like this most mornings, the characters inter-changeable but the outcome largely the same. After barbed words and curses, spittle and fists would fly; hair was pulled and groins were kicked until one conceded or was forced out of consciousness. The utter chaos was abhorrent to Ann. So she would sit as small and tight as she could on her chair, with her elbows tucked in, neat and parallel, and she would arrange her untouched food into tidy separate shapes; porridge moulded into a perfect square, or breadcrumbs nudged into oval islands, soothing herself with the idea that order still existed.

Sure enough, Old Crone clambered to her feet to match the stance of her partner. 'And I have seen *you* stick your dirty horrid fingers into pies meant for the Duchess and suck them cleaner than you would a cock.'

The two small chunks of cheese were now stacked in a neat tower and Ann carefully picked off the fluff of mould with her fingernail.

'Even the most lecherous spirit wouldn't come near you, the most vile of all vile things in this house.'

Ann set the mould on the edge of her plate, but precisely, so it formed the point of a perfectly equal triangle with the cheese as its base.

'Ah yes, I forget you are such a lady, you like someone to lick your arsehole clean after you shit, don't you?' In a cumbersome union, they began to grapple and were soon rolling on the floor, Cook using her bowl to beat at Old Crone's temple, or at least until her counterpart seized her wrist between those slimy gums and refused to let go.

Some of the men skulked from their corners to watch and leer. Ann did not look at them. She never did. Though there were decidedly fewer male servants than female at Ropner, Ann felt them everywhere; crawling up the walls, teeming

13

from nooks and crannies, like cockroaches, one always appearing in the place of its stamped-out brother. She never looked at them, so all their leering faces blended into one, impossible to distinguish from the other. Apart from, of course, Scarecrowfootman, who had forced himself to be the exception. (All Petra's fault, with her lustful sinning, with her wicked determination to drag you down to her shame and sin.)

Petra shouted encouragement as the two women fought and Matchstick giggled.

I should like to tug very hard at my ear, Ann thought, *so it becomes loose, and at once all my body will unravel into nothingness so that little slice of soul left could catch on the wind and twist away from here.*

Somewhere below the table, Cook shrieked.

They were all so unclean, all of them. Their skin blemished and flaky. What little teeth they had between them harboured dark flecks of food, and they were so lewd and sinful. She took great pleasure in imagining how she would cure them all. First, she would take the butter knife, and wipe off the thick streaks of lard and granules of burnt crumbs. (The fact that their blackness was mixed in with the butter made her want to scream, or at least pull her fingernails off.) Then, with her clean knife, she would slowly peel the skin from the scalp of her nearest peer until a sizable plot of ceramic was revealed. Wipe the knife, gooey with fat and blood, clean, and use it as a chisel to make fissures in the skull until it came off like the shell cap of a hard-boiled egg. Then she'd reach both hands in and scoop out the fleshy brain (a rancid, rotting thing) that was dirty from all its owner's badness, and scrub it until it was entirely clean, and its iridescent outer tissue shimmered. Then she'd put them all back together, and when they woke up they would be good and proper.

She would start with Petra of course. Ann watched her, edging along the fray of the fight while she thought no one was looking. But Ann was looking. Ann saw. Ann knew. Knew she was sneaking out to find *him*.

Ann slipped out of the kitchen after her; quick and silent and nimble, while the rest of them foamed and boiled and racketed clumsily over one another.

3

OUTSIDE THE KITCHEN, at the other end of the corridor, the door to the servants' stairwell clicked shut softly.

So Ann was right. Petra was stealing away to meet the man upstairs in their room. She was so uncivilised and lustful that she no longer even waited for the guise of night to unsheathe her flesh and— (And nothing! Because you will stop it, won't you, Ann?)

Ann strode towards the door like some kind of righteous hunter that had picked up a scent. She would stop her. She would stop all the wrongdoings and bad goings-on, quash out all of this sin and badness once and for all.

The servants' staircase was at the margin of the house, and it rose up like a throat all the way to the garrets. A dank column of winding iron and stone, with each step like a great slab of sunken cake; their middles eroded from the scuffing of shoes and weight of bodies carrying laden luncheon trays. Its walls were studded (not frequently enough as the light was always dim) with cubbyholes for candles, many of which had been replaced so carelessly that their meltings overflowed and built up to resemble a mountain range of hardened wax. It was rank and dripping and disgusting. And it had that *smell*, that faint odour of stale piss and rusting iron that all the servants seemed to emanate.

Petra had not made it far. Ann had anticipated racing up the stairs after her, seizing her with such pure conviction that Petra had no choice but to stop dead in her tracks, collapse at Ann's feet and renounce all her misdeeds. But here Petra was, only two steps up, standing completely still and facing the door Ann came through, almost as though she were waiting for her.

Her dry hands were clutching the metal handle of a pail, being bitten red by it. Ann noticed the hot water sloshing around inside, puffing out steady threads of steam. Water for Lady Charlotte's bath perhaps? A sudden image shivered in her mind; the nakedness of the lady from the big painting, curling and curving in between the clouds of steam. What human body bits were the vapours hiding? What dimpled elbows or stretching thighs or slopes of breasts? Would the water ripple as the stretches and rolls of skin melted into it?

Ann swallowed the strange thrill. It needled all the way down her throat and settled far down in her belly. A fucked-up little twist; like a knot of hair.

It was more likely a ruse, this pail carrying, this pretend-ing she was dutiful and loyal. A guise in case someone tried to catch her, like Ann was about to now.

'What do you want, Ann?' There was irritation in Petra's voice, an *I-don't-have-time-for-this* sigh that reduced Ann to an annoying, irrelevant ugly insect, buzzing so weakly that even Petra found it too beneath her to squash.

Ann shifted in indignation. The water sloshed some more in the pail and she caught sight of her reflection wobbling on its shadowed surface.

An ugly little bug indeed. Big eyes protruding out of a gaunt face; sunken and tired and weathered and melancholy and appalling. Unremarkable and unlovely features, slipping, warped and disfigured by ripples and slops. The cleanliness of her face was a small consolation, but why wasn't it that all her goodness and purity was shining out of her? Why wasn't it giving her a countenance that was bonny and *perfect*? Instead she was as ugly and as foul to look at as the rest of them.

Tears stung fast and hard at her eyes. Could she peel off her skin and start again please? Could she peel off her face and find another underneath; one that hadn't been ravaged by exposure to their badness? Because that's what was making her look like this (all *their* fault); she would be beautiful if it wasn't for *them*.

Petra took a step down, closer, and Ann lost sight of the warping waves of her reflection.

'What's wrong, ickle Ann?' Petra whispered. She made her voice high and sobby, pushing out her lower lip in mockery. 'Cat got your tongue?'

Grisly images of witches juddered in Ann's mind; repulsive grins and black swathes of unspeakable magic, vicious cats, and slimy, fat, purple tongues all red and pulpy when ravaged by sharp teeth.

Petra stepped closer again.

'You need to stop.' Ann tried to emphasise each word firmly; show how seriously she meant it. But her voice cracked under the weight.

'Stop what, Ann? Hm?' The bitch laughed. Yes, she laughed, actually *laughed*, right at her. 'You can't even say it, can you?'

Though her lip trembled, Ann raised her chin proudly. She would not be tricked into speaking of such badness, as if she were a co-conspirator in Petra's crimes.

A flash of something like anger crossed Petra's oafish face and she put down the pail. The water oscillated between their two reflections. Splintering them, stirring them so they melted and melded together in a sickening unity. (Not true, not true, if you peeled off your face you would not find Petra's underneath, the water lies.)

Petra stepped closer still. The reek of her breath was thick on Ann's face.

'Why are you like this, Ann?' The mocking baby voice had vanished, and in its place was a cold, expressionless whisper that sounded so unlike Petra.

Ann's breath stuttered. Petra's question had frozen her; its calm utterance, its absurd simplicity, the fact it was entirely unanswerable. She couldn't find a single word, even a single thought that sufficed as a reply; her mouth and her mind were still clogged with liquid reflections and witches' drool and fat tongues and bad, terrible, lustful sins, and her own ugliness that was so tied to them.

Petra took another step; they were almost nose to nose now.

'Poor, poor Ann, who thinks she's so much better than us all. How little you know.'

Was there pity there? Somewhere in the bottom of that cold voice that was so unlike Petra. So unlike her. More like a puppet finally cut free from its marionette strings, free to slump and croak its own wooden mind. Pity or not, the flash of anger came once more across Petra's face, so suddenly that Ann stumbled back, only to find herself pressing against the door she had come through.

Petra's arms lashed out, her fat, awful, chapped and chipped hands seized Ann's shoulders. They squeezed tight, right down to her bones. Ann tried to shrink away more still, tried scrabbling across the wood to find the handle, but Petra was pinning her with such force that her arms could do nothing but flop helplessly to her sides. Petra was pinning her with such force that her bones were creaking and breaking, that everything around her was tilting, threatening to spin. Petra's horrible face filled her vision (so close, too close), the world was nothing but her screaming pores (all full of dirt, all full of rot), nothing but cracked lips, nothing but spikes of nostril hair, nothing but the wide, mad white of her eyes, yellowish and threaded with red. Petra's sour breath was in Ann's mouth, actually in her mouth, she tried to gag, to retch and repel it from her, but her own breath was coming in such great heaves (don't breathe, don't breathe it in) she couldn't. She was gasping for air like she was drowning.

Petra was still cold and unmoved, almost stoical with purpose and coming closer and closer, her face as near as Ann's to a kiss. This was it; here and now Petra would dispel all her sin to Ann, fill her with that sordid dark and deep red; it would rip all of those hollow aching places even wider. It was all too much. Ann could feel her mind, battered by her drowning breaths, slipping away down some gullet of horror.

'You don't even know how bad it's going to get, Ann,' she said. 'And what will you do when all this badness possesses you?'

The wail came about as though it were torn out of Ann. It parted the air into currents, churned the hot water in the pail and rattled the twisting metal of the banister.

Petra stepped back as though Ann's body had suddenly surged with red-hot heat, and Ann crumpled to the cold stone floor, the wail now subsided but her mouth still torn by its shape. She was numbed with horror.

It was an eternity, surely, that she was slumped there for. Her breath rattling with snot and spit, her skin and mind humming *sin, sin, sin*.

Some faraway part of her brain, though, a tiny animalistic part that remained un-numbed, pieced together the sounds around her like a puzzle. That was the scrape of the pail being picked up; that was the meaty smack of a boot connecting with flesh (your flesh, Ann; a kick, right at your middle, another right on your thigh); there were the fading clacks of Petra's footsteps going up and up and up; that was the slam of the door; this now is the sound of silence (and of *ow ow ow*).

Ann would have let the silence last forever, never moved again, expired into its eternity there and then, if there was not the pressing matter of her virtue.

Clean, the rest of her mind un-numbed itself to say. *Cleaned*, it said from under the soundless sobs and blooming pain. *You need to be cleaned.*

She dragged herself to her room, crawling all the way like some loathsome toad. Ann imagined a slime of sin oozing out of her, being trailed behind her. She had to be clean before the housekeeper discovered it.

Why are you like this, Ann? Petra had said.

She had to be like this, she couldn't be like them, she wouldn't. Not with their sinning and fucking and dirt; she didn't want any of it, she had to be like this, she had to be good and clean. She. Had. To. Be. Clean.

In their room (mercifully empty – perhaps you put a stop to her sin after all) the chest-of-drawers had never looked more like an altar, holding on its surface her most sacred instruments. Cloth, bowl, white porcelain jug filled to the brim with water. Ann had broken pieces of carbolic soap tucked in her pocket bags at all times, just for moments like this. She seized one now and scrubbed until her skin reddened and smarted. Her hands, her face (every centimetre that the bitch might have breathed on), even the thick fabric of her sleeves, rinsing them with water from the white porcelain jug.

What will you do when all this badness possesses you?

Her nerves jittered, her head kept jerking to look at the door. She was sure she could hear little, tiny, impossibly quiet giggles, as if their eyes were pressed to the cracks around the door, watching her panic, her frantic scouring, trying to stifle their snickers.

A wave of cramps sloshed in the bottom part of her belly. She tensed and thought of the vinegar smell of blood. She was probably due to bleed again. The chaos of not knowing was as disgusting to her as the sin she was sluicing off, as revolting as her dirty cycle itself. But it was hard to keep track. At Ropner Hall days are not contained, orderly things. No. They seep into one another so that tomorrow is today and today is yesterday and yesterday and tomorrow are each other and for all Ann knew Scarecrowfootman had been coming for weeks, or months, or years, or maybe just days. But somewhere in that tangle of time Petra, quite suddenly, was gone.

4

O N THE MORNING of Petra's dismissal Ann woke to find her parting gift: a putrid smell that she eventually pinpointed to the chamber pot beneath the bed. The china lip curled at the bile in its belly. Ann imagined the stink polluting the walls like smoke, seeping into her bed-sheets and aprons, dirtying them with a perfume that would make her smell no better than the rest of them. Petra's parting spite.

Well, she couldn't get to Ann now, not now she had gone . . . wherever she had gone. Ann wasn't sure if there was anything beyond the grounds of Ropner. Its isolation was almost tangible. It seeped from its walls slowly, like sap, engulfing them all in its amber. Perhaps upon her dismissal Petra had stepped a foot outside the grounds and her and her fat belly of sin had vanished entirely. Disintegrated into nothing. Disappeared as if she had never been. (Serves her right, the whore.) Ann was chief of their room now. There would be no fucking, no sin. It would be a space entirely clean, entirely pure, just like the rooms the ladies of Ropner lived in.

She emptied the chamber pot onto a gum of earth that teethed on the grass from the woods, and looked out across the grounds. The autumn colours of Ropner flushed dark

23

and thick, deep and ugly. But there was a beauty to it too; a stark rawness that was so striking she wanted to bite into it, to taste the mud and earth, to chew on the purples and rusted oranges, waterlogged greys and scrubbed-pale ochres, to let them all fester warm and heavy right in her stomach.

Everything in this autumn seemed heavy; the weight of change, the grasses thick with dew, the hills rapidly growing dense with darkness, the layers of clothes, the mounds of leaves pressing and crushing impossibly rich soil. And the feeling. Not quite like fear, but close; a foreboding of winter. Soon would come the dresses and curtains and coverings to be washed and freshened and darned; the navies and green velvets that were so dark they were almost black.

Ropner itself remained unmoved by the sodden landscape. The Hall seemed to blend into it and at once be something entirely separate. A bone that had pierced up through the grassy skin so long ago that the body of the grounds had evolved to live with it like that, protruding in a way that was wholly unnatural, but still part of it. Ropner rose up stoically, bristling against the soft grey sky. Its front face was the grandest, without a doubt; two wings, shoulders thrown back proudly, flanked an edifice outlined with four pillars. A wooden door lurked between the central two columns, like a dark throat guarded by stony canines. Beneath the entrance door a staircase splayed, splitting into two pincers that curved inwards down to the gravel driveway.

Ropner Hall was cold and distant and unloving. Yet it filled Ann with the unnerving desire to impress, to respect and worship it. Because, without a doubt, it *watched*. Milky glass eyes in their multitudes stared out from the house, some made squinting by their lattices and frames, some creased by fissures of crumbling crow's feet. And she got the feeling sometimes that it wasn't just the windows that were watching her. Sometimes, if she looked at Ropner out of the corner of her eye, she saw faint brushes of motion at the windows; figures moving just out of frame, as if someone, something, had been standing up against the pane, watching her.

She had no recollection of ever arriving at Ropner, of ever living a life before it. It was as if she had been born here, into this exact moment of emptying Petra's morning sickness onto the sodden mud, all the intimate knowledge of the house as instrumental and intuitive as the act of breathing.

Of course, there were vast chasms in her knowledge: Ropner had two floors, four if you counted the crawl space of the servants' garrets and the kitchens in its bowels, and yet Ann had never set foot in the two floors sandwiched between. The first floor was only cleaned by the older servants, those who could be trusted to keep their mouths shut. The second floor, the floor that housed the bedrooms and the painting Ann spied on when she could, was tended to only by Rachel now that Petra had gone. Rachel could be easily relied on to keep the secrets of the second floor, whatever they were. She was a freak, a mute, either by choice or design. Ann saw her infrequently, oafing between doorways, silent and stupid. It was hard to fight the child-like urge to gawp at her. Once, Ann had seen her by the wonky lines of the kitchen garden, kneeling over the ground, her soft body slumped and folded like a pillow that needed plumping. Laying broken on the mud, half concealed by Rachel's doughy hands, was the tiny, feathered body of a spug.

It was odd, seeing Rachel's dopy body in proximity to something so delicate. Even odder still to realise that Rachel was crying over the little bird, silently of course, which made it sadder somehow. Those tears making their way unannounced to plop steadily on its speckled breast. Watching, Ann had felt like a little part of her heart had been pricked by a pin and was steadily bleeding. But she couldn't stop her lip curling right beneath her nose. Ann found herself feeling some level of revulsion towards everything Rachel did; the way she sighed at a lamb heart blubbering there on the counter before she butchered it; the way she waited by the door of the washroom for Ann to hand her the basket of clean clothes, her head bowed and eyes averted, as if Ann were doing something intensely private and Rachel wanted to respect it; the way her big, cow-like eyes accepted any insult hurled toward her without so much as blinking.

She was pathetic, and it made Ann feel grossly aware of her own body, of her bones moving through space, aware of the air on her skin and a faint ringing in her ears. Aware of being human; breakable, vulnerable, something that could be eaten alive.

Despite the hours Rachel sacrificed in the upper rooms, only Mrs Hardy tended to the ladies of Ropner directly. They were secreted away, those ladies upstairs. The Duchess and her niece were folded into the many corners and rooms from which lower servants were forbidden. In that liminal space everything was surely sun-soaked and clean and good, beating like a joyous heart, while Ann and the servants crawled through the garrets above and squirmed in the kitchens below, pumping the organs that sighed and shit and bubbled acid.

The Duchess had supposedly had the happy misfortune of some brother or father or distant leaf of the Ropner family tree rolling over and dying and bestowing Ropner upon her. The niece had come with the house. Rumours and fables and vicious twisted little fairytales grow best in the dark; they're nourished with ignorance and a grotesque case of belief triumphing fact, and the mystery that enshrouded the ladies of Ropner was the blackest kind of dark: optimal conditions for tales to sprout like mould; to fix themselves to crumbs of fact before blooming and crackling to monstrous proportions.

The Duchess sent for a veritable banquet for her daily luncheon. So, then: those million delicate canapés, those hundreds of glazed fruits, those thousands of gloating cakes, had not so much delicately expanded her waistline as swelled her to such epic proportions that Mrs Hardy had to roll her from room to room, feed her and wash her and wipe her arse because her own arms were too confined in fleshy prisons to reach. The Duchess was never reported leaving the house. So, then: she had been cursed by a black-toothed witch as a girl to forever remain in Ropner, for one step of a fat foot outside would bestow a most painful and odious death upon her in which all the noble blood in her veins would harden to stone and she would be doomed to be weathered as a statue for all eternity. The Duchess dressed in swathes of pink silk and spun gold and sat in rooms groaning with priceless ornamentations and all kinds of trinkets and treasures from distant lands. So, then: she had sold her soul to the devil for such riches, and she secretly crunched on the bones of virgins and drank the blood of bairns to be forever youthful and prosperous. All lies of course. The rumours spun out of control so viciously it was impossible to discern fact, or even those that had sprouted from such.

Ann thought of her secret viewings of that painting in the corridor and of the way the Duchess's likeness leaned elegantly to kiss her niece. The Duchess who exuded so much decorum and sweet grace that it was forever immortalised in a painting. *That* was who the Duchess was, no matter what they said.

Her niece, Lady Charlotte, was less of a conglomerate monster of myths and superstitious rumours and more a complete enigma. Even the most spiteful of servants struggled to fabricate any fable for her. If they did, they would be wrong, just like they were about the Duchess. Lady Charlotte would be as pure as an angel.

It was a travesty therefore, an ugly smear on order, that it was Petra who had acted as her lady's maid, Petra who tended her rooms and dressed her and did her hair. Mrs Hardy naturally forbade any gossip about the women above, but one night, when the footman had not slunk in and Ann was feeling particularly brave, she had pressed Petra for details. Her skin had tingled all over with excitement as she lay there in the darkness, waiting for Petra's disembodied voice to perhaps change her life forever.

'I think she is very simple or very lonely, or perhaps both,' Petra began. Ann had held her breath. (How divinely tragic!) 'Because she's a terrible stuck-up bitch who doesn't care for anything unless it's the nose on her face.'

God, Ann hated Petra. She would be glad every single day that she was gone.

Whatever she said, Ann did not let it impeach her fantasy of the ladies upstairs. She dreamed one day they would be seized by some divine omnipotence and discover what a good clean girl Ann was down below, and how it was all Ann's good clean work that meant they could live as good clean gods in that heavenly space. So they would summon Ann to them and Ann would curtsy, and the Duchess and the lady would watch her do so with divinely delicate tears lingering on their cheeks like diamonds. (Because Ann would have such a beautifully tidy curtsy.) They would say, 'Ann, you have made our lives so perfect, we could never live without you, thankyouthankyouthankyou.' And here the lady would extend an impossibly elegant hand, a hand practically glowing, its skin was so soft, and Ann would be permitted to kiss it, and as soon as her lips touched that holy skin she would close her eyes and die happy.

Such things would be possible if she wasn't constantly breathing in sin and halitosis. If she wasn't emptying Petra's curdled vomit onto the soil.

He was by the big clock in the corridor when she returned to the house. *He* had not been dismissed, of course.

Scarecrowfootman was jangling cogs and metal and winding it into order, teasing time between his horrid fingers. Ann's stomach constricted and lurched and fresh menstrual blood sluggishly belched out onto her rag, a wobbling clot that made her shudder. He could probably smell it. (He'll sniff you out the way dogs sniff out bitches on heat, the way foxes, slobbering and grinning, slink around the lame rabbit bleeding out.)

What if Petra had been right? she thought suddenly. What if she had been sacrificing herself to save the rest of them from the men, after all? (*You don't even know how bad it's going to get.*)

God, her mouth was dry; her sandpaper tongue felt like it had swelled up. In fact, her whole body must have swelled, because she was suddenly enormously conspicuous; her shoulders were pushed against buckling walls and her head was wonky and too far forward on her neck like it had been ripped off and replaced wrongly. Her newly gigantic feet played dumb about walking. (Are you sure this is the right gait?) They stumbled. (Should steps be big or little? Are you really so thick you've forgotten how to work us? Surely you know it's left-right-left and heel-toe-heel-toe, you silly girl.)

He turned at the sound of her skirts. How could he miss her? She was simply huge in this tiny corridor, blown up to epic proportions especially for him, so that his mean eyes would not miss any inch of her, would not fail to ravage any speck of her being with their unashamed roaming. He smiled his horrible carnal smile. His head tilted and she saw his tongue flash between the gaps in his teeth like he was licking his lips, like he was hungry. All the better for him to eat her. The hallway was damp and hollow, like a dried-up bone whose marrow had been sucked out; it unspooled before her in spite. She trained her eyes on the stairwell door and walked slowly with her head hardly moving, because surely if she looked at him or quickened her pace he would break into a run after her and she would be hunted and mauled.

He was watching her the full way, she knew it; she could hear the silence that meant he had stopped his clock-winding task, the silence that meant he was staring, the silence that meant he was waiting to pounce.

Why didn't he? Why didn't he launch his gangly frame straight for her, dig his hands into her flesh until it parted and sprang blood, pull her hair, and bite her right down to the bone?

It was on the stairwell that she remembered the secret second key. It winked at her slyly from his pocket. So, then: he was only biding his time.

5

PREPARING LUNCHEON WAS never-ending. They rolled and boiled and burned the spoils of the grounds into delicate morsels that could be held perfectly in a lady's hand (*with* room for the little finger to point out). Mud was churned and juiced until it could steep sulphurous eggs in truffle butter, shell-like tarts were filled to bleed earthy beet-root and slimy swirls of fresh-plucked spinach, pulsating purple rabbit legs baked until the meat fell from their bones and marched upstairs on china plates so delicate and thin that they rang like glass.

It was a yellow afternoon that had settled, squinting meanly into the kitchen from outside, and dribbling in rain. A pan bubbled sluggishly on the stove and the clock on the shelf belched its low tocks like a lazy metronome. All that was missing were gnarled branches growing from the walls, and strange animals shrieking from their pickling jars. It could have been a witch's den from some macabre fairytale, Ann thought peevishly. A witch's den where devils came to dance, and all were cloaked in sin.

She sliced bitter brown lines away from the carrots. She didn't belong here with the likes of *them*, so she needed to always be on her guard in case one of them decided to push her and stuff her into the oven for dinner, or boil her with newt's eyes and a dead man's tongue. Although real witches, she reasoned, probably weren't like these. She peered at Old Crone and Cook and Matchstick from beneath her lashes; openly lecherous and foul. Real witches were probably altogether more shrewd and sly and refined in their hiding, so as not to give away their demonic associations and be burned at the stake. A real witch would be like Mrs Hardy; proud and slippery and silent.

'She's made of the same stuff as the house,' Petra would whisper of the housekeeper. 'How else would she blend into it so well? You think the room is empty and start speaking your mind, and then suddenly she appears like she was always there just waiting for the moment to chastise you. The bitch.'

Ann thought of Mrs Hardy somewhere high above, tending to the Duchess.

'The old cow is probably up there pleasuring Her Grace,' Old Crone croaked like a toad.

Matchstick giggled at her lewdness as she crunched apart cloves of garlic, their sharp smell permeating the room like sweat. 'Oooh, you are wicked!'

Old Crone smiled and itched the shell of her nostril with her fingernail. 'Can't say I'm wrong though, eh? She *is* always with her, far more than a housekeeper should be.'

Cook tutted, Matchstick giggled again and Ann shifted her footing. Sometimes it was as if they had some kind of unspoken language that everyone understood apart from Ann.

Matchstick popped a clove in her mouth and sucked on it like a sweet. 'You think she'll tend to the young lady now, too?'

'What, adopt our dear departed Petra's duties?' asked Cook with a sneer. She kneaded a bowl of mince with sticky knuckles. Ann noted that the little black hairs that curled on the back of her hands looked like the stubble stubborn enough to stay on a pig's hide even after it's cooked. She tipped the carrots into the belching copper pan and thought about seizing Cook's hand and pressing it right there into the boiling water. Letting the bubbles roll over her skin; watching her flesh grow red, then purple, then yellow-white before it would peel from her bones and twist away in the water, like a part-poached egg. She'd leave Cook's skeletal hand in until it was entirely clean of meat and skin. Pristine white, thin and shining, not a callus or hair in sight.

Matchstick nodded her little red head. 'Has she really . . . gone?'

Ann knew this would come sooner or later. The gossip. The malicious, stinging words that knitted them all together to form some kind of great conglomerate beast with a multitude of heads, whose nerves and marrows were so connected that they understood each other perfectly. It made her feel small and vulnerable, and she hated it.

She prayed for them not to notice her, for them not to try to pull her into their nasty little cohort; to peel apart her lips and her eyelids and pry out every slither of information she knew, every incriminating sin she had seen Petra commit. She tried to become marble, like a statue, tried to gooseflesh her skin into stone, stay as still as she could, become invisible in her frozen form while the spiderwebs of whispers spun all around her.

It began.

'You know she couldn't stay; you saw how fat she was getting. Let me tell you, you don't get fat like that on soup.'

Outside the rain began to patter heavier.

'She was a whore, I knew it all along.'

'Aye, and you couldn't half hear it at night too.'

'The old bat'll choose a replacement soon.'

'Fresh meat?'

'Who said owt about fresh, it could be any one of us next.'

'Not me, I won't be going on any chopping block.'

'Someone like you dun't need to worry, I'm sure.'

'Ha! We all know Miss Hoity-Toity is eyeing it up anyway, she has been from the off.'

With a start, Ann realised they meant her. They were all turned to her, leering. She blinked back at them.

'I-I don't know what you mean.' It came out barely more than a whisper, but that wasn't because she was scared of them. (No, it wasn't.) It wasn't because she didn't understand, either. (No, it *wasn't*.) It was just that there was something, a raspy marble of phlegm or something, caught right in her throat, that was all.

The room had suddenly become thick and still, and slowly, very slowly, Matchstick began to slink towards her.

'We all know you think you're better than the likes of us.' The whisks and the knives and the tools were laid down with sly hollow clinks. 'Just admit it, you little slut.'

They were all advancing on every side of her now, their voices prickling on every part of exposed skin, their faces pulsating and undulating closer and closer, it was making her dizzy and hot. The overwhelming static of the rain sounded against the window.

'You would jump into Petra's job as soon as you would her grave.'

Were they hissing that spitefully, or was it just the steam whistling out from the pans?

'Would you jump into her bed too? Hope that the footman mistakes you for her?'

Her cheeks were burning, smarting as if from a slap.

'Be careful what you wish for, Ann. History has a way of repeating.'

'It won't be long until all the moaning and groaning from your room starts back up again.'

There was a knife there, just there, right near her fingertips on the chopping board. She could pick it up right now, and she could stab the nearest of them right in their thigh, where even under all that horrid stony fat there would be a dangerous artery to slice into.

Just at that moment, Rachel entered in her soft and silent and stupidly vulnerable way, holding her apron full of warm eggs. Suddenly Ann was dropped from their jaws, they turned their heads towards Rachel. All the yellow air in the kitchen had turned to tar and Rachel stepped stickily into it. She had no chance; it was hardening like amber all around her. She was as good as dead.

'Can mutes moan, Rachel?' they hissed. 'Can they laugh if they're tickled or groan if they're fucked?'

They advanced towards her as one, their backs to Ann so she could hardly tell who was speaking. They prowled around Rachel, the freak, the oddity, the cursed, all of them murmuring and dribbling and giggling.

'We ought to thank you really, for easing them off our own backs.'

Rachel was motionless. Her head was bowed and only her eyes moved, their brown jellies quivering slightly as they carefully watched the friendly curves of the eggs in her apron. They cackled and coaxed and prodded all around her, but Rachel just stood, her dipped head never moving, and Ann hated her.

'Your hole must be so wide now,' they persisted, cajoling each other to edge closer and closer to the freak, the cunt, the cursed. 'Your hole must be so wide now that if you ended up like Petra, a bairn could just walk out.'

Laughter shrieked and tore. Old Crone had seized a wooden spoon and was brandishing it like a cock, she began to scoop up Rachel's skirts with it, sifting for flesh. 'Go on, let's have a look, shall we?'

Rachel could apparently take no more, and with a wrenching shudder she leapt back from Old Crone and let go of her apron so that the little brown eggs spun and cracked on the hard floor, their dopy orange faces wobbling gleefully.

'You stupid bitch,' they shrieked. 'You stupid bitch.' They pummelled at her stomach. 'You fucking great thorn in our side.' They scratched at the soft flesh on her arms. 'You wretched cow.' They seized her by her hair and pulled her face down to the floor. 'Lick them up till they're clean and gone or we'll take you to the stables and let the men do what they like with you.'

Rachel's face crunched against stone; it was beginning to crack, and that big silent mouth began to open in a threat to scream out. Her stupid bovine eyes looked up and found Ann; they beseeched her for help.

'Eggs,' Ann murmured. 'More eggs.'

She didn't wait to see if any of those pigs had heard her. She ran from those stupid wet eyes, and all the whooping cackles and dirty scratching fingernails, into the slanting rain that was coming down so heavy now, splashes of mud were flaring up against it in retaliation.

They were all demons – licking, spitting, fucking, twisting, burning demons. Little perpetrators of hell. Driving her out into this damn rain that was making this awful grass slick and slippery. Rain that was running down her collar all the way down her back, blurring her vision with relentless grey lines like cobwebs. If they had spoken one word more to her she would have shown them, she would have picked up that knife; oh yes, she would have done. She would have sliced them into halves, into quarters, and barely had to clean up after because everyone knows that demons don't have proper blood. Not pure blood like hers, good and red and juicy and flowing, demon blood is so thick and black it is almost solid. It would move slower than treacle, so you see, it wouldn't even have had a chance to touch the flagstone floor by the time she had finished carving them up.

It wasn't any of her business that they decided to turn on Rachel, she thought, her peevish gait marching to a fury as she got closer to the woods. It wasn't any of her business that Rachel was so stupid and feeble, she wasn't to blame if she didn't want to be associated with that, if she didn't want to have to suck up raw eggs or be thrown to the snapping jaws of the men in the stables.

God, this rain was so thick and wet she could scream, she wanted to wring herself out, to throw up so she had no wetness inside of herself, either. She reached the woods and seized at the bark of a tree and squeezed it so that she could feel the rough of it biting hard into her skin. She opened her mouth as wide as she could into a scream. Wide, wide, wider, so she felt like her skin would split, like the corners of her mouth would rip at the seams and carry on tearing until her outsides peeled back and the purple underbelly of her skin was revealed. The veins on her neck were growing fat and ropy and nearly bursting with the exertion of the silent scream, her stomach muscles were hard and burning. Between each scream she took great shuddering breaths. Again and again and again, until the screams themselves were no more than harsh breaths that began to soften. Growing softer and softer until she found that all the frustration inside her had nearly mellowed to a pristine calm, and she wasn't getting wet stood here in the woods now either, and it was actually like a little air pocket; a cradle of bark and decaying orange and half-hearted green, oddly silent.

She had found order again. They were wrong and bad and she had purged herself from the horror of being in proximity to them and God it felt good. She *was* better than them, they had been right about that, and so what if she knew it. But there was something else that niggled in a little corner of her brain, something else that their vulgar words had stirred.

Petra was gone.

Ann knew it, of course, and was glad for it. (Let her rot or burn or I don't care what.) But it wasn't until now that she realised the significance of Petra's dismissal.

Ropner would need a replacement.

Petra would need to be replaced.

Petra, who had brought the lady breakfast in the morning, who had curled inside her fireplace to clean it, who had dusted each and every precious trinket that the lady's own clean, soft fingers had toyed with. Petra, who had combed the lady's hair, washed it, plaited it. Was there anything else so intimate as standing head above head, close enough to see someone's thoughts, hands weaving and knotting in a rhythm that was like a secret.

Ann's breath grew little and fluttering. Pressed against the bark, she watched the image that had appeared in the middle distance; the niece sat on a cushioned stool, head turned away, and Petra stood over her, her ugly, oafish head bowed in concentration, her ugly, fumbling fingers moving defter than Ann had ever seen, plaiting the lady's hair into a twisting crown.

Ann watched them until her eyes went woozy, until the image distorted and blurred, until Petra's unsightly head and foul hands were replaced with her own. *Her* hands in the lady's hair, *her* head bowed neatly, dutifully, obediently above the lady's own; watching the plaits she had made shine like a halo, watching the curved line of the niece's scalp, so smooth she wanted to trace it with the tip of her tongue. She chewed a slither of her lip and tentatively probed the thought. It felt familiar, that image. It felt right.

She would not be so slovenly, so ungracious and immoral as Petra, though. No, she would treat the position of lady's maid with the respect and honour it was owed. Petra had left behind a fraying moth hole in the great tapestry of Ropner. Ann would sew it up.

She would be perfect.

6

THE CHICKENS AND their shit-covered eggs were kept in a clearing right in the thicket of the woods, near the evil-smelling shed where game was plucked and skinned. The shed was dark and crooked, chickens fussed in front of it, loud and brassy as fishermen's wives, with penny-coloured aprons and prehistoric talons that scuffed the ground. Ann shooed them away from the nearest rotting coop by feigning flicking at them with her skirts and kicking them; she didn't want them near her. She never did trust those diabolical creatures, with those pointed beaks and eye-gouging claws. As for the other creatures; she saw their smoke before she saw them. It curled through the air like a witch's fingers in sharp and crooked loops.

Quickly she knelt low behind the hen coop, with a heartbeat raging right in her ears. If she peeked a fraction of an eyelash over it she could see them leaning untidily against the furthest side of the shed.

A kitchen boy she did not know, and with him a figure she knew all too well.

It was Scarecrowfootman.

Of course it was, of course it fucking was, because that was just her luck. Or maybe he had been sniffing her out, trailing her, hunting her. Thank God for that horrible blue smoke he was puffing, that fusty pong was probably disguising the vinegar smell of her blood, those rotting clots damp on her rag. Otherwise he would sniff her out right now, like a dog, like a pig snuffling for truffle, and she would be as good as dead, crouched here, sopping wet and shivering, nippled with gooseflesh and deafened by her own heart.

He was slouched against the damp wall like he didn't have a care in the world. Even his smoke was let out like an afterthought, escaping between the gaps in his teeth as he spoke, in thin strands that looped and horned about his head slyly, framing his face, not wanting to stray too far from him into the cold air.

The kitchen boy standing with him was a head shorter, with flaccid hips and a face as smooth and vacuous as a larva. They were all faceless at that age; rendered nondescript by their stupidity, by the easy liminality of boyhood that girls were never party to, that liminality that would soon expire as they grew mean and sharp and grabbing and slobbering and wicked and dirty and vile. There was no other way, they never deviated from that narrow path to cruelty, they were all the same.

After a moment, the blood pounding in her ears slowed so that she could hear them talking. That reedy scarecrow voice cut through harshly. 'C'mon, he said he's getting here quarter past the hour.'

The boy coughed on a plume of smoke he had mistakenly swallowed. 'Butler said he's coming with dogs, is that true?'

Scarecrowfootman threw his fag stump to the ground then hawked and spat on it, 'Well aye, he's a groundsman isn't he – he'll be bringing them slobbering wiscous things for hunting.'

Ann could hear quite easily now as he spoke, and easier still as they both, unheralded, began to slowly slope towards the house, along past the hen coop.

'Them breeds can stick their snouts into burrows and tear rabbits right up from their holes.'

Could she burrow now into this ground below her? Or sprout feathers to disguise herself, and grow a pointed beak she could stab them with if they came too close?

'And then what?' asked the boy, fascinated horror plain in his voice.

'Then he'll take them, still squirming and screaming—'

'Rabbits scream?'

'Well aye,' Scarecrowfootman said with horrible knowing. 'He'll take them and snap their necks clean and fast.'

They were getting closer to walking directly by her now: unless she crawled into the coop they would see her. Something in Ann screamed at her to do just that, to crawl into that putrid-smelling hut, to cover herself in all the straw and shit and loose feathers so they couldn't sniff her out, and just lie there forever, warm and sheltered and safe.

But too late.

Scarecrowfootman, who saw her first, gave a horrible toothless grin. The boy, who saw her second, looked towards Scarecrowfootman, as if waiting for instruction.

She snapped her head towards the coop door and thrust in her hands to busy herself with the search for eggs. Their conversation muted to soft mutterings. Ann breathed slowly, ready to run at even the slightest sign they would pounce. A rogue hen moved closer, inquisitively, and gave a low greeting cluck. There was something almost motherly about the cock of her head and the wobble of her red leather cravat. *I'll look after you*, it seemed to say.

She felt the foolish bloom of safety, and clutched it to her.

'He'll snap them like this.' The footman's hands were big and deft and like flashes of lightning in their paleness. He picked up the hen and twisted her neck to break before Ann even had a chance to straighten and step back from his advance. The crack bolted out from the hen so loudly the air seemed to shimmer with it long after he tossed the flopping cadaver at Ann's feet and let out a harsh one-note laugh as she flinched.

Ann watched the corpse, its legs twitching from the echo of its last heartbeat. She would be carving it up soon, on a chopping board, once that poor thing had been stripped down to its tough yellow skin and emptied of its offal. Or if no one brought it in in time it would be left and the cold would get to it, and the rot, and the maggots that would squirm out of its eyes and wriggle inside it. That's if the foxes didn't get to it first, with their slavering snapping jaws just like Scarecrowfootman's.

He took a slow step closer towards her. This was how she was going to die, she knew it. She could feel his horrible hot breath stirring the air near her face.

'Will you show me what your screams sound like, rabbit?'

Scarecrowfootman did not move, but Ann felt his hands around her neck, felt all the sinews round her throat protest and tighten against his pressing hands, felt them give and let her bones splinter and snap, shuddering all down her spine, felt her shivering goose-pimples split to sprout feathers, felt her face harden to a beaked point, felt her new fowl body fall to the floor to lie with her friend in a cold vulgar death. She stood in front of him, scrawny and weak, her eyes were watering with tears. She was crying, God dammit. She was crying right in front of him, and what was worse was that she felt a warm dark rush between her legs that was surely blood but – horribly – might be piss.

This couldn't be happening. She stood in front of him, wet and shivering, and staring hard at the vile twisted body of the hen because she couldn't bear or dare to look at his face. If she did, she wouldn't just cry and bleed and piss, she would be worse than dead. If she gave him even a glimpse of her eyes, no matter how masked they were with those stupid traitorous tears, that would be enough for him to steal through those windows and look for that thing inside her like it was his, like he had been invited to, like she had begged him to. It was too late now anyway: whether he saw her eyes or not, he had already decided she belonged to him and there was nothing she could do about it.

Scarecrowfootman stepped away, barked his ugly one-note laugh again and moved back towards his companion. He whistled as they sloped back towards the house.

'See you soon, sweet.' They thrust the trees apart and plunged into their distant darkness.

Ann stared and stared and stared at the corpse by her feet. This would not be her fate; she refused it. It was upstairs, or it was this hell. She would fill the post of lady's maid before it grew cold; she would become untouchable in her goodness. They would not tarnish her soul, they would not fill her with their rot, this badness would not possess her, she would be perfect.

7

HOURS HAD PASSED before Ann returned inside, or at least it had been enough time for the rain to let up and the others to have finished with the luncheon, finished with Rachel.

The air in the empty kitchen was thicker somehow, it stirred and seethed in the dwindling shafts of light like it was charged with something, the way the world turns static before a storm. The way all that pressing closeness tells you something is going to come rumbling and whipping from over there, just beyond those hills.

So it wasn't with shock that Ann noticed Mrs Hardy was there. Although the room had been empty when she walked in, she had known all along, somewhere in a fold of her mind, that Mrs Hardy was somewhere near. She had felt those black eyes staring at her, pressing on her. (Just beyond those hills.)

It would be easy to say Mrs Hardy inspired a cold dread, a compulsive nausea of fear, but that would only be half of the truth. It was as if, in the housekeeper's presence, everything in Ann were scooped out, so that if you looked inside her you would see a hollow cavern with walls of ribs; blood and bodily goo dripping slowly from shoulder-blade stalactites. If you poked out her eyes so that they plopped to the floor like wet marbles and you looked right into the space behind her sockets you'd see a smooth tacky skull curving round precisely nothing, no thoughts or memories or lies or prayers, so if you wanted you could reach your hand into that space and move her mouth like a puppet. It was not a liberating type of nothingness, there was no peaceful freedom from being disembowelled like that. No, rattling around in her own empty body was excruciating and humiliating.

Still, Ann couldn't help but be thrilled by it. All of Mrs Hardy's cold ruthlessness, her austere observations, the silent, lurking way she watched, saw, *knew* everything, all of it was for the benefit of Ropner. She was its fiercest advocate and protector, and Ann could think of nothing more admirable than that. The housekeeper weeded out the weak and the ruinous, she trimmed away the fat and sliced away the sin for the good of the house, for the good of the ladies upstairs.

Mrs Hardy had in her hands a small black notebook with curling cream pages. She was whistling to herself softly as she examined it. The tune was quiet and eerie, and sounded, in the emptiness of the kitchen, like glass. Slowly she made a thick black mark in her small black book and closed it. It seemed to be a long decision to look at Ann, and an even longer one to speak.

She would have been pretty for her age had her teeth not been quite so many and quite so sharp.

'You are sensible, Ann, are you not?'

Did she know Ann was good? Did she see how dutifully Ann tended to each chore? Or had she seen what had happened in the woods, with the footman and the chicken? Did she know how her mind had burned with the horror of how quickly a thing could snap from alive and pumping blood and breathing air, to dead and staring and blank.

'Are you sensible, Ann?'

Ann had buried the chicken in a quiet place: the soft earth behind that evil-smelling game hut. Thickets of dried ferns, like huge clumps of hair, netted the ground, masking it with slick wet hues of orange and purple. But underneath, the earth parted easily in thick damp clods. She had scooped the black mud with her hands. Against its darkness, the chicken's feathers seemed the colour of pockmarked orange peel, of brown pennies, of the kind of pebbles so smoothed by the sea you felt the need to put their cold weight on your tongue. The grave was shallow, but when Ann moulded the mud back into place it might not have been there at all. She had wanted to cry until she remembered Rachel's tears over that tiny bird. She would not be so pitiful. She had waited and counted to the highest number she knew to put enough space between herself and Scarecrowfootman. The footman's eyes had made her a promise; he was going to climb in through hers and steal everything that she had inside. (No he wasn't. Not if she could help it.)

Are you sensible, Ann?

Had she heard the footman swear to that terrible promise? Did she know Ann would not let it happen, not like Petra, because she was stronger, more capable, better? Perfect. The way a proper lady's maid should be. *Oh, see me,* Ann thought, with all her might, so that the housekeeper might hear it, might feel it vibrating through the tiny atoms in the air. *Oh, see me; how good I am, how pure and devoted,*

48

see how much I would flourish, how I would fly, how I would serve if I worked upstairs. How perfect I would be.

Are you sensible, Ann?

'Yes, Mrs Hardy, I am.' (Sensible and loyal and unsoiled by sin.)

For the briefest moment, the housekeeper cocked her head, as though listening.

'Good,' she said curtly.

And with that, Mrs Hardy vanished.

8

THE WONKY LINES of the kitchen gardens looked especially dark and ruddy in the dwindling autumn light. All around Ann was gloomy and cold, washed out by the fine rain that stained any remaining colours with bitter tinges of blue-grey.

She was safe for the time being. Scarecrowfootman would be having his tea somewhere with the men, or maybe he would be bragging to them of his terrible plan, dangling the second key in front of their faces. (Damn him, damn him, damn him.)

She stomped along the bastardised path between the furrows and troughs. Squelching over the brown mulch, black mulch, green mulch, brown, orange, black, brown mulch. Smaller leaves, too dry and newly dead to succumb to the wet stew under her feet, skittered about her in the breeze. They swirled around her ankles and skipped ahead of her down the path, like they were showing her the way. Ann exhaled in time with the wind, puffing out her cheeks and directing the gusts with her fingertips. Perhaps this was a secret power she did not know she had. Perhaps she could whip up a storm if she really tried. Create a gale to shudder the very bones of Ropner, to sweep up all of its most loathsome residents and spit them back out, far, far away into some distant abyss.

She thought of a hurricane sucking Scarecrowfootman, limb by lanky limb, into its fury. Flinging him about like a rag doll, like a scarecrow, until all of his cloth skin ripped open and his straw spilled out and he was buffeted into nothing by the raging wind. Ann stopped and smiled to herself. It tickled her, that thought; that thought of him being ripped and ragged and torn into shrieking bits.

She stood and puffed out her cheeks and blew a mighty gust to play with the treetops of the woods; watching as they bent and swayed, their leaves flustered by her powers. She turned to the house, to see how far she could make her winds stretch. And as she turned, with a feeling dropping fast and heavy like a stone inside of her, she saw a figure framed by the kitchen door. Watching.

Ann whirled back on her heels quickly. The wet ground squelched beneath her and she marched on as if nothing had happened. She was here to pick herbs and that was all she was doing. There was nothing for anyone watching her to see.

A gross feeling of embarrassment sluiced through her. The sickly entity of it disagreed with her so horribly that it burned her cheeks. There was a special kind of horror about being watched in solitude. She saw a flash of a scornful imagining; that putrid, insipid watcher, whoever they were, running back into the kitchens to shout for the others to *listen to what pathetic little stuck-up Ann was doing,* how they all would laugh with spittle drooling between the black gaps in their teeth.

She marched as fast as the mulch would let her. Past the impatient pushings of bright carrots and grudgingly jovial onions, past the prickling gooseberries and brambles, burrs catching onto her skirt. (Perfect. Just perfect. Now she would have to pick each of the horrible little buggers off the fabric once she was in.)

Ann picked out the thyme and rosemary, shoving them straight into her pocket bags without stopping to smell them as she usually liked. She was still stinging from the indignation of her embarrassment.

Thrust in her pocket bags, her hands grazed the taut skin of her lower belly and it groaned out its discomfort in response to her touch. This nasty curse. She would fetch some nettles from the woods. That would show it for trying to get the better of her. She would make herself some tea to silence that relentless gnawing.

In the woods the ground was less of a petrichor soup and more a great thick tapestry. Hundreds of ferns, thick like hairs of a brush, wove together with tiny flowers and rusting orange shoots, thin and tall. The oppressing canopy of trees bore down over it, condensing the air and amplifying every sound so that even the silence buzzed.

Ann found a thicket of nettles near the riverbank. The plants did not appear as spiteful as their nature would suggest; in fact, Ann thought them tall and proud, the way their leaves fanned in a satisfying gradient and tapered into a fluffy spear. She pinched their heads firmly, dismembering their leaves with a ferocity that scared the sting right out of them.

The dark was coming, but if Ann wanted soup for those rotten cramps, she would need more nettles than were here.

She looked around her. Evening mist was beginning to settle, but the river was unmoved: a vast never-ending plane; an eternity of translucent steel unfurling everywhere. It was so still that its liquid surface seemed only a glass pane, separating her from where she stood and the world that lay beneath. A tree creaking and leaning right over the bank cast a thick black shadow onto the water with its branches. Something shifted below the translucent stillness.

She turned her head away quickly; she did not want to see, she did not want to know of any more horrors that she ought to fear. As she did, the hairs pulled too tightly into her braid pinched at her skin, like sharp teeth nibbling at her neck. A shiver rippled from her head to her shoulder blades. She clamped her teeth together, pocketed the nettle leaves and set off to find more.

The muddy path was oily with deep-set damp, but firm. It followed the curving noose of the river faithfully. The river that, the further she walked, was becoming swollen and seething, ready to burst its banks. It threatened to kiss the path that ran parallel to it, to part the grass with its wet tongue and thrust down its throat in a desperate bid to meet the trees. If she came here tomorrow the steps she was taking now would be under several inches of cold, rushing water.

Wind lashed in the distance like a brandished switch, but the creaking trees sheltered her from its blows. It was trickling away faster now, the light, but Ann was still yet to see any more upright silvery spires rising jaggedly above the rest of the slick, thick greenery.

The groaning ache in her lower belly and back made itself known once more. She pressed on.

What if she walked right out of the grounds? What if she followed the river all the way to . . . to what? What existed beyond Ropner's border? Where did the thick path of land that the river couldn't slice through connect to?

Nothing, said a tiny little voice from her head, or perhaps the voice came from the river itself. It was tiny and terrible in its absolute certainty.

Nothing.

She was afraid of what she would find, she was afraid of how much she wanted to know.

This was his fault; she had never so much as thought of what lay beyond Ropner, of leaving. Yet now her legs were walking on and on as far along the river as she had ever been before. Spurred on by that morbid thought of reaching where the river curved away from the grounds, that savage notion of having to choose between following its path or returning to its noose.

She walked and walked and walked, full dark was still teasing but had not yet mustered the courage to fall entirely, which was a riddle Ann could not solve, because she had been walking for hours now surely? She had become so tired from walking that her gait had now rendered itself nothing more than a heavy trudge, her legs protesting with a groan almost as loud as her belly and back's.

She should turn back. But there, up ahead, was a cluster of nettles that had never before seemed so attractive-looking.

Ann smiled. It was only fair that something finally go her way.

But when she reached them, when she readied to trick their sting by seizing them with pinching, fearless fingers, she found them decapitated, sore and wounded with missing leaves, missing leaves exactly in the places she had pulled from earlier.

She had walked a circle somehow; she had walked for so long that she had lost sense of direction and doubled back on herself.

Impossible. She had followed the river the full way, with it always scoring the right side of her vision. The length of time she had walked for should have walked her right out of Ropner, should have walked her miles away. It should be as black as midnight, and she should be free.

But here she was in the same light, with the same nettles, in the same spot she had started.

She looked out over the river again, and under the gossamer mist something stirred below the surface, just as it had hours before.

The river began to ripple slowly; like a great steely back rolling its shoulder blades. The branches reflected on its surface, twisted and contorted. Whatever was there, whatever was under the surface, was going to leap up, leap out, and seize her in a furious foam of water and pull her into the belly of the river so fiercely that her lungs would burst with the rush of silt forced down her throat.

She stumbled back from the water that was now roiling, succumbing to the buffeting of the winds. A bolt of fear was shooting through her spine, right into the meat of one of her pulsing organs. Her heart pounded painfully and something small and sharp leapt up and bit the heel of her hand.

She had stumbled into the nettle thicket, caught one of the leaves with her flailing limbs. She thrust the red skin to her mouth and let warm spit flood over it, circling the burn with her tongue. And without looking back, without listening to her protesting legs or the yawning ache in the pit of her abdomen, she ran.

9

T HE DRESSER WAS the hardest to move. It was stout, with only two drawers, one for Ann and one for Petra, all that was in it were spare starched aprons, but the red-soaked wood was heavy and its feet gave out rusted groans as they thrummed towards the door. Ann persisted until wood met wood like firmly pressed lips refusing to give away any secrets.

She fell onto her bed, panting. The footman had made his ugly promise and she was not taking chances. She closed her eyes and tried not to think of his filthy face, tried not to let her dread of the night and what it might bring kill her.

In the darkness, Ropner Hall came alive. She could hear it. The blackberry bushes twisting and creaking, sparring with their thorns, the doughy pops of mushrooms pluming from heavy clods of earth, the flowers brave enough for the season sighing, like women stretching, unfurling their heads towards the moon.

The animals were weaving in amongst it all, breathing in the nocturnal purple. Primeval cries were shrieked by owls and nightbirds; the rabbits would twitch and jerkingly hop, baiting the fox who would watch them from the way, his foul mouth itching and his fur buzzing with the tease of the chase.

The river was loudest of them all, a stream of conscious-ness spoken in a stage whisper that feigned modesty. For how could it not be conceited? It lived in the sky and the ground and the bellies of all the beasts and the veins of all the trees, it steeled and sealed its signature on everything in Ropner Hall, living, breathing and dead. And there, in closer proximity, the house itself was waking up.

Floorboards groaned as the house stretched and yawned, things scratched and scrabbled behind the walls, the house whispered and hissed and mimicked her door handle being tried, then rattled, then more forcefully pushed.

Ann held her sheets tightly around her, she pulled them over her head so she did not risk being confronted by some horrible face looming out of the darkness towards her, teeth bared. But she kept her eyes open wide under the false safety of her sheets; every part, every morsel, every pore had to be open and alert and listening.

(Listen to his breathing, the muffled grunts. He's getting *stronger*.)

The drawers pressed against the door creaked and groaned like they were going to betray her and give way.

This was how she was destined to die: cold and alone and angry and afraid. She was going to be unhooked from all her parts until there was nothing left but meat, and then that would be bitten and torn and wrung and ripped, her ribs would be cracked open and all the heat would steam out into the frigid room. A small and involuntary gasp escaped from Ann's throat, that to any listening ear would sound like one of longing. Ann swallowed the sound as quickly as it had come, and found her nose suddenly stung by the coppery smell of game meat, raw and purple and rancid. She crossed her legs tight so the scent of blood wouldn't leak out from between them. (Fuck this stupid curse. Fuck its black brown and red.)

Agonisingly slowly, the pushing and rattling abated. (Don't move, don't check, it's a trick, an evil trick.) She hardly dared believe the sounds of a half-laughed sigh and sloping scarecrow footsteps retreating. So she remained, paralysed, until the sounds of morning, of Mrs Hardy's heels and the clunk of the true key, told her to move.

Every night Ropner repeated the rhythm for Ann. Each beat was hit with such precision there was surely a spiteful conductor tucked away somewhere; a maestro of torture orchestrating it all with his baton. The waltz with the dresser: push two-three, push two-three; Ann shivering under her sheet in a delicate aria; the harsh staccato of the footman rattling the handle, abhorrent music. Throughout it, Ann's heart obediently crescendoed until at last came the four-beat rest, where the jangles and the bangs and scrapes of effort gave way to sotto scarecrow sighs and the diminuendo of footsteps.

It was never-ending, this music, this fucking score. She was sure it had been playing since she was born and it would keep on playing until it killed her.

Upstairs was her only chance of salvation.

10

'A NN!'
She was on her hands and knees in the kitchen fireplace. She peered up from beneath the mantel to see Cook standing over her. Close up, Ann could see the clusters of thick pustules juicing her cheeks that she liked to suppose was all the badness trying to escape from her.

'Ann, you welt, get up when I'm talking to you.' (Shame the badness didn't try harder to get out.) 'Get up!' Cook launched a hard kick at Ann's backside.

Ann got to her feet quietly and hated herself for it. She liked to think it was because she was too dignified to speak to the likes of Cook, but she knew this was only a lie to herself; they all scared her. She pressed her lips together to keep from breathing in all that sin and halitosis.

'Hardy's told you to forage with Rachel.'

A sharp thrill went through her. '*Mrs* Hardy,' Ann whispered.

Cook laughed. 'Don't be such a prude and go lick her arse while you're at it.' Ann felt a fleck of her horrid spit arc and land on her pinafore.

IhateyouIhateyouIhateyou, she thought, as intensely as she could without speaking.

'Pick good ones, or I'll piss in your soup. It's me that has to chop them, and the spindly ones hurt my fingers.'

'I should like to break off those fingers one by one and push them into your mouth until you choke on them. Then I should like to push you in this fireplace and light it until you're roasted like a pig, so I could serve you to the others and watch them all slice you up and eat you,' Ann said.

Only it came out meekly, and sounded a lot more like, 'Yes, of course.'

But what did it matter? *She* was the one who had been trusted with a task directly from the housekeeper, not Cook. *She* was the one who understood the significance of it. She understood that this was a test – no, a chance, a chance to prove herself.

Tonight I will plait my hair, Ann decided. *I will plait neat furrows that knot tidily and tightly and perfectly, so that Mrs Hardy can see I am perfectly prepared to tend to my lady's hair.*

All the hatred for Cook that had filled her gave way as a huge bubble began to swell in her chest, under her cheeks, making her nearly gasp and float. She turned to leave (it would bode well to start as quickly as possible), but someone blocked her way and that huge friendly bubble deflated.

Rachel stood in the doorway, watching it all. She had marks from the last beating. A bruise on her neck and another on her wrist, and a thin, long scratch, not yet scabbed, down her face. She held out a basket in her stupid too-big hands, and Ann felt the most tempting urge to hit her.

The woods crept along the west side of the Hall like a dark menace, and already their autumn seemed eternal. The last of the orange leaves were clinging on to branches for dear life, and though frost threatened it never quite broached. The smell of the earth was so potent it coated Ann's throat with its claggy richness. She stifled a cough. Had she not been so clean and good she would have liked to spit away that lump of fragrance that had lodged in her, straight onto the wet black soil at her feet. The soil that was so thick it caught in glutinous clods that smelt like rain and thunder and lightning, and so dark that the mushrooms were easy to spot, their fawny caps standing out starkly.

Rachel and Ann gathered them in silence. They did not do so side by side, but by moving around each other in wide arcs, skirting each other's company, each glancing at the other from time to time while they gathered.

Rachel, Ann suspected, lived the most miserable life of all in Ropner Hall. *She is as soft as the inside of my cheek*, Ann thought with one glance, tonguing the flesh experimentally. *As soft as a rabbit's foot*, she decided with another, *and her eyes are so big and wet with thoughts that I'm scared for her to look back at me in case I feel them; in case she traces them onto my skin.*

Rachel's soft body sloped and curved, but bent stiffly as if something pained her.

She really was pathetic, Ann decided. No wonder she was hidden away from the other servants; always busy in Mrs Hardy's chambers, or scrubbing and doing God knows what upstairs. Because otherwise they would never miss an opportunity to be on her with the savagery of foxes. Tearing skin and softness and spirit from her until there was nothing left but bone; nothing left of what they didn't understand.

Stupid, sad, pummelled-to-a-pulp Rachel, whose loyalty and blind diligence was so tragic it was terrible. The perfect slave. The perfect servant. Perfect.

The sharp thrill that had visited Ann earlier returned, only this time it was crueller, mocking. Suppose . . . (Stupid thought, don't even think it.) Suppose Rachel was chosen instead. Suppose Mrs Hardy saw how she was as dutiful as a beaten dog, as pliable as a pussy willow switch. Then it would be Rachel whose soft brown eyes filled up with the lady's words and wishes and secrets; Rachel whose big soft hands massaged cold creams into the lady's skin.

'Oh,' the lady would say. 'What a wonderful warm touch you have, Rachel.'

'Oh,' the lady would sigh. 'What wonderful meek manners you have, Rachel.'

'Oh,' the lady would smile. (A smile meant only for you.) 'What a wonderful way you look after me, Rachel.'

Birds squawked from overhead in the half-naked branches; a magpie with his wife and five of his brothers watched sharply, their heads cocking this way and that, spying for worms or crumbs brought from the kitchen. Rachel spotted them and made them a funny kind of quick salute. She turned to find Ann staring at her.

Ann ducked back down quickly and resumed busying herself with the picking. She didn't want to look at Rachel anymore. It had suddenly become wildly offensive now to be anywhere near her, to be in proximity to something so weak and meagre. Ann's lip curled in disgust. *She probably thinks I am like her*, she thought savagely. *She probably heard the way I spoke to Cook and thinks she has found a companion in submission and wretchedness. Well, shan't I prove her wrong, shan't I show her we are nothing alike, that she should be damned for comparing herself to me, and won't she be green once I am lady's maid? And if she tries anything, if she so much as thinks of offering her services for my position, I will kill her, and that'll show her. I'll kill her the way a heel stamps on a spider and squashes it thinner than air, and the ladies and Mrs Hardy will be so thankful to me for sparing them the mistake of appointing her.*

Rachel made a small deep sound, like a cow lowing, and Ann straightened up and turned to face her sharply, ready to strike in the most vicious way she could. She would curse at her now and repent later. Only, what Ann saw rendered her incapable of doing anything as coherent as cursing.

Rachel was crying. She stood, swaying slightly. Her eyes were open, impossibly large, drooping with the weight of fat tears running steady courses down and over her breasts. Her palms were open and facing outwards and her mouth was dragged wide in a most unbecoming manner. That red-black frowning chasm moaned and echoed as if it belonged to someone being disembowelled. This creature Rachel had turned into was all the horror of a weeping Mary, a banshee, a spirit, an omen. Ann felt its eyes boring right into her, rummaging about her organs, sniffing and squeezing at her heart, which in this moment had surely dried up and died. And there, by Rachel's side, reaching a blueish hand out to brush against her cheek, to cup her chin and bring her ear close to his lips, was Scarecrowfootman. He had slunk into the clearing like a fox.

Ann's heart had stopped. Surely she was dead. Or had it just beaten so loud she was now deafened, numbed, unaware it was still crashing away against her ribs?

Could she spit venom if she hawked back far enough? She could feel it burning inside her. Wouldn't that be glorious, for a luminous wad of mucus to propel from her throat and sail to land *splat* on one of his mean eyes, burning and bubbling the skin at the socket, corroding through everything to leave his face a fleshy pulp for Ann to laugh and sneer at the way he had her. (Set fire to him too, burn him slowly still alive, roast him like a pig and leave him for all the rancid things of the black mud to feast on.)

But she could not, and his straw-like limbs moved defiantly, his thin voice went on, rustling harshly into Rachel's ear. Ann couldn't hear, she didn't want to hear. She watched Rachel's skirts bubbling and foaming for an age before she realised it was his scrabbling hands disturbing them. Rachel remained motionless, defeated. Her eyes were staring at Ann but, Ann realised, no longer seeing her. The wind in the trees made a cruel mimic of a door handle rattling, of a frame creaking and groaning.

'Stop,' Ann pleaded to the trees.

Her whisper reached Scarecrowfootman, who paused his rooting through Rachel's skirts to turn and face Ann. His smile opened, and his laugh echoed round all the gaps in his foul teeth. It was wide enough, his mouth, his teeth were bared enough, for him to stretch forward across the clearing and bite into her, feast on her right here, right now. Everything underneath Ann's skin burned, and his horrible breath and horrible eyes smeared dirt and disorder over her so thickly that everything's edges began to wobble and melt. Colours bled into all the wrong colours, and her ears rang so loudly that sound didn't seem to exist anymore. Scarecrowfootman's face loomed bulbous and impossibly large, its mouth wide to show her the dark cavernous space she was destined for, and slowly he raised a finger to his lips. Slowly his lips puckered into the kiss-like shape of a *shush*.

All her outside had peeled away, like the skin of a fruit, and the stone beneath was rotten and loathsome and sweetly furred with mould. She carried that terrible inside stone and ran from the clearing, ran from Scarecrowfootman, ran from Rachel. The woods were vast, a never-ending net of brown branches, drooling sap and rain, its loamy floor slick and bruised with drained colours, murky and rusting. Ann ran and twisted down its undulations towards the river. Conniving roots jarred her ankles and snagged her skirts.

A tree she knew rose up ahead from the sodden soil. Its facade was sturdy, but Ann knew round the other side of its trunk was a hollow mouth, open and moaning and the exact shape of her body once she folded her limbs to something compact. She curled into herself and stoppered the ugly dry mouth.

One little hollow in her ear listened for distant sounds from the clearing, and every other fibre of her being fought furiously against it, tried desperately not to hear anything at all. The guilt was right in her mouth, under her tongue and nestling in the strange flap at its root, it was bitter and arid and stinging. She was the one raping Rachel in the clearing, she was the one killing her. As good as. She should have stayed, she should go back.

She could feel Rachel's sad eyes still on her even now.

Suppose the footman had preyed on her instead: would Rachel have saved her? Would Rachel have torn her from the footman's grasp? Would she have? Or would she have stood back and watched him violate her? Either way, Ann knew that she was next.

11

THE CANDLELIGHT IN Ann's room did not flicker; it was molten on the wall and Ann's shadow swam in it. Smoky grey arms wrestled snake-like tendrils from its head and wound them into hissing submission. The shadow could not show it, but as she plaited, her bottom lip was chewed in concentration, and her eyes stared down at her legs. They did not see, however, how they crossed over the sheets, or how the downy hair bristled in the cold. Instead they saw the topography of a head transforming with knots and twists. They saw earrings flash and sparkle under the coils of hair, harmonising with jewels all laid out neat and shining (because she had only just polished them!) on the dressing table. They saw the lady's reflection watching her work and smiling, eyes swimming with gratitude and pride. 'Oh, Ann!' she exclaimed. 'It's perfect.'

The lady would go to dinner with her hair like this, with the halo Ann had plaited, and the Duchess would gasp and clap her hands in admiration.

'Aren't you so glad Mrs Hardy chose Ann?' she would say to her niece.

'Oh, Aunt, it is the happiest happening of my life! Look too how lovingly she has tended to my gown!' (And here she would spin, elegantly, to show her aunt just how well it was pressed and styled.)

'Let us toast to Ann!' they would cry, raising their crystal glasses. (No, not crystal; make them golden flutes instead.)

They would raise their golden flutes that twinkled underneath the chandelier, and sing, 'A toast to Ann!'

Mrs Hardy would step forth here, from where she had been neatly folded into a corner of the room, head bowed but always watching, making sure all was well. She would step forward and say, 'If I may be permitted to speak?' (So respectful, so aware of her place.)

'Of course, dear Mrs Hardy.'

'I am so grateful that I had the canny foresight to elevate Ann to be our beloved Lady's personal maid.' (And *companion*: by this point the lady will love you so dearly she won't be able to bear parting from you.) 'And companion, of course.'

'Thank heavens.' The niece would nod soberly. 'I dread to think what disarray we would be in should you have chosen another.' Ann watched them bow their heads, all disturbed by the thought of a lesser servant, by the thought of Rachel. *Don't worry*, she whispered to them all. *I won't let it happen.*

She thought of Scarecrowfootman's filthy promise. All she needed to do was make it through the night. Then she would put her plot into place. She would make sure Ropner was guaranteed perfection. She snuffed her candle.

It's uncanny how fear can turn both sound and silence deafening. How it can make the darkness grow heavier and suddenly regale your sense with the realisation of just how mortal you are. In the dark, fear turns you to a rabbit freshly snared and upturned. Beating white belly pulled taut and exposed, fine hairs barely concealing the thin pink skin that would peel open so easily to the teeth of a knife. Or at least it did Ann that night.

In such a state she seemed to hover outside of herself and couldn't be clear what was the cruelty of a nightmare and what was the horror of reality. Was that the crashing rush of blood or the shuddering scrape of the dresser being pushed aside by the opening of the door? And that sensation on her leg: was that the pressure of an intruder's hand or just the gentle movement of the bed-sheet, benignly disturbed? Deep in the belly of fear, her reactions and sensibilities were delayed; it did not dawn on her immediately that this nightmarish vision was actually her reality, that she was really able to see, quite clearly despite the darkness, the repellent face of Scarecrowfootman loom over her. His hand clapped over her mouth before it could split into a scream, the force of which pushed her head back into the mattress until she could feel the metal rungs of the bed frame jostling against her skull.

Did death have wings? Because she could hear something rushing towards her like a raptor. He was pinning her down with his weight and she was going to die. She twisted and flailed and screamed without screaming because that looming death had a grip on her voice so tight that it wouldn't work. It probably never would again, she would be mute like Rachel, whom she had sentenced to the same fate not hours ago. This death, this immobilising, inescapable death. She was dying now while he straddled her, pinning her down so far and tight that she would never be able to crawl free.

The bed frame dug in deeper. And then came the pain, the burning that woke the night. Ann split all along her seams from top to tail. Her insides opened and her soul screamed out.

It wouldn't stop, it would never end, she was being ripped and torn and wrenched and mauled away from the body that had once been her own.

Let me die, she begged. *Letmedieletmedieletmedie. Let me die or let this pain end, please. Please.*

Please.

Death was not granting her release. It refused. And that pain, that screaming, purging, hideous pain would not stop, but she *had* to make it, she had to, it was unbearable, it was abhorrent. It was a pain that was teetering so close, too disgustingly close, to something like pleasure. She clawed at the hand clamped on her mouth until she felt her nails rip and felt wetness on her fingers, but the hand seemed to only push down more, its pressure making it harder than ever to breathe. Her eyes widened to the extreme; surely any moment they were going to burst from her head.

Abandoning that clamping hand, Ann's own began moving madly, desperately; searching for anything to save her; tearing at the sheets, grappling the iron rungs on the bed as if she could wrench one free to deliver a skull-shattering blow she knew this agony would make her capable of. Her fingers scrambled furiously, in futility; at peelings of paint on the wall, the paper-thin pillow trapped under her head, the floor by the bed cold and unyielding, the porcelain jug toppled over by the commotion. They moved on in desperation before some animalistic instinct caught up with them and made sure they grasped the jug and brought it up with alarming momentum to meet the footman's contorted face. Dagger-like shards clattered to the floor and his hideous corpse fell fully atop her. She lay there, paralysed by the shock rather than his weight. Aware distinctly of his blood pulsing thickly down her own face.

That is what Ann saw in the silence and the dark. It was enough to terrify her from sleep.

12

THE STAINS ON the mattress were brown. They had dried and dyed the sheet with ugly fissured blots that boasted smeared and crinkled edges, stubbornly asserting that they had always been there and good luck trying to get rid because even when washed their jaundiced ghosts would still be strong enough to see.

Fuck this stupid curse. Why had she not been spared its affliction? Why had she not been spared that odious blood and sour gunk that dirtied everything, that paid no attention to any attempts to control? Even if she clenched all the muscles in her legs together so tightly they shook, that relentless blood would still blubber out, smearing dirty red marks all over the skin on her thighs, dropping impossibly red spots on her toes when she changed, curdling into black and brown lumps that stunk like a raw sheep's heart and made her think something had died inside her. Surely she was better than that. Surely, without a doubt, there was no rottenness inside her. So why did it insist on coming out like this?

'I take some cotton and paper and roll it into a fat fag and shove it up,' Petra had said to Matchstick once in the pantry. 'That does the job and saves the washing.'

She thought it was the most disgusting idea she had ever heard, shoving something right into those ugly alien folds she could hardly believe belonged to her. They were a continuation of her own body she refused to comprehend, those strange slimy parts of flesh hidden under that hair. Those parts that ached numbly when she bled and twinged into hollow places when she didn't. (And they hurt now – oh, oh they *hurt*.)

She scrubbed at the evidence of that horror staining the sheet. She scrubbed and scrubbed and scrubbed and wanted to scream because for all that she scrubbed it would never fully go away. This great filthy stain was evidence that that secret horrid part existed. She had half a mind to fetch a needle and thread and sew up that open seam all along her pubis bone to stop it from soiling anything ever again. And that fucking dull burning was obscene, it spoiled all of her nerves, it tugged her from her sleep and surged up even now when she was bent double over the wash barrel. She wanted to stop and curl up into a tight ball and groan, the way the pain felt exactly like groaning, until all her breath ran out, so she turned inside out and kept doing so until there was none of her left and she had expired completely.

She retaliated against the pain's demands for her attention by tackling each washroom task with a kind of composed ferocity that bordered on mania. It was as if she were performing a well-rehearsed self-flagellation, hitting the exact same spot again and again with a whip.

She turned the mangle handle in laboriously even counts of five, and on every fifth turn she thought about forcing herself through it. She blued and bleached the sheets, she scrubbed stains and hung up ghostlike aprons and thought

73

about her skin, her body, being soaped and boiled and rinsed again and again, scoured and wrung out and starched. All the different ways to get the badness, the dirt and memories (don't think about them) out, out, out of herself.

She was going to make her body as honed and as stream-lined as an arrow, become strong and straight and true, the perfect instrument for executing chores. The perfect instrument for serving Ropner and its ladies. She had to make sure that the muscles on her arms would no longer just be wiry, but taut and unforgiving, so she could beat rugs and haul slops, strong enough to carry the dead weight of a man. (*Don't think about that.*) Her legs would be lithe, and her back light and supple.

There would be no more badness able to get in. And all that extra work she would be able to undertake would tire her so viciously, so deliciously, that she would sleep heavily and without dreaming. No grabbing hands, ripping, tear-ing, mutilating between her— (Stop! Don't think about it!)

Ann wrestled with strange flashes from the night: copious syrupy blood, its copper smell, soil slicked under nails, wail-ing mouths and sharp, shattered shards.

She would not allow herself to think on it a moment longer; she could not. Thinking on it, remembering it, would mean admitting it happened, and that would make her as bad and as soiled as the rest of them. (*What will you do when all this badness possesses you?* That's what she had said, isn't it!) It was a nightmare, a brilliantly awful night-mare, nothing more. That's all it was from now on. And what use was there in remembering nightmares?

The day dresses needed folding. There were two piles to sort them into: the servant blacks, and the Lady Charlotte's

74

gowns. She folded the thick black frocks quickly and methodically. With the Lady's gowns, she allowed herself a little indulgence. She took her time. It would be hard not to; the colours, their patterns, their shapes and fabrics, were so rich, so delicate, that it was impossible not to let her eyes loiter. Buttery and soft, embroidery so tiny, and tight frosting hems and necklines, lace leaking and trailing from sleeves, skirts the colour of overripe peaches, running juices of silks and tulles.

One stomacher was a smoky lavender, as dusty as the heather that barnacled the moors. Another, a day dress, was the exact fleeting pink Ann had once seen the sky blush. Two skirts and their bodices were green, bottle green, heavy velvet austere enough to ward away cold. A final was an evening gown, the steely blue of the river.

The weak light from outside caught onto it and turned it iridescent; turned it to something alive in Ann's hands, fluid and flowing, searching for a form to slick to. Ann held it to her own; only to make it easier to carry, that was all, not to pretend to try it on, not to imagine herself in it, not for anything like that. Though it was hard not to when it was pressed against her, when she could feel its weight, see her arm poking from beneath the lace of its three-quarter sleeve like it was coming from inside of it.

The lady must be as pure as an angel, wearing these all day. Ann thought of her in it, with her hair all beautiful and curled and coiled in a style Ann herself had woven for her. It was a thought that made her feel full of light, and for a moment nothing throbbed or ached. In fact, she struggled to remember what had so troubled her a second ago, now that she was deliciously lost in the dizzy dream of the lady.

'Lady,' she said into the frigid washroom. Her accent, the accent she so hated sharing with the others, lilted the final syllable; made it chirrup into an *e*.

'Ladie,' she said. 'Ladieladieladie.'

She tried to hold on to the glorious image of her, as tightly as she could. If she did, maybe somehow Ladie would appear right here, right now, and Ann could dress her in the gown and curtsy all the way down to the floor to kiss her feet. But the thought slipped and slid mischievously, flickering the tighter she tried to hold on to it. It grew fainter and fainter, and the washroom swam back into focus. That tucked-away nightmare was starting, slowly and surely, to throb vividly once more. Vulgar colours and lurid images, shards of brilliant white, dark mud, dark blood, screaming tearing hands, awful grabbing, twisting and clawing hands, the same from the woods, frothing Rachel's skirts. In her mind's eye she saw Rachel and those big bovine eyes, wide, so terribly wide, with pure and simple fear.

Rachel was standing there now. Really standing there, by the door of the washroom; her eyes bigger and browner than Ann remembered. They were wet and soft, drooping with something horribly like pity. Something that was horribly close to saying, *I know. I know what he did to you too.* (No, it was all in your head. That mud that you took him to, buried him in, that black, black mud that wormed under your nails and spattered and smeared across his skin and made all the blood smell ever stronger, even more sickly and metallic, that was all just a nightmare. It had to be.) But Rachel's eyes were still staring, still damp, still sympathetic, still citing sisterhood.

Some blood had blubbered out like water, it was dribbling down the inside of her thigh, it would make its way down to her ankle and stain a scratchy line down her stocking.

I'm not like you, Ann wanted to scream out, *I don't want your pity*. But Ann couldn't have stayed in the washroom with Rachel even if she wanted to anyway. She needed, quite urgently, to be sick.

She threw up in the woods. Not as far in as the clearing, or the hollow tree, but deep enough to be hidden from the eyes of Ropner. And there, God dammit, just then without meaning to, she had thought again of the clearing where she had buried the corpse, of the footman and his hands, all over Rachel, all over her. Under her skin, between her legs, then twitching and bloody and peppered with soil.

The badness was bulging inside her, she wanted it out. Whatever rot he had infected her with, it needed to go and go now. She seized at the bark of a tree to steady herself and with her other hand rammed scratching fingers down her throat, tickling a fleshy ridge that flexed in protest, trying to elude the black mud clagging her nails. (The soil isn't there anymore, idiot. You washed it off, you washed it away.) She prodded her gullet harder and coaxed up sluggish bile that burned with a fury for being disturbed. Once more, then twice more after that, then twice again just to relish this total control she had pioneered.

In this moment her body was hers, it obeyed her distinctly, mechanically. Her eyes and nose streamed red from all the retching, but who cared about that. Some of the badness was congealing potently on curdling leaves, away from her, out of her. All her head was fuzzy and ringing and too blithe to remember broken shards of vicious nightmares. Even the relentless beat of blood had dulled. She was in control again now. She had found her footing and made herself as agile as the shaft of an arrow and as sharp and unwavering as its head. She pulled her fingers from her throat and looked at them. They were slimy with mucus, still wrinkled and puckered and freezing from the washroom she had been working in a million years ago. She sucked them until they were clean and warm. She remembered the dress and Ladie with the halo and was calm enough to smile.

She knew what she had to do.

13

THE HOUSEKEEPER'S ROOM was in the short, neat corridor next to the kitchen. Walking towards its door was like walking towards the dark box of a confessional. A chilling, almost child-like excitement skated and skittered above the dark notion of fear. For here was a moment, right at her fingertips, that teetered between one fate and another. The dark door to Mrs Hardy's room shone and pulsed slowly like a just-snuffed candlewick. The magnitude of the moment was so real, so tangible, that it pressed against Ann's cheek, traced along her shoulder blades, pushed at her hips and crushed heavily on her toes. Quite suddenly the moment lurched and tipped Ann's hand towards the door handle; turned it.

Fate was a thing now sealed.

Pushing open the black door was like opening the pages of an ancient book. A breath of fusty air was expelled as it opened, but, just as she expected, the room itself was perfectly pristine.

It was bare in a way that was practical rather than lacking, its scarcity had the air of a holy vow. A press fit neatly into one corner, prim and aloof with neat lines of drawers and canisters and preserves; all fruits and vegetables that had been spared from rot with vinegar and sugar and transformed into bountiful amethysts and emeralds and topaz mined from Ropner's own grounds, each meticulously labelled in spidery cursive. A small fireplace, too polite to open wide into a yawn, held a polished kettle under an empty mantelpiece of scrubbed stone. There was no ornamentation, no unnecessary frivolities, yet the room held in it the distinguished gravitas of a sacred space, one undisturbed by the dirty fingers, the spit and snot of any lowly, snuffling servant. It was not the heart of Ropner – no room that did not house the Duchess and her niece could truly be Ropner's heart – but it was, Ann decided, a vital organ; some fleshy sac or other that was crucial to Ropner's life. Behind Mrs Hardy's desk and chair hung a painting of the house itself, like a shrine. Strangely, the painting seemed in some way familiar to Ann.

The housekeeper sat beneath it now as Ann entered, still and poised as though she were an actor on stage who had been patiently waiting for the curtain to rise and reveal her. Her black skirts were arranged neatly and without crease, one hand folded atop them and the other rested on a small pile of black notebooks on the table, the spine of each pressed with a different letter.

'Ann,' Mrs Hardy said, without a trace of surprise or question. Ann sometimes got the feeling that Mrs Hardy knew the house so intimately that any occurrence or happenstance was a thing always anticipated by her. The housekeeper's eyes flickered to Ann's hair, taking in the tightly woven braids in place of the usual scraped bun. 'May I help you?'

In this sacred space, this instrumental, hallowed hollow resting in Ropner's skeleton, Ann felt it somehow blasphemous to speak. As if she would be disrupting the perfectly balanced order and serenity. But was she not here to ensure the very livelihood of Ropner, to secure its future (and your own), to save it and its Ladies from the taint of rot? So, then: what could be a more appropriate conversation to have right in the housekeeper's room?

'Yes, Mrs Hardy.' Despite the assurances she had given herself, the voice that came out was small, curled and spineless. This would not do, this would not help her case. She rolled her shoulders back and felt their meaty crunch push her to a straighter position. 'That is . . . is to say I have something to confess.'

One of Mrs Hardy's eyebrows gave an inscrutable twitch, and Ann cringed at her choice of words. 'Oh?'

Confess. Roving hands with dirty fingers, rolling skirts to a boil. Running, raggedy breathing. Pain. In the chest, between the legs, pain of being no better than the rest of them. And blood, so much blood. Trickling down his forehead, over her hands, onto the sheets, onto the mud. Black mud. Absolving mud. Corpse-swallowing mud.

Ann curled her fingertips further into the shell of her folded hands.

'I love Ropner,' Ann said. The overwhelming truth of it made her voice thick and sticky. 'I live for every working moment to serve it and the blessed Duchess and lady.' (After this they will be so close, all their light and cleanliness and goodness all in touching distance.) 'Which is why as its most obedient servant I feel it is my duty to tell you of anything that may serve to jeopardise it.' (Most obedient, most devoted, better than them all. You must see, you must know.) 'Rachel, who I know has always been trusted to work hard and work well, I have fear that she may have been influenced by Petra's –' Ann struggled for the right words and saw in her struggle Rachel's own, her tortured banshee scream, its silent horror – 'by Petra's sins.'

In the silence that followed Ann held her breath until she died again and again and again. How stupid had she been to think that this would work, how stupid had she been to not see that this was no better than passing on the insipid gossip the others bolstered their days with. God, what if Mrs Hardy saw her as no better than them? Well, now she had only confirmed it.

'You're sure, Ann, that it is Rachel who has done wrong? You are not mistaken in any way?'

(If she knew about Petra, if she knows about Rachel, like she knows all, then surely she will know about you, too; all the rot, all the badness that he has infected you with.)

Ann forced herself to breathe again, a big breath to steel and steady, a big breath to flood her mind with the honeyed decadence of upstairs, its delicate wonders, its clean, glowing occupants, their perfect manners and pristine hands, reaching out for her own.

'No, Mrs Hardy, I am not mistaken.'

The housekeeper's black eyes did not blink, and right in their depths Ann saw a thin hand extending out towards her, scooping underneath her, lifting her, weighing her, picking between each tooth, peering down her ears, squeezing and creaking each bone; a butcher's hand judging the quality of a pound of bloody flesh.

'Thank you, Ann.' The hand set her back down. 'This will be duly noted. As will your devotion to Ropner.'

14

THE HARVESTFEAST WAS fast approaching.

Harvestfeast was the axis on which Ropner Hall spun. It was the only event that mattered, and indeed the only event Ropner ever held. The Duchess hosted an exclusive list of the elite; of those deemed worthy because somewhere in the roots of their family trees their ancestors had pillaged and plundered and planted an obscene wealth that their descendants could harvest to afford themselves eternal gorging. To forever grow drunk from dancing with no consequence or care, to constantly stamp on bony fingers with fang-sharp heels and command some poor unfortunate subordinate to lick the red blood from the bottom of their soles.

They say there's a whole orchestra that plays for Harvestfeast, with instruments made of solid gold and bows threaded with real human hair. They say that each year some guests can't return owing to the fact they had eaten themselves to death at the previous. They say that dusky smoke-filled rooms glow with winking red devil eyes while guests puff on cigars stuffed with tobacco and truffle shavings and caviar and all manner of expensive things people don't like for the taste but just for the fact they can boast about buying it. They say that dirty old men cajole the wives of other dirty old men into darkened rooms, designed for discretion, and empty their horrid withered balls and spew out horrid plots of how they will paw at the niece and charm her idiot brain and secure Ropner for their own after that Duchess, who has been a wonderful host it must be said, finally dies and the cremation of her corpse sets off explosions like fireworks owing to all the rich food forever churning in her belly. They say that they all do wicked ritual dancing in that big grand marble hall while they guzzle from silver goblets filled right to the brim with blood so thick it's like jelly.

But of course they *would* say things like that.

Of course they would make up such wicked dirty tales and spout such wicked dirty fiction from grinning slobbering mouths, yammering about their view from the wrong end of a spiteful telescope.

Ann knew they were wrong, by the way. She knew they were only jealous, she knew that everyone at the feast was filled with a goodness, incomprehensible to the likes of stupid, snivelling, crawling servants. She knew that if, on the night of Harvestfeast, she were to hold Ropner up in her mind and cleave it in two like a doll's house she would see the servants below, teeming over one another, like bugs in mud, while suspended above and moving so leisurely in comparison, would be the lords and ladies; proper gentlemen and elegant women swimming languidly through the ballroom like bubbles in honey. Twirling their champagne flutes, twirling each other, twirling golden light shows about the room as their beads and cufflinks caught the candles and gas lamps. There would be ladies in the drawing room too, like half-beached sirens, lazing on the chaises longues and sofas, drowning in nets of jewels and beads and lace, laughing and gaily talking in their siren song. All the colours – the glass greens, timid blues, the sparkling yellows and golds, the humble oranges and fat plum purples – would be like their mermaid fins.

Her Ladie would be there, too, of course. She would be in the centre of it all, in that blue gown from the washroom, with its silver-grey stomacher and skirts frothed like a fountain, and everyone would swim round to admire her in it and fight the urge to kiss her feet.

Ropner Hall enjoyed making time undulate.

In all the same moment Ann was scrubbing at the lines on her hands, and scraping at black tar between the fireplace tiles, and peeling the squeaky green leather skin of apples into spirals before she herself spiralled into bed and the hard mattress gave way to deposit her onto a forgotten shard of white jug that sunk its teeth happily into her skin. The blood it drew dripped into the swelling tide of soapy waters to spin and blossom; splashes of scarlet quickly sedated. Seconds later, the skin that split on the teeth of the jug had thatched and knitted to a hard purple that puckered and wrinkled in the thick white steam of the washroom and from the sweat of plunging and pummelling various articles into large pails and against corrugated washboards. Thirteen turns of the mangle handle, fourteen, fifteen ... Twenty-nine china plates stacked neat and high, thin like the eggshells, most brown and freckled, that coughed out jolly yolks floating on near invisible goo and secreted to a universal yellow with a whisk. Two, three, four eggs were off-white, one was closer to pure white than the others. Bright white. Impossibly white.

White like the shard she had pressed into the earth, the one that had bitten her. Into that earth that was so black and had swallowed the bones of the cadaver and eaten all its meat and spat back up for Ann a twist of cold black metal with square set teeth. The second key slyly winking its secret. When she prised it from the earth it smelt of cold metal, like blood, like freedom, like vomit. Like the vomit splattering into the chamber pot now.

It was too dark for Ann to see but she knew it would be a faecal brown. It smelt coppery and under it her tongue tasted like pebbles. She was making herself sick every night now. It staved off bad dreams. It made her so light-headed that it was easy to fall asleep without thinking or seeing anything. It was sharpening her too, the vomiting. After she was sick, her mind became keener. It stopped scolding itself with nasty pictures and sly retrospects of invented nightmares. It proved more attentive to her duties, protected her with a proud stoicism whenever she had to be near the other servants.

Most happily, her skills in imagination bloomed. She was able to take herself away now, vividly, to the imagined heaven upstairs. She could picture the Ladie in every one of the gowns she had seen in the washroom. She could hear her voice, even have conversations with her. Admittedly, Ann thought self-consciously, they were rudimentary, childish ones. But they were conversations all the same; important to practise so she would be ready as soon as Mrs Hardy gave her the position.

She would peek through the door to the second floor on the servants' stairwell and stare at the central figure of the big painting until her eyes blurred and the painted Ladie lifted her head and smiled and waved at her.

'What did you do today, Ann?' Ladie would ask from the painting.

'I gathered firewood to keep you warm,' she would whisper in reply. 'I baked bread and rolled canapés for you to eat. I mended the tears, the frays, the worn-away parts in your dresses. I scrubbed and scrubbed the kitchen to make sure none of their badness would ever contaminate the things sent up to you. I atoned for my own badness. I thought, I *tried* to think, of you and nothing but you, so that I might feel you were standing by me, at my shoulder, like a guardian angel. Or that each thought of you might appear as a physical entity, again and again and again, filling the entire room, blotting out the rancid, the rotting, the vile and the vulgar.'

'Thank you, Ann,' Ladie would reply, and the second figure, the Duchess, would stand up from her kiss and give a dainty little round of applause, just for Ann. 'Thankyouthankyouthankyou. You are good and clean and noble and pure. You have cleared yourself of any badness, any sin.' Ladie said this on the good days.

On the days Ann was tired, when she could not so easily silence sudden spikes of pain, scorches of flashbacks, Ladie would respond differently. She would tell Ann exactly what Ann herself knew to be true. That she was as bad as the other servants. As vile and as contaminated as the rest of them. That she would never be good or pure enough to be her maid.

What will you do, Petra had said, *when all this badness possesses you?* Ann swallowed back recollections of that impossibly vivid nightmare. Of Scarecrowfootman over her, suffocating her, inside of her. Her hands covered with mud and blood and something black and something sticky and something that was a very sharp white shard she had to pick from her skin.

Perhaps she had died, really. Perhaps she was dead and this was hell.

When she was a hundred moments older, she stood in the kitchens the day of the Harvestfeast to hear Butler's brief.

They looked neat in lines of black and white aprons and skirts, black and white, black and white, hands folded away, chins up, hair scraped, ears pricked, black and white lines behind the chairs tucked under the long table, freshly polished after breakfast. They were all so deceptively clean in front of Mrs Hardy that if Ann squinted she could have almost believed them. They were like a fox she had seen once in the woods. A tiny cub, looking like it was sleeping, lying on its side with its tiny orange tummy breathing in and out, in and out. Only it wasn't sleeping, it was dead, it had been dead a long time, and its tummy wasn't full of air or life, but a load of white maggots teeming and squirming so violently they made the unfortunate little beast look like it was heaving with breath.

They could pretend all they liked, but Ann knew as the day went on, as the meals were prepared and steamed and couriered, sweat would begin to eke out. Sly slugs from hip flasks and leaking music would make them jitter and gyrate, and they would expose their decay and let everything fall into disarray. But for now, they were neatly pressed and starched black and white. The men were there too. On the other side of the table.

Scarecrowfootman was not there, Ann noted. There had been gossip about that too, just like there had been with Petra. About how he had left so suddenly.

'Gone after his bastard baby, I suppose,' they said.

'But without a word of warning?' they whispered.

'Just disappearing into the night like that?'

Ann had swallowed, and nearly choked on bile that coated her throat like thick black mud, and burned like the terrible tearing scream she had been too scared to make while he was atop her. (Don't think about it. A dream. A nightmare. None of it real.)

Butler stood at the head of the long table. He was a crooked old man, quite literally; his entire torso was off kilter owing to a curved spine, so he always leaned precariously to the left. His knees were bowed enough to let through a whole parade of fat-for-the-slaughter pigs, and even his fingers, brittle and white with age, stuck out at anatomy-defying angles. He was fast going deaf, particularly in his right ear. To combat this, he stuffed the respective lughole with tubular tufts of straw, supposedly to channel the sound as an ear trumpet would. Naturally, this only assisted in increasing his deafness twofold. Mrs Hardy usually took it upon herself to make the briefings, morning or otherwise. She only called upon Butler for special occasions such as this. It was a ceremonial gesture, nothing more, because as far as announcements were concerned, he was, quite frankly, useless.

'All here? Right, to business with it. I'll start today with an announcement I have for you,' said Butler. Only it actually came out as '*Ere rait busnezzwiv i'all for announc' a-ave fu ye*'. His broad accent flattened his words to entirely guttural sounds that came directly from his throat, without the shaping provided by his mouth, owing to the fact he was usually as drunk as a fish. Butler let out a hiccup like an arthritic squeak. '*Rai', wo was aye?*' He opened his mouth to continue but seemed to forget what he was about to say, so clapped it shut suddenly.

His brow crumpled like paper and he wobbled dangerously as he turned his head to find Mrs Hardy. He blinked at her, like there wasn't a thought left in his head at all. Mrs Hardy was unfazed. It was almost as if she had been waiting for it, standing as she was right by his left shoulder, counting down the seconds until his marionette strings were due to fray and snap.

'Thank you, Butler,' she said smoothly. She stepped in front of him and addressed the rows of black and white. 'You each know your duty to this house. I request and expect nothing less of you than to perform your duty to the highest standard. Understood? The guests arrive from six o'clock onwards, and the feast will begin at half past the hour of nine to allow the final toast to align with midnight. Now then, *iterum in scaenae alas* – once more to the wings.'

She clapped her hands together and the show began.

15

THE FOOD WAS a cocktease. A dizzying display of gluttony. Hungry eyes all followed the trays that were twirled
up the kitchen stairs and towards the heavens by footmen's
hands. There were parades of warm bread that blew plumes of
yeasty steam, gloating cream cakes adorned with flamboyant
icing in various shades of simpering pastel. Plate after plate of
shining mounds of fruit, armies of wooden sticks standing to
attention and spearing concoctions of golden cheeses and
pineapples. Silver platters were sent away displaying unfurling
hams and salami and chorizo splayed out like a magician's
deck of cards mid-shuffle. Troops of bowls followed one
another from the kitchen; sulphurous eggs steeped in butter,
nightmare-dark caviar that dared to drool over the lip, frosted
drifts of sugared lavender and Turkish delights. And with
great pomp and ceremony, the bronzed and brazen form of
some unlucky beast with various delicacies shoved into its
orifices that required three footmen to carry.

'It's like agony watching it all disappear and not getting so
much as a crumb.'

'Aye, I hope they all get sick from it, start spewing up
everywhere; coughing up their lungs and shitting out their
hearts.'

'Ha! I don't, I'll be the one having to mop it all up.'

'Anything they leave on their plates I'm having, I don't care if they've slobbered all over it.'

'It's torture, isn't it?'

It wasn't torture for Ann though; oh no. It was a wonderful privilege to watch all this food, to feel that raging groaning empty space right inside her, to circle her arms and hands around her middle and thumb the edges of all her ribs. A wonderful, wonderful privilege for all those smells to drip down her throat into that empty clean space in her belly, to remind her that she had abstained, that she had not fed any of the badness inside her by stealing crumbs and nibbles like the rest of them. She instead let herself be made full on happiness; delicious honeyed thoughts of her Ladie and the Duchess and all of their wonderfully good friends eating and enjoying it all.

She shut her mind's eye and pictured all the slow-moving decadence, the glass clinking like diamonds, the fronds of flowers and twisting wreaths snaking along the dining table, snobbish pillars of white candles rising up from the thick linen tablecloth, the chandeliers above, swaying and tinkling with the music. It was like parting milky clouds and peering right into heaven. It was delicious, this cradle of thought, so rich and indulgent and consuming; getting pulled away from it was like a wound.

They had to pull her away from it, of course. They had to ruin it. They ruined everything. One of them had propped open the stairwell door so that the music from the dining room leaked down and they could steal it for themselves. The thieves. The foul bandits. They muddied it with their stamping feet and caterwauling laughs and howls, their rolling eyes and flaring nostrils, their furiously fast dancing, their spinning and stumbling. More of the footmen came back down as course by course was finished; they seized at fabric and squeezed flesh underneath. They were all spinning so fast it was making her light-headed. She didn't feel safe when they were like this; when they were happy. They felt even more dangerous than usual, even more unrestrained and unpredictable, like feral animals. It was impossible to tell what they would do when they were high on happiness like this, when they were there to egg each other on. Ann glanced around, looking for soft, sloping shoulders. But Rachel's stupid, silent silhouette was nowhere to be seen.

She tried to swallow a bitter lump of panic. What if, right now, right as she was stood here buffeted by the lewd uncouth words and moves of the servants, Rachel was in Mrs Hardy's room, listening with an ardent look of triumph in her wet eyes as the housekeeper spoke to her so fondly and told her that there would be no one else more suitable to take Petra's place?

Impossible. She chewed that rancid lump of panic until it was a purée that she swallowed like spit. It was far more likely that Rachel was in Mrs Hardy's room, listening with a crumpled look of shame in her tear-filled eyes, as the housekeeper admonished her ruthlessly. Ann imagined Mrs Hardy beating Rachel into submission with her tongue. More satisfying still was the thought of the housekeeper beating her properly. Actually beating her, with one of her black notebooks, or a poker , Rachel cowering underneath the blows, further and further to the floor until she melted into it and disappeared entirely.

Then Mrs Hardy would come and find her and tell her that she had been chosen. (Of course you have, who would be more perfect?) Ann breathed in sharply; vindictive triumph that was like a blast of fresh air. She should go upstairs and pin a new pinafore to her dress, so that when Mrs Hardy sought her out she would be presentable and perfect for the occasion of her promotion.

Ann rounded the first turn in the servants' stairs and nearly fell back down with shock. There, sitting right on the step of the green baize door, was a woman crying.

A lady.

Ann would have taken her as a ghost, and blacked out or died from fear, if she hadn't been so solid, so colourful, so . . . beautiful. She could have only been a ghost if ghosts were made of bygone sunrays instead of dust and malice; Ann had never seen something so breathtaking in her whole entire life. It was impossible to breathe. Oh God, this woman was choking her. Her presence was tightening round her neck like a belt and blocking her windpipe. Her vision was going so blurry, that all the thousands of jewels in the woman's hair and on her gown and pressed on her eyelids and falling down her cheeks onto her lap were shining in streaks of light. The way stars do when the night is very dark and you squint at them very hard until your eyes are almost shut. This woman's silk-gloved hands, long and soft and elegant, were choking her. This woman's thickly coiled hair was wrapping around her neck and stopping her from breathing. This woman's pristine skin, her squashy, curved, fuzzed skin, was filling Ann's mouth and nose to completely block them off.

What a wonderful way to die. To suffocate from something so completely wonderful. With sleepy, dying eyes, Ann slowly realised what the woman was wearing.

It was the gown.

The blue gown, her favourite, the one she had spent hours, possibly decades, of her life washing and wringing and mending. But it was only now that Ann saw that the dressmaker must have prised a piece of the current from the river outside and sewn its steely shape together with a sharp edge of the sky to make it. Because how else would the colour be just so? How else would the skirts ripple and cascade and foam at the hem? How else would the pearl-grey stitching meander so serenely over the bodice and belly?

And now there was a body, a person, a woman, in it. Under the folds of the skirts footsteps pattered, ones that were light and soft and that could dawdle and race on command. And beneath the bodice was a heart that beat and pumped and swelled next to lungs that could be left breathless from a laugh or a sob. There was a body, a person, a woman that shaped the dress, pulled the fabric taut so its silk shone with each breath; supported the skirts so they cascaded to the floor and swirled like currents. The dress was filled with life.

So you see, the woman couldn't have possibly been a ghost, because she was so beautiful and alive. She couldn't have possibly been a ghost because she was more like an angel, actually. She couldn't have possibly been a ghost because ghosts can't speak anyway, their tongues are glued to their mouths so they can only moan and scream and rattle from their throats.

But this woman spoke. Quite suddenly she became aware of Ann's watching. She looked up and stared straight at her through the iron spokes of the banister and said, 'Oh! You frightened me.'

She sniffed. Her voice was thick with fluid, and her eyes were every gentle shade of grey Ann had ever seen.

With horrific embarrassment, Ann realised she had been standing and staring open-mouthed. Her tongue felt very wet against her little bottom teeth and the back of her throat was all crackled with dry air. She tried to swallow and it made a wet little frog-like sound. She wanted to die.

'Sorry, my lady, I . . . I . . .' Ann baulked and made to step back down to the depths of the kitchen.

'It's quite all right.' The lady sniffed again. 'I probably gave you a turn sitting here all forlorn like this.'

Her skirts were puffed oddly around her; she looked like a nesting hen, and so impossibly tragic and lonely Ann wanted to cry. Or fling herself to the floor in sympathy and kiss those pointed pearl-encrusted shoes. There were pearls in her hair too, jammed in at every angle like fairy teeth. Teeny-tiny strands of hair had come loose, and they caught the evasive light of the candles and glowed orange and iridescent, feigning that they were on fire; it gave her a kind of mischievously molten halo that you would miss entirely if you weren't looking for it. But Ann was looking for it, because she was sure, beyond belief, that the woman sitting in front of her was her Ladie. Sitting right there as if she had stepped out of that big painting on the second floor, dusted paint chippings from her shoulders and come right here to sit and wait for Ann.

Perhaps she was only imagining it. Perhaps all those conversations she had conducted in her head and under her breath had manifested into an incredibly realistic hallucination. But Ann knew that was impossible, because she could never have imagined something, someone, so beautiful. Never.

This was the moment she had been rehearsing for. This was her chance.

'Yes, you did, my lady.' Why was her voice coming out so quiet? This stupid piddly whisper that hoarsed and croaked as if she had only just clawed her voice back from some terrible curse that had been rendering her mute for years and years. 'I should say M-Mrs Hardy should not like to find you here.'

The moment swung between them, thick and pendulous, weighted by the wait for the other to speak. Me or you? Me or you? Tick-tock, tick-tock, like a clock.

Her Ladie's mouth was open slightly from the sobbing, in a perfect pitiful O, and Ann imagined strolling into it, into the soft pink, looking up at the cavernous red roof, that was sloping and ribbed like the inside of a whale's belly; she imagined counting all those shiny teeth slick with spit and so well-tended that none of the gums had nests of black or jammy gaps and even the far back teeth were only the palest yellow. Ann tried to smile at Ladie apologetically, comfortingly, but she must have done it wrong because Ladie shivered in the stairs' dankness.

'Yes, you're right, I . . .' Salty water crept back into her voice so that it cracked under the briny sting. 'It was the only place I could think to come –' the tide was swelling – 'to come away from it all. All the beastly . . .' The waves broke into crashing wails and its foam spat salt spray onto her face. The stairway echoed out the sobs like a seashell does the sea.

Ann watched her crying, motionless. Of course she had messed it up, of course she had. *You stupid girl, Ann, you stupid girl.* How could she possibly win the favour of a lady when she'd been downstairs with *them* for so long? (They've all rubbed off on you, she can smell it on you, she wants nothing but to be far, far away from you, see how she's crying, see what you've done.) *No, no, no, all I want is for her to like me,* she thought. *I want her to love me. I want her to look at me, to let that make her crying stop, and to look at my heart that is so red and shiny and good, and say, 'I love you.'*

The thought was pounding out like a drum (*like me like me like me*), like the rhythmic plucking of daisy petals (*please like me please like me please*). She was being half chewed and swallowed whole by this wild desperation, she was festering in the pit of its stomach, dissolving slowly in its acid. But what did she care if she was eaten to death? All that mattered was that Ladie should like her. All she wanted was that in this moment Ladie should like her and think her pleasant and good and clean and proper and worthy of her love.

Emboldened by this desperation, Ann hurried towards her, pulling at the handkerchief tucked to her wrist. 'Here, shhh, here now.'

The kerchief had all kinds of colours of dirt on it; sweat and blood and mud and food, things a lady never should see. She ripped it so the whitest bit was isolated and handed this part to her Ladie. 'Here, my lady.'

'Thank you.' She took the handkerchief. 'How kind.' She did not bring it to her face but scrunched it further in her gloved hand. 'I'm sorry, I rather hoped no one would find me like this. I must look in an awful state.' She peered at Ann pointedly through her lashes.

'No! Not at all.'

The Ladie looked at her expectantly. Ann faltered; her imagined conversations had never gone this far before.

'Your dress . . .' she continued shakily. 'It is the most beautiful I have ever seen, it . . . it looks like a piece – a piece of the river outside.'

Ladie seemed to sit up straighter, and even her skin seemed to suddenly resolve to glow a little brighter.

'Yes, it rather is like the river, isn't it! That's why I picked it from the others; you ought to see it in the candlelight; everyone was staring.'

'Oh, my lady! I can imagine! And all those pretty jewels in your hair too, they look so beautiful.' Ann was a miserable bag of bones in comparison, she was scrawny and ugly, and she would splinter away at the slightest gust of wind, she had that little pitiful life in her. But she was happy to exist as something horrid, as Ladie's ugly antonym, if it brought Ladie joy, if it let her see how glorious she herself was, how healthy and vibrant and full of rich colourful life.

'Wonderful jewels, aren't they? But oh! My hair must have fallen out by now surely.'

'No, not at all! Well, just a strand here . . . Let me.'

Ann's hands moved in quick darts, re-threading the stray hairs through pins and weaving jewels back into formation. Her heart was wringing itself very hard, so all of its liquid made her skin burn red. What was she doing, touching a lady, her Ladie, like this, without permission, without restraint? She was going to be fired away from Ropner on a bolt of lightning, straight into hell where she'd sizzle lonely and unloved forever. Such brash daring was only worthy of such damnation.

'You're much gentler than Mrs Hardy, I have to say,' Ladie said. 'I hope she finds a replacement for the last girl soon.'

How stupid she was to have thought this would damn her, when it was the moment she had been waiting for all along. A chance to prove herself, to show that there was no place for her in the bowels of Ropner, crawling like a beetle in the undergrowth, to prove that she belonged with Ladie, in all the light and purity and goodness, to show Ladie that she *needed* her.

She stepped back and tried very hard not to tremble, which wasn't easy, not when she was stood so very close to the edge of something very grand and very tall, on the brink of falling or flying into a world of unknown perfection.

Ann gave a small curtsy but kept her head bowed low; she wobbled only slightly. There was a rustle of a dress as Ladie stood and her heart thrummed out: *Ladieladieladie.*

'That will be all.' And that, that moment on the stairwell, that pocket of a moment, is when everything changed.

16

THE COAL SHED was so cold that Ann's entire body had stiffened and the skin of her face was pulling so tight that any moment her bones would surely crack it. The shovel was brass, and underneath the black dust it showed something warped that resembled her face.

She shoved it hard into the mound of coal.

All she wanted to do, all she wanted to think about, was Ladie, her Ladie. Her Ladie on the stairs, smiling and crying and looking right at her, right into her. The memory of it was so tantalising, so delicious, she wanted to bite into it, to shove it all in and masticate like an animal. God, it was driving her mad, all this yearning, this retrospective pining and dreaming and aching. It was agony, this aching, practically toe-curling, so practically toe-curling that she had to check her toenails hadn't fallen off.

One more day of that and she would pull them off herself. Or maybe she would just eat herself. Put herself out of this misery, the misery of this likely invented memory. But when she bared her teeth to bite down onto the bones of her wrist she found them squeaking against the torn fabric still tucked into the sleeve of her dress – her half of the handkerchief – and the sheer wonder of the interaction consumed her once more.

All through the sweat and stone and splitting skin, Ann thought of the kerchief's sister; of Ladie pressing her own scrumpled piece delicately to her eyes. While Ann bent and scrubbed at the shit and spit and smatterings of spilt stew, she imagined Ladie patting that soft white leaf to the neat little corners of her mouth to catch any stray smears of food (that of course would never be there because she even ate so good and neat and proper).

When Ann's arms burned, stomach groaned, blisters bubbled and burst, while the bones in her knees creaked and cracked, Ann thought of Ladie holding that scrap of hand-kerchief. She thought of those delicate gloves, those grey eyes, the unblemished skin. The absence of rotting insides really made people so perfect, didn't it? (If you weren't stuck down here breathing in all the rot, you could be perfect too. You *know* it.)

When would Mrs Hardy tell her, God dammit? Surely Ladie had spoken to her by now, told her of their encounter, told her how wonderful Ann had been; surely they had both agreed there was no one better, and that Ann should be granted the position immediately. So why was she still down here? (Maybe, maybe, Mrs Hardy has found out about Scarecrowfootman.)

Ann shook her head; found out what? It was nothing more than a nightmare. So then, what if Ladie had not found her wonderful and perfect? (Impossible.) What if Ladie had seen her for what she really was: an ugly, scrawny servant who lay in the dark without sleeping, and at any given moment was thumbing at scars inside her throat? Who was scared of ivory white shards, and who kept scrubbing at invisible blood and mud under her nails? Whose life was so splintered she herself struggled to make sense of it, struggled to hold on to it and arrange it into something that didn't constrict her whole chest and rob her breath?

Ann thrust the shovel once more into the mound of coal and quite without warning her arm froze. She was completely unable to draw it back, unable to pull the shovel out from the pile, because without knowing how, she was unshakably certain that there was a corpse buried underneath.

I will pretend I can't see it, she thought. *I will pretend that it's not there and that I can't see so much as a straw-like hair on its head.* But even the voice in her mind trembled and her arm stayed frozen.

She could not move it. She could not take the chance that she might reveal the blood-covered body (sticky and lumpy and peppered with white shards like tiny bones) that had extracted itself from the mud to follow her, to surprise her here. She would have to remain frozen like this for eternity.

She imagined flakes of black ash falling from the ugly ceiling of the coal shed. Tiny drifts of coal catching in her hair, clogging the hollows of her collarbones, her elbows, her palms, her knees. (Skin dark and wet, hair matted around deep gashes – Don't see it, don't see it.) The snowing coal dust was sticking to her eyelashes, too heavy to be kept from falling into her eyes. It was *stinging*. (A bluebottle twitching on the pink shell of one ear, gelatinous blood oozing slowly . . . Don't!) The coal had fallen so fast it was all around her, squeaking like chalk, filling her nose and her mouth and her eyes so everything was black black black like that soft black mud. (Don't!) That soft black mud that was still under her fingernails. She was going to be buried with the worms and the leaves and the secret bones, buried along with the—

'Ann?'

The blackness vanished and the corpse under the coals twitched. Mrs Hardy had slunk from nowhere, and now she stood right in the doorway of the coal shed. The grey light from outside streamed so fast from behind her, her face was entirely disguised by shadows.

Ann let go of the shovel handle and stood sharply to attention. The shovel stayed speared into the pile of black boulders, mercifully concealing the corpse from view.

The whites of Mrs Hardy's eyes had transformed to a dark grey, almost black, rendering them deep pits impossible to discern anything from.

Ann's absence of voice choked her. Suppose those black eyes had seen her on the stairs with Ladie. Suppose Ladie had reported Ann speaking out of place and those black eyes had narrowed in fury, steeled with the readiness to send Ann away from Ropner, reeling away from the world into nothingness. The black eyes blinked and the lips below parted to bear those sharp teeth, too many to count. Ann's neck prickled at the notion of feeling them pierce skin. But with a shock, she realised that the teeth were, in fact, bearing a smile.

'You are required upstairs, Ann.' Mrs Hardy spoke, still smiling. Alarmingly, her tone was genial, like she was disclosing a specially exciting secret in the way one would confide in a friend. That familiar sharp thrill pierced the length of Ann's back and her skin tingled all over.

'Lady Charlotte has requested your services.'

17

Mrs Hardy's black skirts rustled and hissed over her silent steps as she walked. Ann followed at a respectable distance, trying to keep her head bowed, her eyes trained on the hem of the housekeeper's dark skirts, but it was impossible, there was too much to take in.

The corridors upstairs were very long and highly polished. All the colours – in the lacquered wallpaper, in the thick tongues of carpets, in the flashes of wood – were deep and dark. Scowling reds, austere purples, and heavy golds. It was hideously ostentatious and Ann drank it in, because any second now she would wake up, she would wake up and realise that it wasn't nerves or anticipation that was making her stomach crackle and heart pump so fast it was filling her head with hot steam, but a fever she was suffering from. One that had sent her spiralling into some madly delicious dream where she was walking upstairs, through the very same corridors as her Ladie, when in actuality she was tossing and turning between drenched sheets.

Yes, she was locked in some fever dream, she had to be. Though those clean citrus smells of potpourri cut through so sharply it felt real. No, it was a dream, surely. And in this dream all the doors along the corridor were shut, but their handles were molten gold and shining. They pressed the lips of their doors tightly together, hiding their innards from her. Paintings and hangings lined the walls. They whispered of false lands beyond Ropner; pretend habitats of gloating white houses, of terracotta streets with gloomy donkeys, of garden gates choked with flowers, of burnished ochre deserts, of screaming blue lakes so tranquil you could see right down to their stones.

There were none of Ropner's dark moors and stinging weather and miserable churned earth. Nothing of all Ann knew to exist. She began to feel woozy and leaden. It hurt her head and the soles of her feet itched to think of places beyond Ropner. To her it was a discernible fact that only Ropner existed. Anything beyond its grounds was non-existent.

She thought of Petra dismissed into that nothingness. She thought of Scarecrowfootman who would never step foot in Ropner again. Something little and dark and hard inside her laughed, and as soon as it did a half-rotting corpse began to follow her along the corridor. It peered at her from behind the thick curtains, its decaying limbs trailed and thumped along the carpet, and its hideous half-gone face wobbled and withered along each curve of the door handles. Its straw-like hair was dirtied with clumps of mud and its rattling breath fogged the windowpanes as it whistled out between the gaps in its teeth.

Mrs Hardy seemed unperturbed.

Go away, Ann thought, as hard and furiously as she could. *Goawaygoawaygoaway.* But it was stubborn and it would not. She saw huge eyes staring at her from the end of the corridor and would have screamed out loud if she hadn't realised they were the eyes of a painting and not those of the bulging, horrible corpse.

The painting at the end of the corridor was large and dark and one Ann had spied countless times, but had never really seen, no, not like this.

Up close, the big painting revealed its full and unadulterated spectacle; up close, there were dark green fig leaves and burgundy cuckoo birds embossing the painted wallpaper, there were rubies as round and shocking as welling blood studding the fingers of the Duchess, there were dried flowers and their skeletal leaves scattered at the feet of Ladie, and the armchair she sat in was a soft, plush velvet that was surely tangible. The detail stretched even as far as the painting within the painting; there, at some of Ropner's windows, were tiny little silhouettes looking out.

But Ann had eyes only for the central figure; the lady with her head bowed and her eyes looking dead ahead, looking impossibly, but surely, right at Ann. It couldn't be that this figure was made from paint; there was something so alive about her – the strands of her hair, the slight openness of her lips inhaling and exhaling, the intensity of that gaze and its mercurial emotions.

It was the most wonderful thing Ann had seen.

'Lady Charlotte with the Duchess,' Mrs Hardy informed her, following her gaze.

Ann wanted to cry. She wanted to fall to her knees and kiss the floor beneath the frame. Her heart was swelling so big it was warming up all her insides, and she knew at that moment she wasn't dreaming: never in her wildest dreams could she have imagined something as beautiful as this.

Lady Charlotte and the Duchess, there before her in all of their glamour and glory. In her wet-eyed entrancement, Ann failed once again to notice the third figure.

After allowing her a moment, the housekeeper continued to walk down the corridor, and Ann, as quiet, content and obedient as a little lamb, followed.

18

L ADY CHARLOTTE WAS sat very erect at her dresser, which had on it a mirror that was actually three mirrors fanned out to scoop her in an embrace. The room seemed dark even though it was not yet midday, but the corner she occupied was very light, as if the mirror were reflecting the white-yellow of the sun. She faced her three faces, her eyes flicking between them while she brushed her hair; as though she were trying to catch one of them out for being too slow, or not mirroring her properly, or for not really being a reflection at all. When she turned to see Ann enter, the three other Ladies turned their bright heads too.

Ann had summoned the memory of the stairwell so often that it had grown smooth and flat, like a worn penny; her mind had been unable to hold the volume of Ladie's beauty. Seeing her again now was so overwhelming, it was like seeing her for the first time. There was no recreation of Ladie's beauty that would do it justice, no mind, no memory, no words, no painting.

In fact, Ann was startled by how little Ladie looked like her portrait in the big painting that hung in the corridor. She saw now that the painting was a gross insult in its attempt at creating Ladie's likeness, it had come nowhere close. The painting was aloof and dead. Here, the girl it pictured was very much alive. She sat straight and attentive, her body sloping and curving in a way that was rich and full and decadent and glorious. Her face was open and alert with buoyant cheeks and grey eyes that looked right at you. From far away, Ann heard Mrs Hardy introduce her to Ladie, and regale pragmatically that Ann would be unlikely to disappoint her standards. Ann wondered if she should speak; explain how suddenly she was struck by the thought that she would rather cut her heart out at its seams than fail to impress the mistress at the mirror. But Mrs Hardy brushed the silence aside like a cobweb as quickly as it had been spun.

'Your bath now if you please, Lady Charlotte.'

In the bathing room Ladie revealed her body with the kind of effortless pride Ann would expect of a fairy queen. Her naked body was not sharp and abhorrent and ugly; the plump softness of her skin, the tenderness of it, covered any notion of bone or sinew so lushly that she didn't really seem naked at all. She allowed her nightgown to slip fluidly to the floor, and Ann expected, at any moment, for her to vanquish Mrs Hardy into an oily black puddle with a mere flick of one hand, and to summon tiny pixies in her wake with the other. To stand godlike as the bright little things pressed petals into skirts and wove beads of dew into necklaces. Such fantasies seemed capable of existing upstairs in Ladie's proximity. The air around her seemed to weather its own climate, an early morning haze weaving opaquely through her soft hairs that stood to salute the coldness of the bathroom. It rendered delicate and wonderful magic a possibility.

Ann bundled up the soft dough of the nightgown. It was crisp and clean, but the traces of Ladie's warmth that clung to it brought to Ann's mind hot, sticky figs. She held it to her chest like a bairn for as long as she dared before Mrs Hardy's curt nod commanded it into the wicker basket. It dropped soundlessly, like a ghost. Ann held its scent in her breath while she stood neatly, watching but not watching, not looking but looking, as Ladie stepped into the bathwater.

Ann was ashamed to stare, to even glance, but she could not help herself. She stared at the smooth unbroken lines and curves of Ladie's body. Her eyes furtively sought after a dark smiling groove like her own and found it brazenly there, unabashedly detailing the origins of the world. Its thick curve, its unforgiving deepness, refuted vulnerability and refused the unconscious shame Ann's own inspired. (Why should it not? Ladie's are not soiled and spoiled.)

While she bathed, Ladie's ceaseless chatter filled the room like music. She spoke dreamily, watching the water ripple over her skin, her voice ebbing and flowing in unison with its lapping waves.

Ann could hardly hear; Ladie's words were immediately absorbed into the atmosphere that framed her. They turned into a soothing hum of white noise, a distant heartbeat vibrating through barricades of skin and bone. They thickened all the air and turned it to amber, so everything seemed to move in slow motion: the milky water cobwebbing her skin, the floating tendrils of hair, her laugh – that laugh, that laugh, that laugh, ethereal like gold and homely like warm wood. It bounced from wall to wall, extended luxuriously by the slow, sticky fossilisation of time. It all hurt so fantastically, so wonderfully, that Ann wished she could be granted the release of crying. That would be the only way to rightfully worship something like this.

Only the dull horror of Mrs Hardy touching Ladie's skin marred the tableau. It sickened Ann to watch the housekeeper sponge her shoulders, lifting the hairs on the nape of her neck away from wetness with a tenderness Ann never expected her to be capable of. There was a vulgar greed that glinted in Mrs Hardy's eyes as she did it. Even blacker than her pupils.

Ann watched it with a horrified fascination. The housekeeper's scuttling fingers, her sharp darting eyes, were like the ominous threat of scraping violins, dementedly screeching under an orchestration of the softest woodwind, breaking through like shattered glass to let in howling winds of terror. She was overcome by the urge to seize one of the shards and pierce the blackness in each of Mrs Hardy's eyes, to saw at each hand until they thumped to the floor and she was left with nothing but bloody stumps, incapable of ever caressing Ladie's skin again. The hairs on Ann's arm prickled and her nipples hardened as if scowling from cold. She shivered uncomfortably.

Ann held out the towel and Ladie, dripping and distracted by her own ever-spinning tongue, stepped into it. She was unbelievably close, so unbelievably close Ann could feel the warmth coming off her, as if the sun had seen her stood in the snow and cracked open the clouds to offer her a peek at one of its rays. She could smell figs, sticky and sweet. She became suddenly, terribly aware of the memory of their first meeting and found she could no longer look at Ladie.

'Forgive my horrid hands,' Ladie said, obliterating her own nakedness with deft folds of the towel. 'So dry and cracked, not at all becoming for a lady.'

Ann braved a glance. Ladie's hands were lined and the milky eyes of old calluses blinked from between them. They were a little like her own, Ann thought.

Ladie smiled, and all at once, everything was so wonderfully perfect.

It seemed Ladie was never not smiling. She smiled as she dressed in rich colours – humble oranges and browns, goldened ochres and baked berry-reds. She smiled as she sat expectantly, back on her little dressing stool, slipping on silken gloves and waiting for Ann to at last tend to her hair.

Mrs Hardy issued a stiff, curt nod and Ann gave a quick, neat, curtsy and rushed to Ladie's side as if to demonstrate her willingness to succeed. Mrs Hardy slunk into the shadows by the door and the room shrunk so that it was only the size of the dresser, Ladie's stool, and the little square of carpet for Ann's feet.

She began at once, parting the hair into thick sections and very carefully weaving them together, just as she had practised. With each twist and loop, Ann questioned fervently whether or not she should say something.

The moment on the stairs seemed a lifetime ago now, and it was almost embarrassing to think of it in Ladie's presence and under those pressing black eyes that watched somewhere from the darkness. How much she had talked, without permission, how familiar, how tactile she had been. God, she had even given her that repulsive handkerchief.

She wanted desperately to make it up to Ladie, to leave some kind of impression that she, Ann, was worthy of attention and affection and praise. Or at least prove she was very kind, very clean, very good, very obedient. The more she thought of it, the more her hands felt light and loose, like they were becoming slowly detached from her body. They shook and dropped a loop of hair. The darkness held its breath and grew more solid around her. Ann forced her mind back down to steady her hands.

Over, under, twist, over, under, pin.

It had to be perfect.

Over, under, through and pin.

The room was very quiet.

Twist.

The room was very quiet but for the clock ticking and the clink of metal on glass as Ann picked and dropped pins from their glass dish. It seemed there was a grave bass underscoring each tick, so low it was almost impossible to hear, but it was there, threatening like unchartered waters, blacker and vaster than night, watching for something exposed and alone, waiting to swallow it whole.

Through, over, under, pin.

Ann, slowly and surely, without seeing, became very conscious that all six of Lady Charlotte's grey eyes were staring at her through the three-faced mirror.

She felt like a pinprick, one that you barely notice at first, but that, without warning, wells with a big fat drop of blood so that you can't help stare at how stark the red looks on your skin.

'I've just realised,' Ladie said suddenly. 'How silly of me! I don't even know your name.' Dignified purple crescents curved under all six eyes and each blink seemed like a little smile.

'My name?' Ann whispered.

Ladie nodded encouragingly.

'My name is Ann, Lady Charlotte.'

Over, through, twist, pin.

Ladie's smile remained as sweetly encouraging as ever. 'Is Ann short for anything?'

Over, under, pin.

'No, Lady Charlotte, just Ann.' It was an ugly name, she thought, An *e* looped neatly on the end would have been more becoming, made it seem more elegant. But Ann abandoned of an *e* was like a grunt, or like that dark green space between leaves in undergrowth where you know the earth is lurking but can't quite see it.

Over, under, pin.

'Just Ladie is enough, Ann.'

The word suited her perfectly, it was fussy and fine and delicate and effervescent; pink sugar frosting that laced the lip of a fluted glass. If the tiniest fragment of that would rub off onto Ann there would surely be so much more colour in her life.

The dusty curtain of silence had fallen heavily again.

Through, twist, over, under.

Ladie's scalp was so pale that her hair follicles, all hundreds and thousands of them, looked very dark; like little fleas crawling amongst ashes, like how the bits of dark mud looked flecked on that smooth ceramic jug. The floor shifted ever so slightly and Ann knew it was threatening to tip up and spew her into that shallow grave where she would lie broken and dismembered with the cadaver and those sharp skull-like shards.

But then Ladie, sweet Ladie, spoke. The floor obediently righted itself, and there she was, still standing at Ladie's side with her hands, that were mercifully and firmly attached to her arms and her body, in her Ladie's hair. The trenches of partings mapped out the surface of her skull: smooth and clean and solid. Ann fought the urge to trace them with her tongue.

'I ought to apologise for my humour the other day,' Ladie said, at a whisper. 'It was rather silly of me, but the feast was tiring me so, and all the people there were so beastly you can't even imagine.' She lowered her voice further still, and Ann felt the darkness press all around, leaning in to listen. 'Sometimes I rather feel they are all laughing at some grand joke that I don't understand, or that everyone has been told apart from me.'

Ann swallowed a little gasp in her throat and a warm prickling rushed up her spine. *I understand*, she wanted to whisper. *I UNDERSTAND*, she wanted to scream. *I know about being laughed at so cruelly, laughed at until you feel so stupid and confused you can't even speak. You're not alone, Ladie*, she wanted to scream. (You're not alone, Ann!)

Over, under. (You're not alone!)

It was nearly finished.

Twist and pin. (But it couldn't be, not yet, not *now*.)

'I keep thinking once I get older I'll understand,' Ladie continued. 'But I somehow don't even think that's true. It's as though I'll just be stuck how I am forever, at odds with all the frivolities. Like this damn calf lick here, can you see?' Ladie lurched forward quite suddenly, with a little laugh, to paw at the loop of hair pressed firmly to her scalp and growing in defiance towards her crown. 'It does always ruin my hair something awful, I quite hate it for behaving like that.' The Ladies in the mirror frowned at the upturned strands.

'Sorry to have missed it, Ladie, it's really no problem. Here, let me . . .'

Twist and pull, under and pin.

'Oh! Oh! What a marvellous little creature you are, Ann!' The heads turned back and forth like the slow winking of a butterfly's wings. 'It must only be you to do my hair from now on, no one else, I won't allow it. You make for a marvellous conversation too – like a little sponge, I feel like you've soaked all my worries from me. Now, do be a cherry on top and tell me how I look.'

Truthfully, Ann had never seen anything so radiant. But it was hard to translate what she saw into phrases equally as shiny. Her language was clunky and heavy-handed, words fell doughy and dull out of her mouth. She tried her best, but such simple words felt insufficient. How could you do a face like that justice when all you knew how to say was it looks nice and neat, but all you could think was how much you would long to look in a mirror and see that very same face looking out at you? It was like describing the moon merely as being white; it would not be wrong, but it would be so far from the entire truth.

Still she tried, and at each attempt Ladie clapped her little gloved hands appreciatively and held them to her smile as if Ann were the brightest little smudge-faced child in her class. Ann took the moment and swallowed it like it was a hot pip. It nestled comfortably in her belly and her mind made it bloom.

Branches sprouted and leaves unfurled each pre-luncheon visit: Ann learned that Ladie liked her tea lukewarm and hated early mornings. The trunk thickened with bark and became broad: she learned that Ladie was never to be without a pair of her ice cream-coloured silk gloves, that Ladie smelt like fresh sheets and hot figs and a tiny twist of lavender. Roots deepened: Ladie liked cards; Ladie hated red wine and the way it stained her teeth black; Ladie liked her parting slightly to the left. The seed had grown so much that fig-like fruits unfurled from vines with rich plops and nestled amongst crooked leaves: Ladie liked the plaits that had their insides out so that they looked embossed onto her scalp, and every time she pinned her hair Ann wondered if she could push the pins right through her fingers into Ladie's curls so that she would be fixed to her, joined at every seam like a shadow.

19

ANN PRACTISED BRAIDING on herself every night, in the dark, in her room, twisting her own hair tight until she got it right. So tight that strands smarted and snapped and pulled tiny pieces of her scalp with them. The blood sometimes made her fingers sticky and her skull screamed out. (So what? They need to be perfect.) She went down to breakfast each morning with black blood, like tiny little seeds, crusting the curling roots of her perfectly perfect plaits. It made her sit straighter, as if her plaits were attached in some way to the ceiling, or they were being drawn by some magnetic force to their sisters, twisting in Ladie's hair up above. Or maybe it was pride making her sit straighter now, knowledge that all the beastly others would know she was better than them.

She still hated them (they justified it with their revolting slavering, their hideous faces, their vile language, their common tongues, their rotting, curdling insides) but she tried to look down on them in a martyrish way, the way saints look at the peasants kissing their stained-glass feet (pity and disgust thinly masked as love and benevolence). Because one day, perhaps soon, she would come down for breakfast and all of them – Cook and Old Crone and Matchstick and whatever ghastly beast had taken Petra's place – would all turn their ugly little faces towards her and smile genuine, albeit gruesome-looking, smiles and chorus, 'Good morning, Ann.' And they would watch her, eyes brimming with adoration, as she graciously took her seat and looked down at the food they had laid out for her. It would be food she could nibble on contentedly without ever having to worry about it infecting her like them, weighing her down and nudging all her sharp corners into overbaked blubber.

Clean, nice food like the food Ladie had; dollops of bramble jam with seeds in, and salty anchovies laid out in a can-can line, a mug of hot milk. They would let her spread her napkin and their mouths would be sagging open a bit in awe (because she was so neat and dainty at doing things like that) and one of them would say, 'Let us all bow our heads and give thanks for our adored Ann, give thanks for how lucky we are to have her in our presence. Our adored Ann, whom we have always taken for granted these years because we have been so wicked and short-sighted, and are so deeply sorry for it we would gladly slit our throats if she ever would ask.' (Maybe she *would* ask once she finished her hot milk.) 'Our adored Ann, who is so good that now she is able to spend time with our fine lady and tend to her hair and tend to the wonderful rooms in that special golden place upstairs. Thanksthanksthanks.'

It was true, Ann had been granted the honour of cleaning upstairs now, which meant her breakfast time with them was often cut mercifully short. Thank God, because sometimes she heard that rattling phlegmy sound that meant the corpse from the corridor had sat its half-rotten self down at the table, too, and was— (Stop it!)

All the rooms upstairs were like wedding cakes and Ann loved them to the point of blushing. Each day she walked about them, she kept her breathing shallow and light, trying hard not to disturb any of the magic of the glossy plants that dripped like chandeliers and snaked haughtily from finely scalloped pots; of the piped-icing skirting boards and window ledges; of the jigsaw-piece paintings strewn right up the walls towards the teetering ceilings; of the furniture and ornaments so serene and delicate they seemed to hold their own breaths too, waiting patiently to be released from the spell cast upon them. The spell that stopped the china ladies from twirling their ceramic dresses, that stopped the foot-stools from yapping about the room on their stubby golden legs, and stopped the chaises longues from unfurling like tongues to loll comfortably on the cloudy carpets at last.

The corpse never seemed to follow her about there as much. Although sometimes, if she was dusting that little milkmaid ornament that decorated the mantelpiece of the music room (which was painted a bright light blue to make you feel like you'd stepped out of the cut-out corner of a cotton ball cloud languishing in the sky); if she was dusting that little milkmaid, say, that little milkmaid with her yodel-ling mouth and hard, white milk jug hugged to her breasts, she would come over far too hot, as fast as a rash, with beads of sweat popping up on her forehead, and she would know, sickeningly, that the benign lump in the curtains was actu-ally covering a body. She would know that if she looked over at the curtains and their conspicuous lump, she would see turned-in feet sticking out the bottom, with one ankle chewed entirely to the bone. Ann made a little note to one day pluck up the courage to put that little milkmaid and her jug, however innocent and lovely she might be, under the ash in the fireplace.

She usually lost the corpse in the library, where she was able to dust thick brown books in peace, and wonder, undisturbed, which of the golden titles Ladie had read. She polished the windows perfectly alone, squeaking cloths over the glass only after she had pressed her face greedily to every one to see Ropner through Ladie's eyes. By the time she reached the second floor it stopped following her, by the time she reached the corridor and the big painting in it, by the time she stood and stared at the portrait of Ladie for as long as she dared, she stopped thinking about the corpse entirely.

It sometimes found her again in the drawing room. It was always darker in there, and the soft low throbs of the grandfather clock summoned its rasping breaths. (Unthink it, dammit.) The metallic squeaks and sputters of the gas lamps alluded to rattling handles, to scraping wood, to black mud and— (Shut *up*!)

Solitude was to be found in the entrance hall, that cold austere room made entirely of marble, so open and empty and well-lit there was nowhere to hide for anyone, half rotting or otherwise. The only decorations were intervals of solemn statues standing along each wall. She imagined Ladie looking at them all, and tried to think which one might be her favourite. She decided it would be the one poised next to the doors of the dining room. It was head and shoulders taller than Ann, a twisted woman, forced into a state of half-undress by invisible marble wind. Scraps of a dress covered her modesty but plump shoulders and legs were left unprotected, tantalisingly bare. Thighs rose so high that, under the thin scrap of fabric, Ann could see where they met like in the crook of a Y. She wondered if there were milky folds of marble flesh under the fabric too. (Dirty to wonder about that.) Ann wanted to peel back the fabric and see if they looked like hers, to make sure hers weren't wrong in some way, especially after all that blood on the mattress from that night, all that black-brown— (Shush!)

The marble woman had no hands to peel back the fabric and show Ann herself; they had been snapped off at the wrists either by design or some long-forgotten accident. A few rabbits with hollow little eyes surrounded her feet, standing to attention or nibbling at a basket of spilling fruit; marble figs and grapes and cherries. The inscription on the statue's base named her Hermia.

Hermia, Ann whispered. *Hermiahermiahermia.*

She whispered it again and again and again and again with each brush of her duster, like a spell.

Its magic summoned her ever more to Ladie's side, to weave plaits into her hair, to sit with her while she embroidered or read, to stand by and smile encouragingly while Mrs Hardy prepared her for luncheon, to walk with her along the path that traced the outline of Ropner Hall, in an outside the magic had rendered as glorious and crisp and fresh as an apple.

Months sprawled out into infinite days or ordered themselves into delicate bite-sized rows that dissolved the second they touched a tongue, hour after endless hour snaked into a perfect circle so that everything that had passed, no matter how quick the month or how infinite the second, came back around to pass again. Ladie spent hours talking, Ann spent eternity listening. Everything was wonderful.

She made herself sick less often now. Nights were better too, now she had more solid imaginings of Ladie to distract herself with. Better than imaginings even. She had real memories that she could pore over again and again.

When she was caught up in those retrospective trances, everything that had happened with Scarecrowfootman and Rachel (Ann hadn't seen her in what felt like forever. Never once had she run into her upstairs) seemed so distant that they could have happened to someone else entirely.

Or perhaps they hadn't happened at all. (But you know to avoid that patch of mud; you remember, every night when Mrs Hardy locks you in, that the second key is tucked safely away in your drawer.) *Don't think of that*, she would tell herself firmly, instead think of how Ladie had noticed that your plaits were an exact copy of her own, how she had reached out and stroked the ridges of them and the touch had dripped all through your body like cold oil.

20

S HE TOOK LADIE with her everywhere in her mind. Ann imagined her here now while she scrubbed the entrance doorstep. Ann's fingers were brittle with soapy ice and the underside of her eyeballs were dry and frozen. But Ladie stood warm and serene, smiling down on her industrious friend.

'You and I, Ann,' she would say, 'could have our own kingdom. Perhaps one day, when I own Ropner, it'll be like that. We could rule over it together. How wonderful we would make it. Not a single day would ever be dull and dark again. You would no longer slave away downstairs or sleep in the servants' garret. We would have wonderful balls and invite all types of exotic guests; fire eaters and ballerinas and string quartets. And we would have days of just picnicking, you and I, in the woods or the meadows. And you could sleep curled up at the foot of my bed like the most precious pet.'

Ann struck through the neat circles she had scoured with harsh lines, perfectly parallel, and suds winked at her as they popped. They made little faces with mismatched eyes that smiled wobbly and sweet. Here she had her own little kingdom. This step, this soapy water, this dirt, this scourer, they were under her rule, her command. That satisfaction made everything hum. Finally, finally, perfection was something Ann could reach out and touch. Its softness was sacred, she could pick it up and hang it round her neck like a rosary, like a talisman. Life, finally, finally, was good.

A weak light from the sun escaped the trappings of grey clouds and broke into a run over the grounds; towards the forest. Ann watched how the light caught in the cold and dew on the grass and formed a silver haze that hovered over the fields, providing each one with its own climate of wintery mist. Watched to see a figure, birthed from the furthest bowels of the woods, begin to trudge laboriously towards the Hall. The figure was seemingly contorted; a hulking back from which extra limbs swung sinuously. Plumes of blueish steam pulsed and bloomed around his head.

As it advanced across the acres now, its features became more apparent. The hideous hump; a bag slung across a back causing it to stoop; and its sinuous limbs; some kind of game freshly snared and not yet stiffened. It was a man. A poacher? There had been warnings of such before; the forest was rich with game. But Ann never heard of any caught, or even sighted. The man stopped abruptly, letting his pack drop to stand and stretch before he deftly lit a pipe. Tilting his head back to exhale the first drag, he turned suddenly away from the forest to face the house as if he were aware of being watched. And, seemingly unfazed, he stared back; towards Ropner, towards Ann. She froze. Slowly, lazily, he extended an arm and waved.

Without the pack he stood to his full, imposing height and the angles of his broad back and taut legs outlined him violently. She could just about make out his face; it was wide and sharply cut, like a prism of glass. He had deep-set eyes whose colour she could not see.

She had never looked at any of the men this closely before, she had never dared. But something now was making her look. That same something was making her stare. It was making all the world around her slow and silent and all the flesh inside her fast and roaring.

Yes, she had never looked at any of the men this closely before, but still she knew that this man was new to Ropner, because even she would have noticed him before; she would have noticed that his face, though dark, was too bright to look at, like a beacon. The hand he raised in a wave was wide and thick. Ann could imagine it strong and roped with veins. The hole between her legs itched and buzzed and the hollow above it ached angrily. Blood dribbled like snot. (There's the badness starting to come out.)

Ann turned suddenly. In her panic she tossed her bucket of water over the steps, obliterating her kingdom. The suds rolled off the marble, splattering dark stains onto the surrounding gravel.

The steps shone clean but Ann shook with nausea. This moment of panic, this careening of control was abhorrent to her. These bad, dirty thoughts were foreign and vile and most certainly not her own. (*What will you do when all this badness possesses you?*) They did not belong to her. They were coming from all the rot, all the badness that *he* had infected her with that night. All the sin that abhorrent Scarecrowfootman had passed onto her, it was making her think terrible (lustful, burning, aching, oh God) thoughts. She wanted to bleach her skin, she could not stand being looked at by these men anymore. She could not handle that unruly fear it struck up inside her. As soon as one was struck down another sprouted in its place. (Fuck him. Fuck them all.) They all blended into one nameless man who had one mean face with staring eyes that she knew were making quick darts to try to unpick thread and unravel clothes and find flesh to consume and chew and spit back out again with foul and hungry mouths. God, this awful fear made everything in her so disorderly she had to fight against herself not to scream.

She threw the bucket to the ground and ran to the outhouse. There was a folded sheet she had hidden under the loose floorboard especially for moments like this; when she needed to order herself back into something sharp, something controlled and narrow and pointed. She extracted it carefully and smoothed its folds flat against the floor. Then she knelt on it, tucked her hair and methodically began to scratch at the fleshy pulp in the back recess of her throat.

She threw up five times because today that was a pleasing number. Each stinking surge of retching allowed for a flood of relief that calmed and cleared her head, it almost brought her to laughter. God, it felt good. That acidic burn was a satisfying testament to her victory, to her determination, to what she was willing to sacrifice and suffer for order, for purity, for perfection.

She washed her hands at the pipe. She lathered up the red bar of soap she carried with her until its size was at least halved beneath its own suds, which she massaged into herself so furiously it was as if she were trying to reach bone. Out, out, out stupid spots of rot and blood and black soft mud, out from the dry skin, the raw ugly skin all craggy and cracked with a hundred and a thousand hair-thin lines all on her fingers and her knuckles and the backs of her hands and her palms.

The lines on her palms were deep and if she stretched her hand wide they grew fatter and more saturated and seemed to pulse. One of the lines had fissured and cracked so deeply it opened up a little red mouth that blubbered out blood like a tiny crying baby. *Oh, poor baby*, the carbolic soap jeered, and then squirmed its suds mischievously to make sure it stung extra hard.

'So what?' she said to the soap. 'You can hurt me all you like and I'll only be pleased. You can get right under my skin and burn and burn and I'll only be happy because that way I'll be all squeaky clean inside too.'

You can't be clean with all that blood and black soil under your fingernails, the soap whispered back greasily.

Don't be stupid, Ann, she scolded herself. *Don't be stupid, soap can't speak.*

Still, she sunk her fingernails right into those creamy suds and scrubbed until they nearly ripped. *You can't be clean with all that blood running down your face and getting into your eyes and dyeing their whites red.* She needed to wash her face anyway, it wasn't like the soap's voice was real, or that she was doing it because it had told her to; no, she wasn't. It was just that she had washed the copper earlier and then brushed some hair back from her cheek without thinking, so now some dirt or a streak of grime was sitting evilly right on the point of her chin, lurking until it was ready to sprout into raging pustules as bad as Cook's, as bad as Scarecrowfootman's. (Don't! Don't think about him.) She chastised herself by scrubbing her face extra hard. (Don't think about it.) In her desperate fury, she wasn't careful and those leather-smelling suds spiked viciously right into the jelly of her eye.

You're still not clean. The stupid hissing frothing bubbling piece of red soap was half its size now but twice as loud. *You can't be clean with all that bad food inside you, sliming all the walls of your throat and your belly so thickly you can't even ever sick it up.*

It was right. It was ringing in her ears. All that rotten stale and mouldy food was leaking out of her in foul smells or congealing to fat that screamed out sins of gluttony. Before she had a chance to think, she clapped that spiteful little know-it-all bar of soap right into her mouth, and she chewed its waxy body into a million tiny pieces. She nearly choked on the foam and the froth but she swallowed every last piece, sucked in every last sud. Let something try to tell her she wasn't clean now; all the badness was out from her fingernails, from her face, from her belly. All that blood, rot and mud was now so deftly scoured away, even some wicked witch magic couldn't read it from those miserable lines on her palms.

It would all have been fine and order would have settled quietly like a sphinx if Rachel hadn't been standing there when she turned to go. Contriving, conniving Rachel, standing there in her stupid, silent, sad way with her down-turned eyes staring, confessing that they had seen everything. She held out a wicker basket for Ann to take. It was all relentless. Today was yesterday and yesterday was tomorrow and tomorrow would never change. She thought of Scarecrowfootman, she thought of the man from the woods.

'It's never going to end, is it?' Ann said.

Rachel just stood and stared and blinked at her with her big sad eyes full of knowing.

If it wasn't for Ladie, Ann thought, she would be sure she was in hell.

21

I T WAS ALREADY mid-morning, but the air was still cold and the paving slabs shivered excitedly, squirming with grits of moss and mud that grew in their gaps. Ann watched them and rolled her shoulders back and forth in inscrutable circles.

She looked out over the grounds, at the clotted-cream sky and solemn trees and swathes of stiff grass. If she stared too hard the world wobbled, twisted into a psychedelia; pulsations of saccharine green, slices of dying green, peeks of grey-blue, of clouds (white like skulls), beating branches (snapping bones), damp and hard paving slabs (with black mud under their fingernails), rough clouds, sickly leaves, white skulls, mist, blood, bleeding, grass, damp. She had the itching urge to throw up, that burning compulsion, to spew her guts on the stone, to untether herself from this damn place.

But no, not anymore; Ladie was here.

Ladie glided towards Ann in a thick navy cape that was a shade away from being too dark for her. Underneath, a dark kerchief crossed neatly over her embossed corset; a dusky lilac that reminded Ann of heather bristling in bloom. Ann felt her parts become mismatched and dwarfed next to Ladie. She felt the ugly way her skin stretched over bones, the way it ballooned into cracks and craters, the way it lurked under thorny patches of hair. It made her sick.

'I thought it would be tremendously lovely to have ourselves a little autumn picnic on our walk today!' Ladie called brightly as she made her way closer. She raised a wicker basket threaded through her arms. 'To stray from our usual path and walk through the summer gardens. I asked Mrs Hardy to organise us a basket!'

'What a wonderful idea, Ladie. Here, let me.'

'No, darling Ann, I shall carry it, I like the feel of it, it's as if I were a peasant woman from a book.' Ladie let out a laugh and a few rays of sunlight fought through the clouds. 'I don't suppose you have ever seen a great deal of the gardens before.'

'No, Ladie,' Ann responded dutifully.

'Well, then.' Ladie smiled proudly. 'You *are* in for a treat today! I shall be your tour guide!'

The east side of Ropner blushed with the half-dead autumn sun. The weak gold sharpened every colour and eked out a beauty from the beginnings of decay.

They worked through the neat lines of the summer gardens that split and segmented into angular patterns almost mathematical in nature. Ladie narrated every perfectly trimmed bush and trained wisteria. She pointed out each pear tree and cherry blossom and white beech and little bay tree standing to attention. They watched the ornate bird baths and fountains carved full of fishes and nymphs. She talked about how wonderful everything would look in spring and summer, if the two ever showed face.

Gosh, she was witty like that. She had a canny knack of saying out loud what Ann had been feeling all along in her bones, and the unity in her observations was so joyful that Ann felt as though the summer gardens were already in bloom.

One cross section led to a little glasshouse, domed and jovial and sweating profusely. Inside Ann marvelled at the lush green foliage that crowded every wall, clawing and fighting their sisters to press against the glass panes, as close to the sun as they could get. Little white iron posts spelled each of their names.

'*Rhapis excelsa*,' Ladie read, and '*Phoenix canariensis*,' and '*Spathiphyllum wallisii*,' and '*Brugmansia*'.

They sounded like spells, Ann thought. She closed her eyes at each one and let their sound soak over her, enchant her. She imagined all the vile people watching all this magic from the kitchen with jealous eyes. (Ha!)

At the very back of the summer gardens was a gate that opened into a sweeping meadow rolling for miles and miles like an ocean, before dipping right down into the river.

'I thought here would be perfect for a picnic. You're not too cold, are you, Ann? No? Then perhaps you would not mind giving me your cape. I know I shall catch a chill the moment we sit down. Thank you – oh, and there's a blanket tucked in the basket. You can spread it out for us to sit on.'

Ann obeyed and watched as Ladie feasted on all the food she had prepared. (Oh no, I couldn't possibly eat a bite, Ladie, I'm not hungry at all.) On asparagus crackling with pepper and rolled in bacon, on cubes of cheese every colour of light, and chalky green grapes as fat as friars. On cloudy buns and (Thank you, Ladie, but it fills me enough just to see you eat and enjoy) salivating chunks of melon, on strips of smoked salmon rolled up like roses. The gaping chasm in her belly yawned wider than Ann ever thought possible. (Good and perfect and clean and crisp.)

She smiled. We will stay here until the grass grows over our heads, Ann decided, and no one will ever find us. We will sleep under a blanket of tea towels all sewn together and sip from acorns and be clever enough to manipulate stray leaves into a gutter and sticks into a little chimney for our fairy flame fire. Everything will be tinged green from the light shining through the fronds of grass, and we will have little rabbit friends that bring us food so we never ever have to leave. Eventually our skin will turn to marble and we will be frozen into an eternal embrace with a name plaque at our feet; one name for us both.

Hermia. Hermiahermiahermia.

A light breeze tickled over them and Ladie sighed softly. 'Do you ever wonder, Ann, if there is any more to life than this?'

Ann almost laughed. What more could she want than to be right here, right now?

'Sometimes it's almost as though everything is too much the same, too perfect,' Ladie said without waiting for an answer. 'Sometimes I think I crave a thrill.'

There was a little catch that snagged in Ann's throat. A thrill was a thing dark and forbidden, a secret taste of badness that needed to be spat out. Surely Ladie could not mean that.

'Like this!' Ladie laughed, and without warning seized Ann's hands, pulling her to her feet. She began to run and dragged Ann, stumbling, with her.

'Come!' cried Ladie, as they broke free of the summer gardens. She pulled Ann over the miles and miles of grass that mixed with the sky in a dishwater blur. They buoyed over the slick stone entrance steps, falling against one another, using their conjoined appendages as crutches, and into the marble entrance hall, panting and sweating and burning all over. There Ladie dragged them on slipping feet and promptly flung herself onto the cool marble floor in Hermia's shadow.

'Ahh!' She shrieked, rolling and writhing to press her cheek, then her wrists, then the nape of her neck to the cold, supremely unimpressed stone. 'Ann, Ann – oh, you have to try it!'

The blood was pounding hot and fierce in Ann's cheeks and chest so that they began to itch. She had no choice; she and Ladie had become conjoined, after all; she had to do whatever Ladie did, her own brain had no say over her limbs. She threw herself ungainly to lie at Ladie's side.

God, Ladie was right. (Was she ever wrong?) The glossy floor was so deliciously cold it made Ann gasp and then laugh and laugh. Here with her burning blood, and the soaring ceiling that echoed their laughter into one, and the hot pip and fig tree in her belly, this must be happiness. It was a feeling almost too big for her, it pushed at all her edges and made her want to cry. The two women rolled and laughed and hugged and shrieked, their arms tangled together and their chests heaved in partnership, one breath an echo of the other, again and again and again.

I am ready to die now, Ann thought. *Here in Ladie's arms. I am ready for my heart to burst with contentment, to be killed by my own joy, and to remain for eternity here in this embrace. Kill me, Ladie, so I can die happy.*

Probably, she was already in heaven.

Ladie moved closer to Ann until her face eclipsed the marble room entirely. So close Ann could see every bolt of grey fibre in her eyes and feel Ladie's breath warm and foreign in her own mouth.

'Ann,' she breathed. Her eyes flicked from side to side conspiringly. 'We're being watched, Ann.'

Ann felt her smile grow stiff and freeze on her face so suddenly that her muscles twitched. Something cold was dropping down, down and further down in the depths of her stomach. The great moon of Ladie's face was supremely solemn, her eyes wide enough to show complete circles of white. Ann could not look away, she had become horribly aware of the marble statues all around them, with their eyes, cold, never-blinking hollows.

'They're like the paintings,' Ladie said. Her voice was low, so forcibly hushed that the only way Ann could distinguish words was by watching the pink lines of Ladie's lip and the wet purple flicking of her tongue. 'I don't like the way they follow me, with their eyes, the way they watch . . .' Her eyes had aged in this short moment, made pained and desperate with all the thousand years and horrors they professed to have seen. Ann realised with a start how tightly Ladie was clutching at her shoulders; her nails were smarting Ann's flesh even through sleeves and silken gloves. Ann lay paralysed by the steely grip, by this sudden stranger that had appeared from Ladie's skin. She felt something move in the room around them and could not bring herself to look. Surely it wouldn't appear here, that half-rotting corpse, not now, not while she was with Ladie.

But Ladie seemed to hear nothing.

'Oh, Ann,' she said. 'You don't know what I'm talking about, do you? How could you? I hope –' she gave a little gasp, surprised to feel prickling tears in her eyes and in her nose – 'I hope you never do.'

Without warning the tears hardened to stone and Ladie swung one hand away from Ann's shoulder to strike her hard across the cheek. Ann yelped in shock and immediately Ladie recoiled with mortification.

'Oh Ann, oh Ann, I had to check, I am so sorry, I had to make sure, you see, that you're not one of them.'

As suddenly as she had slapped her, she clutched at Ann like a drowning man and began to heave great racking sobs over her breast. The marble beneath them was deathly cold, like a tomb. Ann stared at the ceiling, too scared to look anywhere else lest she see the corpse, lest she see any marble had moved, lest she look at Ladie and see again that face she did not recognise, or worse, see her own fear reflected back at her.

She lay below Ladie, as still as a corpse with death set in, her heart pounding in rhythm with Ladie's shuddering sobs. She was crying like something broken, never-ending. Ann felt the thick heavy tears seeping through her own clothes, making her own skin warm and sticky. Sickly goosebumps were rising on her chest to meet the brine.

Perhaps this was death.

She tried to comfort herself that they were entombed together, but the comfort would not come. For the first time Ann could not bring herself to search for a sisterhood, a kinship, a hint of like-mindedness between them.

She wanted to peel Ladie off her, to crawl and skid across the marble floor, scramble away from her. Because the entity atop of her was one she recognised. It had curled up with her in the hollow of the tree, she had held it in her hands as she clawed at mud, she had breathed it in in the darkness of night and coaxed it from her throat in the grey light of day. It was with her always, but never here, not upstairs, never with Ladie. Until now.

The shock of it all was so paralysing that Ann did not hear the footsteps enter and approach. They were muffled and disguised under the eerie ringing in her ears.

Words were spoken by a disembodied voice, but they were blubbered and blurred, as though Ann were under-water. She caught the rhythm of them though; hushed out like the beat of a lullaby. And then, slowly, laboriously, Ladie's weight was lifted from her.

She could breathe again and she gasped like she had broken up through the ice of a frozen pond. Ann sat bolt upright in time to see the housekeeper guiding Ladie from the room. Ladie was huddled and slumped, smaller than Ann had ever seen her; somehow suddenly birdlike and fra-gile. Her walk was so weak and stumbling that Mrs Hardy was half dragging her. They disappeared up the staircase.

Ann was entirely alone in the vast marble tomb, but it was as if a weight were still atop her. She could not move, she could only just breathe. She stared at nothing and could not take her eyes away from it. Perhaps she had stayed like that for hours and days, perhaps only a minute. By the time Mrs Hardy re-emerged she was still sat on the floor, eyes wide, hardly blinking, heart hammering beneath the dark wet patch staining her dress.

'Lady Charlotte,' the housekeeper said from the stairs, 'is having one of her delicate days.' Her voice was as matter-of-fact as ever, unperturbed, always the professional. 'She will be taken care of.'

Get up, Ann, her tone of voice said. *Nothing must deter you from your duty. It is not a servant's place to judge, to ask questions, to even think. All you have to do is obey.*

Ann unglued her eyes from the enticement of nothing and sought out Mrs Hardy.

She was standing halfway up the staircase, hands folded neatly at her middle. From Ann's position below, Mrs Hardy looked like a great cloaked harpy suspended in mid-air. The light fell sharp and unflattering from above, casting shadows on her face that warped and twisted her features. The shadow from her nose hooked and curled her lip, making those hundreds of little sharp teeth snarl.

'Return to your duties, Ann, while she rests.'

Ann left the entrance hall, unable to look anywhere but her feet, the disturbed skin on her cheek still stinging.

22

'Reckon she's gone mad?'

'It probably runs in the family, we all know fat old Aunty is half-gone and all.'

'Shhh, you don't know where Hardy is, she might hear.'

Ann was hiding in the pantry, pressed against the wall by its door, listening to them talk about Ladie in the kitchen. Her Ladie, her poor Ladie, who must be so lonely and missing her so terribly.

If justice were a real thing, there would suddenly be several loud thumps from the kitchen and she would walk in from the pantry and see all their lumpy bodies laid and splayed dead on the floor . She would step over each of their odious corpses and gather Ladie's breakfast things onto a tray, stepping over them again on her way out to the service stairs.

A shelf was digging a deep groove into her shoulder, another gouging a red line into her forehead. She could feel her plaits brushing against the smooth ceramic of the plates on the shelves and the feeling made her shiver. There were four thin plaits at her crown, tracking down the side of her face, joining together behind her ears so that four became two: two thick braids that looped down towards the nape of her neck, gathering hair as they went, so they always stayed tight to her head, then rising to meet perfectly in the middle, like an upside-down heart. She had been practising every night, all night, for each day she had spent without Ladie. Plaiting tight and neat, then unhooking each twist and starting again with a new pattern. Some looped in shell-like whorls, others twisted round each other like wicker, one or two dripped down her neck in loops like a chandelier. Those less practical styles would only be for Ladie, for when she wanted to look particularly special and beautiful and lovely.

It won't be long, she told herself solemnly every night. *It won't be long until you can show her, until you can see Ladie wearing them; see her three reflections clap their hands so gleefully and smile with their teeth and all six of their grey eyes.*

Today marked the longest she had gone without seeing Ladie since she first watched Mrs Hardy bathe her. Ann had not tracked the days. No, it was too great a pain to score in with a measure of time so broad. Each second was agony, so that is what Ann counted. She grouped them into little pockets of tens and added them up each night while she plaited in the candlelight.

The servants did not talk of Ladie in front of her, so she was reduced to hiding round corners to hear their awful idle gossip. She knew it would be horrible and make her want to scream, but she couldn't help but listen, just in case, somehow, someone knew something. 'Well, she hasn't been going for luncheon; all that's been sent for washing is nightgowns.'

'Maybe she's dying.'

Ann stifled a sob.

She had only seen Mrs Hardy once since the incident. The housekeeper had accosted her in the music-room corridor and asked her to fetch some fresh towels and iced water and bring them to Ladie's door. Ann had never moved so fast. That spiteful thing called hope made her really believe that she was going to see Ladie again, that she was about to tend to her; press cool towels to her temples and whisper words of remedy to her. But Mrs Hardy was waiting outside Ladie's door when Ann arrived there, heart hammering, breath rasping.

'Thank you, Ann,' the housekeeper had said curtly, taking the bowl of water and soft folds of cotton from her. She had turned on her heels and shut Ladie's door behind her with a metallic clunk. Mrs Hardy had slipped through the door so slickly that Ann couldn't catch so much as a glimpse of the room. It was like some kind of cruel torture knowing that Ladie was just out of reach. Just behind that door. It took a long time for her to come unstuck from where she was standing alone, hands empty.

That night, Ann imagined she had asked Mrs Hardy how Ladie was, that the question had not dried on her lips. She twisted strands of her hair rhythmically and imagined that Mrs Hardy had smiled with her pointed teeth and said, 'Please, Ann, come and see for yourself how Lady Charlotte is. She will be so pleased to see you.'

The housekeeper would have swung open the door and revealed Ladie laid on her bed, the sheets tucked neatly at her chest, fragrant sprigs of flowers and bundles of smelling salts peppered all around her. The gentle waves of her hair would have been fanned out on the pillow like a halo while she lay as still as marble, eyes closed as though she were in an enchanted doze. Ann would have stepped into the room and Ladie's eyes would have fluttered open, spying Ann, just as light peeked through the curtains, shining right on Ladie as she sat up, smiling and more well than ever.

'Oh, Ann!' she would have cried happily. 'How much better you have made me feel.'

She will be better soon enough, Ann told herself sternly. *Ladie will be well soon, and I will be called for again, and everything will go back to how it was, exactly how it is meant to be.* She told herself it again and again and again, with each twist and loop and knot of her hair. But she could not deny that she was scared. Not just of something bad befalling Ladie, but of all that was rising to the surface in Ladie's absence. In the candlelight of her room, little beasts had begun to dance and twist on the walls; flames and shadows twisted and pulsated, transforming into obscenely forked tongues and curving horns, lewd gestures and exposed bodies. They leapt between orange and black, and within the noises of Ropner at night – the creak of the floorboards, the sigh of the sheets – Ann heard the echoes of their distant caterwauling shrieks and hideous bellows, the clop of their hooves and the weight of their bellies as they danced and slithered closer to her. When she snuffed the candle, if she dared, she would lie back and shut her eyes and feel the horrible pressure of a body atop of hers; warm wetness seeping from it onto her chest like blood or tears.

She was sick with memories and nightmares that had been dug up from the undergrowth of her mind. She retched again and again, watery bile that betrayed just how little she was eating. But she couldn't possibly eat when she was constantly on edge like this, scared of every corner in case the corpse had found her again, scared of eyes in paintings following her, just like Ladie had said. Every time Ann swept and polished and dusted in the entrance hall, she did not feel safe. Every time she looked at the statue of Hermia (Hermiahermiahermia) she saw the white whorls of Ladie's eyes, the poisoned horror forming on the tip of her purple tongue, her own fear looking back out of her. And above the mineral coolness of the marble, she could smell the corpse's half-rotten odour, pungent and diabolical. She heard all the statues whispering like the servants whenever she turned her back, ready to transform into bloated cadavers just to frighten her.

A cackling laugh broke out from the kitchen and burst through her thoughts.

'Look here, she's red like a beetroot! Told you she'd been making eyes at him.'

'Have I hell, he never comes near enough for me to give him so much as a look.'

Ann realised, with a lurch in her stomach, that they were talking about the man from the woods.

'Well, he ought to watch out going too near to you. Before he got a word out, you'd be opening your legs.'

'Well aye, we don't often get the likes of him. He's so tall, and arms and legs that thick, he's like a tree that one day started walking.'

'Hark at her! I suppose you're wondering if all his parts are in proportion?'

Peals of vulgar laughter shrieked down the corridor and Ann felt her lips peel back over her teeth in a grimace that was like a snarl.

Ann had caught only glimpses of the man since the day on the entrance steps. But somehow she had learned so much about him. She knew he was the new groundsman.

She knew he started not three weeks ago, and that he never ate with the other servants, men or women, but with the dog he had brought to Ropner, both of them tearing at scraps of food in the game hut in the woods. (Right next to the mud where X marks the spot.) She knew that each morning when she cleaned the windows in the library he made the walk from the woods to the stables across the lawn. And by the time she was dusting the sills in the music room, he was making his way back again. He walked with big strides, his back straight and arms still, never swinging; like a proud soldier, head thrown back before the firing line.

But she did not know this by choice. No. She did not spend a second thinking about him, she had assimilated this information by chance and happenstance. In fact, she did not think about him at all. She never ever thought of him, because she was not a vessel of lust or badness, she was not wicked like the others. She was the lady's maid and she had taken great care to purge herself of all sin (with soap and sick and mud) and she would continue to do so until Ladie was well again and she was back next to her goodness and light.

23

TWO HUNDRED AND two thousand and twenty seconds. That's how long it had been since she stood in the pantry, a nice round number. Tidy and even; that was a good sign. The day would be good to Ann. She made a whispered wish, then resumed scouring the black gums of the sitting-room fireplace and counted the seconds again. She counted them in groups of ten, and she was on her thirteenth set, unrolling the hearthrug, when Mrs Hardy slicked to her side, silently. There was a moment, half a beat, when Ann anticipated the worst. She looked at Mrs Hardy's solemn face and felt the brocaded wool slip against her fingertips and she clutched it tightly so as not to drop it. She couldn't afford to make any mistakes in front of the housekeeper.

'If you're finished here, Ann, I'd like you to bring Lady Charlotte's breakfast tray to her. I'm happy to say she is feeling much better today.'

'Of course, Mrs Hardy.' Ann gave a small curtsy, barely more than a nod of her head, but she did not trust herself to keep balanced to execute the formality properly; her head had become light and dizzy and all her blood had been replaced by air and her heart was beating it round her body so fast she was about to lift up from the ground.

She shook the hearthrug and laid it flat and perfectly straight, biting her cheeks to stop from grinning. She gathered the box of scourers and brushes, bowed her head and tried to force her feet to move at an orderly pace, tried not to run and skip from the room.

But before she had walked even a few paces Mrs Hardy grabbed her suddenly, just above the elbow. The shock of her touch made Ann give a stifled yelp. Even through the material of her dress, Ann could feel the coldness of the housekeeper's hands, the strength beneath the skin, like stone.

Ann swallowed.

'Ann,' the housekeeper said, tightening her grip ever so slightly. 'Do not mention the incident to Her Ladyship. It would serve you both well to forget it entirely.'

Ann bowed her head gently. 'It is forgotten, Mrs Hardy,' she said to the floor. The housekeeper released her and Ann walked placidly to the door.

Breakfast was ready and still steaming by the time Ann made it downstairs. She narrowed her eyes and looked at the laden tray, hunting carefully for any fleck of spittle, any curling rogue hair, flakes of ashy skin or any tangible sin infecting the food.

They could not be trusted. From now on *she* would be there to watch Cook and Matchstick and any of the other scurrying kitchen maids prepare the food, she would stand over them to supervise as they loaded the tray. She could not risk Ladie being exposed to sin, Ladie becoming unwell again, Ladie talking madly of being followed, staring with screaming eyes and – but of course she would not think of that, she would not remember that it had happened.

The centrepiece of Ladie's breakfast was a deep bowl of bone broth. The liquid gold was swimming with thick cuts of iridescent carrot and celery, translucent petals of onion, and smooth slices of bone with honeycombed marrow appearing as they bobbed up and down. There was a glass of thick warm milk too, and fat slices of toasted sourdough with their soft middles showing open mouths drowning in butter. Ann's stomach groaned and she breathed in deeply through her nose, taking in all the warmth and flavoursome smells, filling up on it.

Yes, this would be good for Ladie, this would help her get better. Ann would watch her eat it. And if she left anything when it was time for Ann to take the tray, she would carry it to the servants' stairwell and sit on that little lip she had first seen Ladie on, and gnaw all the rejected crusts, following the bitemarks of Ladie's pearly teeth; she would sip at the abandoned soup and neglected milk, placing her lips on the glass and spoon just where Ladie's had been. It was not bad to do that because it would be worse to waste it, and even worse still to have the others fight over the scraps like hyenas, gobbling it all down with the taste of Ladie's breath and tongue.

She swallowed a sharp twist of excitement down into her stomach and carried the tray up to Ladie's room. Where she belonged.

When Ann swung open the door (Ladie had called 'Enter' with such a dear cheer in a voice that she must have recognised your knock), Ladie was laid on her bed almost exactly as Ann had imagined her; like an illustration from a storybook. She wore a white nightgown, and light from the window dappled her skin. Her hair was loose, running down her shoulders in two long streams. Ann thought of touching it again and her fingertips tingled.

'Ann!' Ladie said with a weak smile. 'Come sit by me while I eat. I've been so lonely.' Her voice was low and creaked with a drawl, as if she were too tired to bother to speak properly. Ann set the tray over Ladie's lap; its legs sunk into the bed either side of her so that it made a little bridge. She pulled up a little stool, right by Ladie's side, and sat on it delicately, hardly daring to breathe.

In a downbeat way that was almost akin to boredom, Ladie began to sip at her broth.

Outside Ladie's windows, the grounds were blue-grey in the cold air, the woods were coloured a wicked bracken, their darkness heavy with edges outlined in an eerie dusting of frost. They swelled as the trees obeyed each wild breath of the wind, Ann's quickening heartbeat gladder still to be shut away from it. She thought of the groundsman, wandering through those same foreboding woods and wondered if he ever caught a chill. Quickly she remembered herself and caught back her breath. 'You look so well, Ladie,' she said gently.

Ladie let out a puff of air that was somewhere between a derisive snort and a sad little sigh. 'I shall feel it once I am dressed and I have had you do my hair.' She dropped the spoon into the broth with a loud clack and tore into a hunk of sourdough as though suddenly agitated. 'Though Mrs Hardy says I am still to be restful; to get dressed only in my day dresses and to sit gently with some sewing or a book – I shall be awfully bored, so you will have to sit with me all the while.' She was somehow like a contrary child, petulantly picking out her food with her lower lip sticking out, and Ann felt a glow of motherly fondness. She, of course, would sit with Ladie, would look after her as if she were indeed mother to her.

'But I do have to say,' Ladie began again after a long gulp of hot milk. The lilac tip of her tongue flicked out and cleaned the milk frosting her upper lip like sea foam.

Ann remembered how Ladie had wet her lips in the same way in the marble room, right before she said— (Don't remember it, it was nothing more than a dream, another nightmare.)

'This . . . sickness has had its benefits. It has spared me from luncheons with Aunt! Mrs Hardy thought it would be too taxing for me to go in my current state.' She had become more animated, slightly brighter, as she began to speak of luncheons, with a kind of morbid excitement in her eyes. 'Oh, Ann, if only you knew how loathsome they are. How terrible it is to be in my aunt's company for even a moment. Thankfully, luncheon is the only time I see her. She keeps herself quite tucked away in her bedchambers – which are simply sprawling you know, I snuck in once just to look.' Ladie's countenance changed again, to something slow and unreadable. 'The things I found in there . . .' Her expression had something of the view outside in it, Ann thought; brooding and dark. Troubled. 'You wouldn't believe me if I told you.' She gave a shake of her head and a false little wooden laugh. 'She is so unbelievably rude to me. I doubt anything gives her more satisfaction than embarrassing me and pelting me with jibes the way she does. It's fortunate that I know her rudeness is only because she is grossly jealous of me, otherwise I should be quite upset at her cruelties.'

Ann was bewildered to the point of silence. She had seen the rich tapestries of food sent up to furnish the table and it was almost inconceivable to think someone might not enjoy that. And never could she have dreamed Ladie would feel such a way about her aunt. She thought of the beautiful woman in the big painting, cutting such a fine figure in that intricate dress, those decadent jewels, kissing Ladie's head with such tender love and affection. But with that conviction, with that hurt in Ladie's voice, how could she not begin to think less of the Duchess?

Still, the apparent shortcomings of the Duchess only stood as a testament to Ladie's goodness; made her perfection even more of a wonder, because against all adversities she had managed to rise up to be good and kind and pure. (Just like you.)

Ladie had fallen back into a stupor again, exhausted from her sudden burst of speech. She picked listlessly at the remains of her breakfast. 'I think, Ann,' she said, in a low voice that was almost like a groan, 'I may have to close my eyes for a moment.'

'I think that may be wise, Ladie. You mustn't over-exert yourself, it's so important that you recover properly.' Ann stood up and reached for the tray smoothly.

'Yes . . . Clear the tray, then come straight back so you can be here when I wake up. I don't want to be by myself again for more than even a moment.' She gave a shaky little laugh, Ann took the tray and pretended she didn't see how scared Ladie had looked.

*   *   *

The dregs of milk were lukewarm, but as thick and rich as cream, golden drops of butter could be sucked from the crusts before crunching into their cracked brown backs. Ann finished every last morsel of Ladie's breakfast on the service stairs like she promised herself she would, sat on the lip of the steps where she had first met Ladie.

Slowly she licked the spoon until it was so clean it shone. This was friendship, Ann told herself happily. Though really, they were closer than friends, closer than sisters even. They were one and the same; Ann and Ladie, Ladie and Ann.

24

MORNING AFTER MORNING after morning Ann carried the breakfast tray to Ladie's room; she would feel her heart pulsing stronger, knowing that its other half was near. She would sit by her while she ate, tingling with the anticipation of devouring the leftovers on the stairs; sit with her while she embroidered, while she read, while she slept.

Even in her sleep, Ladie wore her gloves. Ann sat by her side on the little stool, watching her chest rise and fall, stroking the smooth soft silk of her fingers. It was worth the suffering she endured downstairs, and all its horrors, just for this moment, for feeling the rich silk under her own fingers and the warm flexing flesh beneath. There was more goodness in Ladie's fingertips than all of the stinking servants combined.

Downstairs Ann was too weak, too starving, too meagre and tired and worthless and lonely. She was awfully aware of each inch of her body taking up space, how jarring her being was. Upstairs . . . upstairs she was free. She was as close to free as she believed possible. With Ladie she had found the personification of her own soul, and in its presence Ann felt everything about herself was just right. How could she be too much or not enough when Ladie existed in the exact same way?

When Ann walked in with the tray and Ladie's face broke into a wan smile, Ann was overwhelmed to think how much goodness one person could hold.

'I thought we might walk in the summer gardens,' Ladie said one morning.

She toyed at the fat slugs of grilled peach with her fork, dragging them through the yoghurt and swirls of honey. The thin grey light of the morning dribbled over her face and hair, which Ann had already darned into plaits; braids that traced her head tightly before dropping into lace-like loops. ('Oh, Ann, I look almost like a princess,' she had said, which was good, which means it was worth pulling out all those great clumps of your own hair and scalp to learn how to do it.)

Ann fought not to itch at the scabs under her hair.

'Mrs Hardy thinks fresh air might be good for me. I can't tell you how awful it is to be stuck in like an unhappy little linnet bird. How I've longed to be free again. Please say you will walk with me. I would much rather your company than Mrs Hardy's!'

Ann felt herself blush furiously. Not that she was condoning the remark about the housekeeper, or agreeing that she was inferior company for Ladie – no, she would never dream of it. She was just pleased, that was all, pleased that Ladie thought so highly of her, and it would be wrong, wouldn't it, to disagree, to defend Mrs Hardy even though order probably dictated she should?

'You are too kind, Ladie, I would be more than happy to, should Mrs Hardy allow it?'

'Oh, I've already asked! When you take my tray down, you can go and fetch your coat and we will go. There's nothing like morning air.'

The morning had still not warmed by the time they had made their way to the neat maze of hedges that made up the summer gardens. Ann had made sure to dress Ladie in as many layers as she could; rolling silk stockings up her bare legs, letting her breath tickle the nape of Ladie's neck while she buttoned the petticoat, pulled at the short stays, bowed the ribbons of her skirts. Ann had swaddled her in the overcoat she herself had darned at the elbow (see it flashing now as Ladie moves her arm, winking at you like a special secret), and placed the rabbit fur hat over the dripping plaits (so clever to have chosen that style for today: they pair with that sweet hat so well they could be part of it).

Though Ladie had protested, Ann had insisted she wear her long wool cloak, too. Ann adored the cloak: it was a dark grey, like smoke, and the way it brushed over the brown of Ladie's skirt was a pleasing echo of the colours in the fur hat. *Really, Ann*, she told herself, *you have outdone yourself, and how wise you were to add the woollen chemise, for the cold is raw and bites; the type of weather that could freeze a lady to an icy statue, one with smooth skin and white marble eyes that*—(Shhh, it is forgotten.)

The frigid weather had rendered the summer gardens bare and haughty. The little fountains and ornaments were fuzzed with blue, and slicked with a dangerous black shine where water still dribbled. Some trees had kept their leaves stoically, but even then they seemed to gather them closely to their boughs, afraid the grabbing hands of the wind might tear them from them. Other plants and trees were completely bare; black and spindled; angular and scrabbling like spider legs. Worse were the smaller plants; they had been rendered a despairing rust with drooping arms that mourned the loss of their once beautiful fastenings.

There was still a refreshing neatness to the garden though, as pitiful as the winter had rendered some of its occupants. It was still uniform and tidy, there was not a singular stray leaf or dying arm that flopped onto the straight paths. It was entirely commendable work from the groundsman.

Ann caught herself with a little inner lurch. It was wrong to praise a man; praise would only lead to like, to adoration, to terrible lustful thoughts that ought to be burned along with the body that thought them. Even now, with just a thought of his work, she was swallowing images of his wide, calloused hand, raised high in a wave, hands that had dug into the earth that she was stood on, a brother of the earth that had covered those other hands, pale and spindly, that had crawled up her legs, in between the bones and crevices of her skin, polluting and dirtying and pleasuring. (No! Never that.) A wave of sick was rising involuntarily, begging to be expunged and purged, along with the intolerable thoughts, but it couldn't, not here, not with Ladie.

'We could sit more comfortably in the winter garden, Ladie, if you find you are too cold, or displeased by the nakedness of the plants?' Ann said.

They had walked around the whole garden twice before they took to the iron bench they were now sat on, in front of the trained wisteria, skeletal and starved. Away from the sharp neatness of the summer gardens, over the well-trimmed hedges to the distant landscapes. The same blue that fuzzed the fountains billowed over the meadow and fields beyond the river like a gauzy veil of the lightest fabric hanging from an impossibly thick grey sky. The ground was no longer green and brown and sodden and rich; it had bled out all of its colours until it hardened to a bitter mono-chrome. A sour black scowled in crooked lines and gritty groups of rubble where it had scratched away at the green-grey grass.

'Please, Ann, stop fretting so,' Ladie said, with a cross little furrow on her brow. 'I am perfectly fine. In fact . . .' She paused, as if thinking what words best to use next. 'Have you ever walked through the woods, Ann?'

'Oh yes, Ladie, we often go foraging in there. Mrs Hardy says that nothing feeds Ropner like that which we reap from its own grounds.'

'Oh, how charming!' Ladie smiled, extra sweetly, that little frown disappearing entirely. 'I think I should quite like to finish our little jaunt with a walk through the woods over on the west side; I can't say I have ever really been in them.' Her big grey eyes blinked at Ann innocently, expectantly. She was clearly waiting for permission.

Ann thought of everything over to the west side, where the woods were: the kitchen gardens, and the stables, the coal shed and the hen coops, and the game hut. She thought of whom they might stumble across, lurking there. Her stomach lurched. It would not do well to have Ladie exposed to them, to any of them (with their dirty cursing and fuck-ing and black tongues and reeking cigarettes). And what's more, suppose Ladie saw the likes of downstairs and assumed that Ann was no better than them? Decided she wanted nothing more to do with Ann? (Then you'll be done for. You'll be banished back downstairs forever, for so long that all the badness will get inside you and pucker all your insides like rotten fruit, and before you know it you'll be sinning like it's your birthright.) It was unbearable to even think.

'Is it . . . ahm . . .' Ann flustered. 'That is to say, are you allowed to . . .?'

'Well of course,' Ladie said flippantly. 'They are *my* woods after all, and I don't see why the outside there should be any worse for me than the outside here.' The cross little frown returned and Ann felt a prickle of panic. She would not ruin their carefully curated unity for the sake of a silly little walk. She gave a nod that was halfway to a shrug, and Ladie cheered and clapped so happily, Ann almost didn't feel that queasy feeling of foreboding.

25

I N THE WOODS, the leaves on the ground were curled
and fringed with mouldering damp, and the soil underfoot was hardened to bone with cold. That was good; that
way Ladie would not get her boots dirty.

The sun was so weak now it had turned the air grey.
Nature had forgotten the lightness and brightness of spring,
and in its lapse of memory, stripped to a skeleton of its
warmer self, the ugly underbelly of its essence was laid bare
beneath a bleak, drained sky. The trunks of the trees echoed
the ruddy colour of the earth, and bare branches webbed
their surroundings, so as they walked further along the forest
footpath, they seemed to be entering some vast, never-
ending haze of cold brown and grey.

Ann trained her eyes to the navy of Ladie's coat and the
rhythmic flashes of her milky-blue glove. She dropped back
ever so slightly, hoping it would remind Ladie of the house
and inspire her to go home. But it only seemed to drive
Ladie on.

Brown, grey, black, brown, brown, grey rolled on and on,
trundling slowly past the corners of Ann's eyes. But there,
just then, was a jerking shiver, a strange flit of something big
and dark and solid. Ann's head turned automatically to

follow it before she could tell herself not to look, not to give in to the promise of horror.

But nothing was there apart from the brown, grey, black, brown: bark, branches, bare and immobile.

'It's almost as if Ropner is cursed with an eternal autumn.' Ladie sighed. Ann turned back to her quickly and watched Ladie's grey eyes squint playfully. 'Tell me, Ann, what's it like? Downstairs, I mean.'

Ann's mind raced over waves of dead animals, of dust and of dirt and purple bruises, and of cold stone, and red-raw burning skin, of whorls of potato peel, and hours and hours falling like sand, of black iron bedposts, of the beating rabbit's heart of fear and of a fur-white ceramic. They blended into a tidal scream that Ann could not translate into words, let alone something palatable for a mistress to hear.

'It's . . . well, it's hard work, Ladie. But it's good work, I'd not change it.'

Ladie chewed on this, then out of nowhere let out a loud peal of laughter. 'Ann, I do believe you are an abysmal liar!'

Ann's face went up in flames and she sputtered, choking on the smoke.

Ladie ploughed on in delighted ignorance. 'What are the people like? Are there simply hundreds of servants? I imagine you all sometimes. Like little black beetles in your uniforms, the corridors teeming with you while you scurry about your work as I sleep. It would be nice to know those little beetles have names and faces; I could imagine then I had hundreds of friends and was not so lonely.'

(Imagine them all, shrieking with pain as stiff, hairy feelers cracked their skulls to sprout out of their heads, screaming for mercy while their backs broke and turned inside out, and the bones fused together and became shiny and black. Ha! Imagine them glittering on the floor, right before you crushed them into nothing with your heel. Ha! Ha!)

'I cannot say I know all their names,' Ann said. 'I strive to work at all the hundred hours of the day, so I keep myself to myself for the most part.' (Keep away so the rot doesn't spread.)

'And so chid the hasty-footed time for parting you,' Ladie said, pleased with herself.

Ann gave an empty laugh in return.

There it was again: in the corner of the other eye this time, a shadowy figure marring her periphery like a scar. Ann tilted her head slowly, to look at it without Ladie noticing. Her neck creaked rustily in her ears and a strange scrabbling noise sounded in the distance. But nothing, no one, was there.

'Well . . . you must know some names. Tell me them.' There was a strange keenness in her voice that made it sound more commanding than jovial.

Ann righted herself. She thought of Old Crone's black tongue, of Cook's pus-riddled face, and felt as though she might be sick. Why was she doing this, bringing up all the horrors of downstairs when Ann tried so hard to keep them at bay? Was she trying to torture her?

'Well, there's Mrs Hardy . . .' Ann began, buying herself time.

'Ah! I know, I know; the less we speak of her the better.'

Ann faltered momentarily, then pressed on. 'There is Rachel, the kitchen maid. I see her some—'

'Rachel?' Ladie interrupted, testing the taste of her name; the way it rolled from back to front, like a fat toffee too rich to chew. 'What colour are her eyes?'

Ann thought of the smell of milk and of open-mouthed sobbing, felt burning guilt and big eyes that saw too damn much. (What was this stupid game?)

'A thousand browns.'

Ladie nodded as if this were what she expected. 'Go on.'

'And . . .' Was this a trick perhaps? Would Ladie do that to her? Ann looked at her, her perfectly rapt, perfectly inno-cent expression 'And you know of Petra too?'

'Petra?'

The heat of a gaze flooded over Ann, and the rasping tongue of fear licked the inside of her skull.

Someone was here.

Someone was watching.

'Yes, Petra. She . . . ah . . .' Ann fought to stay focused on Ladie's cool grey eyes. 'She no longer works here, but once used . . . used to . . .'

The words died in Ann's throat. Mrs Hardy was there. Right between those two trees – no, not those, that tree *there*, with its dismembered branches tearing great slashes all down its grey bark. She was standing right there and watch-ing, her endless black eyes staring right at Ann, right into her. She made no move to acknowledge that Ann had seen her.

Inexplicably, Ann felt some frantic desperation, a need for Ladie to remember Petra so she could say, loud and clear enough for Mrs Hardy to hear, 'Ah yes, Petra! She was ter-rible. In fact she was perfectly beastly. I hated her, but it makes me realise how lucky I am to have *you*, Ann. So lucky.

I want for you to come and live with me and sleep at the foot of my bed like a cat.'

Mrs Hardy would see then that Ann had no rot or badness like the others, that her place was here, right by Ladie's side.

Ladie herself remained oblivious. It was some kind of trick of her imagination, it had to be. (*She's made of the same stuff as the house*, Petra had said. *How else would she appear like she's always been there, just waiting to chastise you, the bitch?*)

The housekeeper was still there, still staring. Ann could feel that hollowed-out feeling starting, scooping at all her insides. But, quite suddenly, Mrs Hardy blinked at Ann one last time before she stepped behind the tree and disappeared.

Ladie, still noticing nothing, seemed deep in thought, a little curve on her brow like a tiny frown. 'I cannot recall,' she murmured. 'Isn't it horrific that we forget? That memories are so slippery and distant, like soap bubbles, like dreams. How can we be sure they were real at all? We'll never know, we'll never see them again, and how frightening that the part of you that once knew it was a certainty, that was living it, whose reality it was, is gone, that you can't ask them for confirmation or proof, because you've forgotten them too.' She gave a tinkling little laugh that didn't seem like a laugh at all. 'What if all my memories are just stories I've told myself so many times I'm convinced that they are real? Some I can see so clearly in my head, but as soon as I try to write them or speak them, I can't find the words. Like a dream: the longer you stay awake and the harder you try to think about what happened, the faster you lose any sense of it.'

Ann didn't speak; she had heard Ladie's every word, but she couldn't process them at all. Not while Mrs Hardy's shape burned fluorescently on her eyelids every time she blinked. The world wobbled so harshly she felt as though almost the entire earth had fallen from beneath their feet, and all that was left was the thin, shell-like layer they were standing on, and that too was ready to crack and fall at any moment.

Suddenly Ladie linked her arm through Ann's, and mercifully the world righted itself and each of Ann's blinks showed only blackness. 'Well, never mind that now,' she said, in a voice that sounded so much more like her own. 'I have two more beetles, dear beetles, to remember.' She counted them off on the gloved fingers of her free hand. 'Number one, Rachel, and number two, Petra . . .'

Ann prickled. Why was Ladie so much as wasting her breath with their names? Why was she talking of them as though they were no different than Ann herself? Ann's face grew hot, and the skin over her cheeks felt uncomfortably tight. 'Well, Ladie,' Ann said with forced evenness. 'You need not concern yourself with them. For one thing, Petra is no longer—'

'Yes, no longer beetling around Ropner Hall. But I spy a third beetle to take her place. Number three, this fellow here.'

A silk finger threw Ann's gaze over auburn leaves to a distant figure weaving through trees like a needle, whose eye winked in and out of the nets of brown and grey.

He was not slowly meandering as he had been a million mornings ago when Ann first saw him. No, now he moved with a purpose that shifted the dead leaves about him so suddenly they seemed to growl. She baulked to start back but he was already upon them.

The man looked for all the world like he was shaped from the earth itself; had sprouted up from its belly like a tree, before unshackling his roots and starting to roam of his own volition. His work shirt was muddied and his boots and trouser legs wet with dew. The skeletons of leaves clung to his ankles. Their yellowed transparency was stark against the brown fabric that made him up. His eyes, Ann could finally see, were brown too. Brown, brown, brown, like a heart-beat's deep bass. From his right hand swung a bleeding rabbit; its matted fur stuck out from between the calloused fingers that clasped its neck tightly. Its body swung supple and heavy. It was still fresh, death's rigidity had not set in. Ann wondered how many of the dark marks on his clothes were not dirt but blood.

He spoke first.

'Well, well, snared two more rabbits, have I?' His voice was quiet, he did not seem to care to speak, but it had a weight to it that made you listen hard all the same.

'Good morning,' Ladie replied.

'My lady.' He made no effort to touch his forelock or even dip his head, but stared unblinkingly into Ladie's eyes. She looked right back at him and did not break her gaze. How dare he talk to her? Ann was absolutely rigid with shock. But Ladie was unperturbed; she smiled, and pointed to the dead rabbits as if they were fur stoles at a market.

'Our dinner, I see.'

'No, Ladie. For me, these.' His bluntness was gritty and brutish, like the short edge of a brick. And he needed to stop *looking* at Ladie like that – who did he think he was? Staring at her with his brown brown brown eyes, all pointed and sharp with a meaning Ann could not decipher. He had not once looked at Ann, beastly creature that he was; she would not want him to look at her anyway.

If she was called to, she could summon the strength to snap his neck, right here, right now. Like Scarecrowfootman had with that chicken. Make a crack like lightning and laugh at the dribbles of blood and foam stringing from his mouth, then put him in the darkness, vanish him with black mud that had swallowed that corpse whole; all those big white bones and shards, soil so dark blood doesn't show.

She was swaying on the spot slightly, like she was seasick. She dug her fingernails into her palms.

'Shame,' Ladie mused. 'I take it you're the new grounds-man and not some opportunistic poacher. Ann?' Ladie turned to her.

Ann stopped swaying abruptly, her nails dug in deeper. She did not want to speak, not in front of this man. She couldn't. What if she felt the sharp stab of his gaze and it pricked her with a wound that would never heal? She looked into the calm grey of Ladie's eyes and tried to swallow that stupid feeling of fear (of want).

'H-he—'

'Wey aye. Marcus Jameson.' He extended his palm; it was rough and webbed like leather. Ladie did not take it. Ann watched it drop heavily back to his side and the bottommost part of her stomach flexed.

'Perhaps you might catch some more for my dinner.'

Something in his jaw jumped and clicked. The grounds-man issued a non-committal grunt.

Ladie studied his reaction softly. 'Or perhaps, you would rather take me to hunt, let me catch my own.'

At this he smiled his slow, lazy half-smile that unfurled on his chin like a sail from a mast. 'Per'aps.'

The air was very thick.

She had done it, Ann thought. Ladie had sentenced herself. He was going to come for her in the night now. He was going to climb up the cracking walls of Ropner like a spider and creep silently through her window while she was sleeping. He was going to leap onto her bed and tear open her throat and try to fuck any available orifice.

'Well, careful as you go, like. Don't want you getting caught in one of my snares.'

'You don't?' Ladie's voice was sharp and careful; as if she were scoring something very precisely with a knife.

Ann wanted to shake her, to tell her it was a foolish, dangerous game, and yes, Ladie might have stopped her own murder for now, but it was only a matter of time before he pinned her against some tree trunk in a dark corner and ruined her entirely, leaving her as soiled as a servant.

She had a horrible urge to crack her palm against one of Ladie's perfectly perfect cheeks and tell her this was not how to handle them. You had to seem so spineless and demure and disengaged that for them to conquer you would be such an insignificant victory they wouldn't bother at all. You had to starve yourself to be sharp and spiky so that they wouldn't want to swallow you in case you got stuck in their throat and choked them.

But she had half a mind to crack her palm against Ladie's other cheek and wail that it wasn't fair, and to beg her to explain how she talked to them like that, how she charmed her way out of being laughable prey and into feeling the sharp stab of that brown brown brown.

Again came the man's lazy half-mast smile. Ladie tightened her grip ever so slightly on Ann's arm, and in one body they turned and walked away back toward the Hall.

Ann could feel his eyes watching them both as they walked away. Had she always stepped just so? At this pace? Right before left? With how much weight on each leg? With her spine held like that? She imagined him when they were out of sight, how he would slowly slope back into the thicket of bruised leaves, rooting through the undergrowth to follow trails of rusting blood and find more snared game, either dead or still squirming. The thought of his gaze seemed to spur them both on, so that their pace quickened and the driest leaves flurried in their wake until they were running as much as their skirts would permit. As a shrieking beast with three legs and three arms and two cherry-red faces.

26

THAT NIGHT, THE house sent Ann dreams. She was in the woods, the moon was hiding and the trees turned gleefully sharp and inky in its absence. Ann weaved through their wicked boughs as light and as simple as the wind, for in this dream that's what she was. She was fluid and free, slipping, whooshing, tickling, blustering, wonderfully supple and liberated in her invisibility. She breezed and delighted in fluttering the last of the leaves from their branches to meet certain death with their skeletal sisters on the forest floor. All along her transparent, ever-twisting spine, a sound carried. No more than a whisper, but it reached the undulating curve of her ear, which at that moment was sweeping over moss in the hollow of a tree.

Help me, the whisper hissed.

Her being trembled and ceased its playful whipping to silence every sound it stirred.

Help me, came the whisper again.

It called to her. She spread her wings, and in a torrent of gale sped towards the cries. Huddled at the base of the darkest tree was a figure, ghostly grey in the moon's absence. It writhed and twisted as if in a nightmare, and Ann felled flakes of bark and branches in her hurry to fly closer. Ladie's eyes were shut tight and her soft curves were rendered hard and harsh by strange convulsions that seized her, her mouth clapped and contorted in ceaseless cries as, there, twisting over her breast, was a great, dirty serpent, its fangs sunk deep into the cavity of her ribs.

Ann fumbled in vain to seize it with hands she no longer had. Whirlpools of leaves swirled in their wake, but the snake held fast, barely a scale was affected by Ann's howling rage.

Help me, Ladie cried. *Helpmehelpmehelpme.*

Ann tried to clap her palms to her ears, to curl up and block out the endless cries. But she was the air that they were cried into: she could not escape. They vibrated waves of terror and pain along every fibre of her being, they screamed right under her skin and sunk their sharpness into her soft see-through belly. She was defenceless, helpless, all she could do was watch as the spiteful inky trees spat out the groundsman at Ladie's feet.

He stood right inside Ann, stoical and painful and immovable, like a tumour. She pushed him with all her might, tried to banish him from her air, but he stood fast, only the hairs on his head stirring, like the leaves at his feet. Swiftly he lunged towards Ladie and plucked the snake from her breast like it might have been an apple on a tree. Ladie, in a movement more fluid than even wind could muster, rose from the floor and threw her arms around the groundsman. All the trees grew horrible marble eyes and watched as they sunk together to the ground. Ann was useless and abandoned, and the rattling mouth of the half-rotting corpse sucked her in through its lips and swallowed her whole.

27

I N THE EARLY dark, Ladie's room turned an intoxicating
honey-brown, the kind that only exists in places that
shelter you from white-cold winter nights. The fire crackled
and the glistening high points of the chestnut furniture
seemed to glow. Dapples of light, borne from the opalescent
mirror and Ladie's jewels, smugly nestled in their glass boxes,
threw themselves across the room to dance at the merry fire's
command. They twinkled and turned the floor to a slowly
shifting stained-glass window, whose innards recalled shattered sheep and hills and shards of saints, all glowing bright
in soft golds and wine reds.

Even the tiny faces in the painted tableaux framed at
intervals along her wall seemed to be smiling. There was
such a deep comfort from the warmth and the colours that
Ann felt it thicken the air around her, holding her close in
an embrace. She could have wept, or slept. Maybe hope was
this exact shade of brown; or love. Yes, surely, with its sonor-
ous bass, a heartbeat would be this colour.

Ann drifted softly through it all, smoothing the fine bed
sheets taut, and running her fingers through the potpourri
to shift the dust and sift its fragrance, making everything
perfect for Ladie's return from luncheon.

She had begun to attend the afternoons with her aunt again. Ann's heart ached at the memory of how much Ladie had declared to hate them. But it was Ladie, as sweet and proudly dutiful as ever, who had, a few days after their walk in the woods, asked Mrs Hardy if she might be well enough to take luncheon with the Duchess again. She had confided in Ann (only Ann, only ever Ann) that in her sickness she had lost weight in a way that was quite unbecoming, and looked forward to the luncheon food restoring her feminine curves.

Despite their closeness and Ladie's ever-growing eagerness to confide in her, neither Ann nor Ladie had ever spoken of the moment in the entrance hall. Ann had obeyed Mrs Hardy so intently that she had never even thought of the moment at all. The memory of it was growing fragile, like a robin's egg, its brokenness an inevitable future accepted by its being. Or like a snowflake doomed to melt and die by the mere biology of Ann's existence. Ann wondered sometimes if Ladie remembered it at all.

'I *hate* it here!'

Ladie returned from her daily luncheon with sugared dramatics a thousand million miles away from the marble hall. In one motion, she had swanned through the door, swept up her shawl, furiously spun it around her person and flopped with a thud onto her bed.

'The walls seem to be moving closer to me day by day, it hurts my head,' she said. Her eyes roamed over the wooden engravings carved in spirals on the roof of her bed, trying to spy if one of them was a secret doorknob that would unlatch a trapdoor so she could clamber up and away from Ropner. (Or maybe she was looking for a door that would take her to *him*.)

Ladie had not mentioned the groundsman, just as she hadn't mentioned the marble room. Perhaps she had forgotten him already. Or perhaps she knew, like Ann did (because you are so similar, after all) that the man was bad, that no good could ever come from him.

'And the food makes me feel so heavy and sleepy,' Ladie continued, 'like a big horrid pig getting fattened up for slaughter. But even that is nothing in comparison to Aunt. Honestly, she is such a *beast*. I'm sure they could write hundreds of books on such an oddity, should anyone have enough stomach to observe her. I always have *such* a ghastly time in her company, you can't imagine what she is like. Ah, me! And to think she is quite likely my only living relative. Abysmal. Ah, *me!*' She struck her heart with such a passionate flourish Ann could hear the echo of skin meeting skin and bone meeting bone.

Ann felt herself scowling. It was a gross injustice, a smite on order to have a thing so beautiful be made to feel like a pig. To have someone as delicate as a swan and as lithe as a cat be made to feel no better than a reeking, abysmal sow.

She had still caught not so much as a glimpse of the Duchess, but her perception of Ladie's aunt had changed dramatically ever since Ladie had first complained about her luncheons. And whatever Ladie disliked, Ann faithfully disliked too. Really, she had always thought Ladie looked uncomfortable receiving her aunt's kiss in that big portrait; really, she truly had. And she had always thought the Duchess's dress and ornamentations to be far too ostentatious in comparison to Ladie's natural beauty, and her elegantly simple gown. So it wasn't as if Ann *needed* to alter her opinion really; she had had the same thoughts and impressions as Ladie all along. *Say the word, Ladie,* Ann thought. *Say the word and I'll hunt down the Duchess. I'll go through all the forbidden rooms until I find her, and I'll seize her head and slice it off from her shoulders, and we can mount it on the wall and have our own happy luncheons underneath it.*

Ladie laughed half-heartedly from her position on the bed. 'A fine idea, Ann.'

Ann's mouth suddenly became dry and tacky so that it was hard to open. She had only meant to think those things, those nasty awful things, not to say them, to . . . Surely, surely she had not spoken them out loud?

Ladie rolled over suddenly, her back towards Ann, as if she might go to sleep. Ann floundered. Ladie had never been so cold with her before, had never turned away so heartlessly. It was what Ann had thought (said?), it had to be; she had given the game away. (Stupid girl, couldn't get the rot out, could you?) And now Ladie had seen it, had smelt it, had heard it, she was scared the rot was contagious (and it is, you know it is); scared that Ann might infect her in some way. All that time, all the ways she had opened to Ann like a mussel, and yet here she was, shell petals firmly re-met. This couldn't happen, Ann could not lose this. She made a desperate stab. 'Would it make you feel better to play court cards, Ladie?'

The silence seemed to last for days, and in the cold weather between them Ann's skin grew leathered with frostbite, pulling painfully dark and tight over her bones.

'I suppose we could.'

There, mercifully, the yellow eye of the sun returned and blinked blearily between them, weak but present. As if her body were the heaviest thing in the world, Ladie rolled over onto her back. Ann could see the crescent of her face again. 'Though let us just play on the bed here, I feel too heavy to move. The playing cards are in the third drawer of my dresser, on the left.'

Ann could move so quickly now that the sun reminded her of her soul and thawed her body's grip on it.

The drawer was empty but for the deck of cards and a stout black notebook. Ann brushed its leather skin gently, as if her fingertips might be able to read its contents like Braille, and shoot its secrets up through Ann's nerves, straight into her brain. But the little black book remained stubbornly shut and silent. Ann sifted the courtiers from the pack and left the rest of the deck with the little black notebook that stared at the back of her head as she walked away.

Ann handed Ladie the cards and she began to spread them out on the bed between them. All the men had spindly moustaches that besmirched their upper lips and made them look pathetic, like half-dead weeds. All the queens looked solemn and sad, like Ladie in her painting. Their eyes were big and round and set deeply in their hollows. Paper hands folded neatly around their respective suits; iron-saturated red or ink black.

'They look very grand, don't they,' Ladie said of the queens. She laid them out on the tray in their diamond formation. 'I like to think of them as friends who all live together while their kings and jacks go about all the boorish courtly duties.' She pressed the kings and jacks slowly into their own places.

Ann let her win.

*　　*　　*

It wasn't until hours, or maybe days later, once Ann was darning, cupped in the armchair and its corner, and Ladie was picking at her embroidery, that she spoke of the woods.

'Tell me who our third beetle was, Ann.'

Ann hesitated. 'The man from the woods?'

Ladie gave an absent-minded nod; her eyes watched her blue and ivory stitches, but she had grown very still, like a hare on its haunches, ears swivelling and whiskers twitching.

'He is the new groundsman, I believe,' Ann said. (He is poison and vile, and badness leaks from his every pore like a rancid smell. Give him an inch and he will turn it into a mile to wrap around your neck and choke you, such is his nature.)

Ladie looked up and blinked, waiting for more and dwarfing Ann's information to inadequacy. She had dropped her needle so it spun like a draught-caught spider from its embroidery web.

IhatehimIhatehimIhatehim, Ann wanted to say. *He stares with eyes that see too much and never shy away. He stares in such a way I can feel it on my body long after he has left, a gristly residue that stains like the mark of Cain. He is a man as bad as any man, if not worse, because he has all the wildness, all the lawlessness of outside to boot, and he has that vicious power, that magnetic pull that conjures sin and terrible thoughts. I hate him, I wish him dead.*

'He lives in the game hut,' was all she added.

'He lives *there*? In that evil-smelling hut in the woods?' Ladie said, crinkling her nose as if she could smell it right then. 'How odd. He must be told he is welcome to stay with the rest of the servants.'

'Well . . . I shouldn't think he wants to, Ladie. I can't see him liking the house much, I rarely see him inside it.' It was true, Ann thought bitterly. He refused to enter the house as if plagued by some sort of curse, strictly orbiting the grounds and the woods. (Good. Let him stay out.)

'Well I can't say I blame him,' Ladie said. 'How exhilarating it must be to live in the near-wildness like that.'

She set her embroidery aside completely. It was a picture of two little rabbits, their faces and ears poking out between a myriad of meadow grass and wildflowers. Ladie looked at them and stroked their stitches absent-mindedly.

'I am envious of game meat sometimes,' she said quietly. 'Of hares snared and torn at by the dogs, or slipped open by a wicked knife. I keep feeling . . . rather, the feeling swallows *me*, for it is too great to be something I just feel. Yes, I am swallowed by this feeling, this desire to be consumed, like meat, to be bit and torn into, to have my flesh wrung and ripped, to have my ribs cracked open by strong arms and have the heat from hands pressed against my insides. It is as if something inside me needs to be let out and that's the only way it can happen.'

Without being aware of it, Ann was holding her breath. The room was, too. She could feel the pressure weighing on her ears, making a funny sort of high-pitched ringing that sizzled the silence between her and Ladie.

'Ann,' Ladie said. Ann breathed out gently, though the room did not. 'Ann, do you know why man started to snare and kill the hare?'

Ann had thought of the scraps of rabbit she had tried once, the way they had tasted, how they looked in the fields; earthen and leaping and twisting and fearful. She could still feel the meat twitching and flinching in her mouth as she chewed, as if there were a non-dead part of them still trying to escape. It was like gnawing at her knuckles until she tasted her own blood.

'They killed the hare because they thought them to be ghosts of witch women assuming their form to enter fields and bewitch the cattle and crop.'

'Please,' Ann said. 'Please stop, Ladie.' She could still feel that trickle of dread now, flowing sluggish and cold.

'Why? Does it scare you, Ann? This talk of witches? Witches are only women wronged.' Ladie lunged and clasped Ann's hands so suddenly Ann could have screamed. 'For all we know, Ann, we could be destined to be witches, or already are . . .'

Oh God. The thoughts in Ann's head thrummed. *Oh God. Oh God. Oh God.* She had nearly always been safe with Ladie, but sharply that feeling of safety grew precarious, as if it had been an illusion all along. All it took were a few words.

Ann tried to hold them delicately in her mind, suspended away from any associations, from any horror they might remind her of. Words could be so fickle and evil; quite un-expectedly they could give way, like a trapdoor, and send you screaming and falling to land on something wholly more sinister. Here she was, about to fall down, down, down into the memories of the marble room, of Rachel and Scarecrowfootman, of blood and soil as black as the gaping mouth of a corpse.

'Please,' Ann begged. The floodgates in her head would not hold. *Stopstopstop.* Ladie squeezed so tightly it was as if she were trying to part flesh and reach bone. But just as suddenly she dropped Ann's hands and laughed.

'It was a game,' she said lightly. 'Only a game.'

Ann watched the yellow-white marks Ladie had left behind, watched the layers of skin slowly unstick themselves from the bones they had been pressed to. The blood squirming back to the places it was pushed from, blooming colour back in its wake. She listened to its steady thump and gush in her ears. It made her voice sound very quiet and far away when she spoke. (Why say it then? What was possessing her to come out with such a thing, such a dirty bad thing?)

'I used to think bleeding meant I was a witch,' she said. 'I thought the house had cursed me.'

Ladie took a very long time to answer. 'The house?'

Ann's nod was slow and small and her voice was smaller still, like it was coming from some distant place inside her. 'I was scared of it, I think.'

Ladie nodded soberly. 'Sometimes I can hear scratching, especially at night.' Her whisper came so low it sounded hollow. 'As if the walls were filled with hundreds of mice and rats all teeming over one another, clawing to get out. Sometimes I lie awake for hours not able to get the sound and the thought of what it is out of my head. Silly, really . . .' The blood still thumped and gushed, so the silence between them didn't sound like silence. 'The bleeding . . . That's not the house. You know that now, don't you, Ann?'

'I do.'

'Sometimes when I bleed there looks like clumps of flesh mixed in with all the blood, and I stare and stare at it on the rag and think of how I made that, that was part of me and now it's not and yet I'm still alive.' (So Ladie had rot, too, Ladie had horrible folds of flesh that burned, and if marble could be moved Hermia would have marble folds too.)

179

'Sometimes my blood is so brown it looks black, like tar, and I think I must be dying, but I'm still alive.'

'Maybe that's what all the blood is for, to say we're immortal – like witches, ha! See! We are witches.'

'Good witches?' Ann pleaded, and she hated herself for it.

'When we want to be. Witch sisters bound in blood.'

It sounded less scary when Ladie had said it like that; it sounded like feeling less lonely.

It was impossible to be lonely, now that she knew her and Ladie were intrinsically one.

28

ANN SAVOURED SILENCE now; it had become special because there was no longer any discomfort in it. Any moment of silence between her and Ladie had become a hallmark of trust and kinship; it showed the strength of their bond, showed it was one that did not need to be qualified with idle chatter.

Ann treasured the silence that came when she tightened Ladie's short stays before luncheon. She relished the aching creak of the strings pulling the bones into submission. The way Ladie braced herself against the chest-of-drawers, her gloves sometimes squeaking against the smoothness of the wood. The little sharp intakes of breath. She loved, too, the small sounds of the bath; the squidge of the sponge and the deluge of water it released down Ladie's back; how it gurgled back into the water, lapping placidly around the dough of her middle. Ann could see, faintly, the nubs of Ladie's spine beneath skin. They did not stick out angrily like hers did. It was as though every part of Ladie, even her hardest corners, most delicate bones, were soft and cushiony.

Ann traced the hidden stepping stones of her spine with the suds and used the space that silence afforded her to memorise the way the colour of Ladie's skin changed under the pressure of the sponge and its release, the friction of its gentle rub. She wondered if all bodies could be this beautiful, or if only Ladie's had this power.

Even when Ladie spoke less, Ann understood her more than ever.

'I am growing so restless,' she had said one day, and Ann knew that she meant she was bored of her room, so she took it upon herself to rearrange it while Ladie was at luncheon that day; changing the cushions on the divan, filling the little china bowls with new potpourri, dragging the partition screen to a different spot. Ladie had come back from luncheon and clapped her gloved hands together in happiness.

'Oh, Ann!' she had said, walking over to the screen in its new place and stroking its Paris green fabric. 'I can't tell you how perfect this is.'

The screen was in front of the left window now, whose wide facade looked impassively towards the half-mast curve of the woods. Ladie had taken to sitting at it often, right on its sill with her feet resting on a little stool. Her head turned away, resting on the windowpane, so all Ann could see of her face was the curve of her cheek and the soft flesh of her ear, the light from outside burning the pink shell orange and catching on the fuzz. The thick sinews of her neck twisted as her chest and body were facing Ann. Ann watched the skin of her chest moving up and down. Sometimes her breath seemed to skip and Ann wondered if those little skips she observed were actually the beat of her heart.

'It's funny to watch all this space and still feel a caged thing,' Ladie had said once. She spoke without warning, still facing the window, her breath fogging the pane with abstract shapes.

Poor Ladie, Ann thought. How that horrid isolation from her bout of sickness had affected her. 'You are free to do as you like now you are well again, Ladie,' Ann reminded her gently. 'Think of how you have enjoyed our walks in the gardens, how liberating it is to wander through such wonderful spaces.' She was darning another one of Ladie's capes; they had been taking so many walks outside recently that Ann thought it important to keep them in good condition.

Ladie's head shifted; her chin dropped slightly as if she were pressing her forehead harder to the window. 'Not entirely free.' Her voice was muffled against the glass so that Ann had to strain for it. 'That feeling of liberty only comes when my heart no longer feels an absence.'

'But I am here, Ladie.'

Ladie turned to her (just like you knew she would, look at how your words have comforted her), and smiled like she had only just remembered that Ann was there at all.

'Yes, Ann, you are.'

Sometimes, when Ladie was at luncheon, Ann sat in the same spot on the windowsill, pressed her forehead to the same place watching Ropner through her eyes.

Whenever they were apart, Ann conjured an imaginary Ladie to be beside her. Ladie was there while Ann picked at breakfast in the morning; Ladie was there while Ann plaited her own hair at night. And while Ann squeaked cloth over windows and watched the jagged figure of the groundsman trudge from the woods, Ladie drew her head high and walked right outside to meet him, to tell him she wished to never speak to him again, to see him no more on Ropner's grounds.

Ladie was even there when Ann cleaned her rust-stained rags, and why wouldn't she be? There was nothing to be ashamed of, not now they had spoken of blood and let it bond them as if one heart beat it through both of their veins. They had peeled back each other's skin and bore the naked ugliness of each other's bones. They were one.

One morning, though, everything changed.

Ann brought up the breakfast tray as usual; Ladie's room was as faithfully familiar as ever, with only one discernible change. The sheets were chewed and twisted on the bed, the mattress was cold; the room was empty.

It smelt strange in the morning chill, in the absence of Ladie's warm body. The light was grey, dreary, and dribbling in reluctantly through a chink in the curtains. Everything was cast unfamiliar and empty. So empty. As if no one had ever lived there. The house clicked and ticked all around.

Ann's arms began to fizz under the weight of the breakfast tray, it seemed to be growing heavier every second, twanging all the tendons and muscles in her arms, as all its foodstuffs slowly transfigured into mean, leaden versions of themselves.

She watched every morning, in solemn silence, as Cook piled on waxen fruit and ladled globs of porridge. It was naughty, but she had begun to wonder: wonder what it all tasted like. Cook tonged ovals of bacon that shone dark pink onto plates and mingled their fat with the grease of the fried eggs. As Ann locked her sharp wrists and elbows around her middle like an embrace, fresh saliva spurted into her mouth, slimed under her tongue. Wonder what it would be like to bite into the thick leathery strips. Pastries with flaky coats and yawning yeasty middles, dusted with flour or sugar that was so white it would make Ladie's teeth squeak to bite. Wonder what it would be like to chew and chew until it turned into a great globule she could suck into nothingness and disappear into the flavour of it all.

Her stomach was groaning. The crystalline glasses made their golden juices look so beautiful they ought to be in a church, and thick flakes of burning pink salmon oozed under chunks of melting salt. Wonder what it would be like to have it all warm and gurgling inside you. She wanted to fling back her head and groan in harmony with her roaring belly. (You could steal some now and no one would know.)

Ann put the tray down on the bed quickly and took a step back, marking a safe distance between the food and her mouth. The temptation to eat it was terrible. It was some kind of mortal sin, wasn't it? To be greedy like this? To hanker so carnally after something not your own? (Why should it not be yours? You're no different really, Ladie even said so.) It was a terrible sin. (It would be good food). She would sizzle and twist and burn. But everything on the tray glistened enticingly at her in the dim light. This was not the kind of food she would have to sick up, this was not the kind of food that threatened to turn to rot once it was inside you. Banquets like this, feasts like this, would convex mean corners and soften skin and put colour all over but especially on the high points of your cheeks, like Ladie. (She won't want it anyway.)

It was true. At her past few breakfasts, Ladie had taken to pushing her food round listlessly. Cutting it into smaller and smaller chunks, like she was trying to make it disappear without having to eat it. Ann couldn't understand it, this sudden, strange little change. She would act like she didn't realise, too scared to challenge her in case it pushed her away somehow, disrupted the closeness she had cultivated.

So she quietly submitted to adapt to any which way Ladie behaved, studiously noting each and every change in routine; how much longer she spent dressing behind the green partition screen, the picking at breakfast, the ever quieter mornings, the long moments of Ladie sitting with her cheek pressed to the window, not breathing a word.

But this – Ladie not being here at all – was new and foreign and unruly to navigate and Ann didn't like it at all. Still, what could she do but try.

With what felt like a great wrench, she stepped away from the tray and hurried to the curtains to open them.

The grounds they hid were bleary and damp. Their vast expanse gave nothing away, their stoical immortality denying evidence of something so futile as time, as fickle as human wishes and emotions. The clouds sighed and stretched above them and they remained entirely unperturbed by the slow sticky panic beginning to congeal inside of Ann. Grey light irritated the room to order, black shadows prickled to a lighter purple and everything in it was suddenly, mercifully, not so secret.

Perhaps Ladie was hiding somewhere in here? Perhaps it was all a game. *Only a game, Ann.* It was all a joke! Yes, one of Ladie's tricks. (Cruel and spiteful and spoiled.) Ladie would laugh that golden wooden laugh once Ann found her crouched under the dressing table, she knew it.

But she was not there. Nor under the bed. Ann lifted each cover and pillow carefully. Ladie was not under any of the sheets. She slid open each dresser door, checked the fold of each curtain, even looked into the scrubbed scoop of the bath.

No Ladie.

The room was empty, completely empty. Ann was completely, utterly alone in it. She had to find Ladie, she couldn't be alone, it wasn't safe. Suppose Ladie wasn't safe.

Suppose the man had got her.

The sticky panic was proving like dough, expanding and bloating, tacking all the way up into her throat, her lungs, and the room purred all around her.

No. No, it was impossible. She would *know* if something bad had happened to Ladie, if she had fallen prey to the man, if she had – worst of all – abandoned Ann. She would feel it. Underneath all that heavy panic would be something hard and concrete and certain. They were joined almost as one; any pain Ladie had, any suffering or strife, Ann would feel too.

She tried (it was hard now, all the doughy panic was baking in her brain) to be rational, to think that Ladie might have taken a walk to one of the reading rooms. (Not without Ann, never without Ann, what reason would she have? He has taken her, surely.) No, perhaps she was with her aunt. (She despises her, idiot. Luncheons are excruciating enough.) No, with Mrs Hardy then, telling her what a good, clean, loyal and devoted companion Ann was proving to be, how Ann should be removed from the dank servants' pits, the festering garrets, and allowed to be forever by Ladie's side. *It's what you deserve, Ann,* she told herself solemnly. *If you are like one with Ladie, sisters, like she says, you should live in these spaces, eat all the good proper food, wear all those lovely dresses.* Ladie would know that too: know that Ann was always good, had always been good (the dark mud?) and pure, and clean (white shards, right there in the corner of your eye), and so dutiful (bloodbloodblood).

A light pinprick niggled her neck, the soft vulnerable exposed bit, right where someone's watching eyes might be felt. She had forgotten to check in the wardrobe!

Ann narrowed her eyes towards the thin black space between its doors. Squinting for Ladie's grey eyes blinking back at her. But when she pulled the doors open, Ladie was not there either.

There were six gowns hung inside. Six skirts with their bodices that all shivered like leaves. Four day dresses, oh so sweet in shades of fruit and flowers. Two stoical outdoor dresses and their loyal coats dark enough to ward off winters. The luncheon gown of the day led the line, slightly turned out of the wardrobe so that the fabric of the skirt fell towards her, like it had draped itself deliberately so; to titillate, to invite. She let herself run the skirt through her fingers, one hand still holding a wardrobe door open, so she could shut it if needed; if the gown spoke too loudly, or Ladie came back.

The skirt was ivory cream with a fine brocade of blue-grey winter foliage and bursts of deep-pink berries. It had a thin layer of gauzy muslin apron as its uppermost fabric; not soft like silk, it made the skin on her fingers buzz. Her other hand loosened on the wardrobe door. She seized the skirt with both hands and they grew greedy. They unhooked its matching jacket from the hanger, still prickling. They pressed it against her, and now there was a strange effervescence bubbling through her body that made her so light she could float to the mirror. The colour looked just right against her, just the way it did against Ladie, the pattern so delicate and feminine.

Ann pulled her shoulders back and let them relax down so the points of her shoulder blades bit into the meat of her back, the way Ladie held them, the way it looked like she had no weight on them. And she widened her eyes and tucked her chin so her cheeks looked rounder and younger.

God, she looked like Ladie.

If she had more to eat, if she didn't throw up the little she had, her cheeks would grow fuller. Perhaps if she dabbed piss on her eyebrows and spent more time outside they would go lighter and her skin would grow darker, like Ladie's had from all the sun, from not having her head stuck underground and in fireplaces. That would make her eyes look wider, too, she imagined, the way Ladie's did. The likeness between them was growing more and more every second Ann held the dress against herself. She laughed a little, from that bubble of happiness the thought made. But she made sure to do it the way Ladie would. So light and carefree that it always sounded a little fake and dull.

'Ann!'

Ladie stood dazed and flustered, as if she had just landed from being whirled in a hurricane, entirely unstuck from the earth's mantle, and was confused to find herself back to what she had so savoured being untethered from. Her eyes were glazed and unseeing.

'Ladie! I . . .' Ann thrust the jacket far from her body and fumbled to right its lifeless form and reinstall it in the wardrobe. 'I was just making sure everything was in order for the day.' The fabric hissed against its sisters and nestled back to its place, smug with Ann's secret. 'I thought perhaps you were in the one of the reading rooms . . .' Ann tailed off, because it was obvious that was not where Ladie had been.

She was still in her nightgown, but its lilac silhouette was rumpled and stained lightly in places. She had on a pair of her silken gloves, and outdoor boots. With the delicate dress, the boots looked overly large and offensive. It was all sadly comical in its mismatch. The odd, washed-out look it gave her was only exacerbated by wisps of her hair curling out haphazardly from her night plait. She looked like something blown in by the wind, a sprite or a waif, her eyes big and heavy in her head.

The notion of her being in one of the reading rooms still hung in the air; it snickered at them both. Ladie listened to it and seemed as if she were weighing up how to answer.

'I was quite seized with a desire to walk, Ann,' she said, 'I must confess. I felt almost as if I had a fever.' She followed Ann's eyes to her bare arms; her silk hands toyed with one of the stains on her nightgown. 'I needed to cool, and in my half-awake mind, well, I suppose I did not give much thought to attire . . . Goodness, imagine how I would look for luncheon if I had to dress myself.'

Ann wished Ladie had not tried to joke. It made it more obvious she was keeping something from her. 'Oh . . . yes. Well, I have your breakfast here, Ladie. It might be pleasant for you to sit and eat it by the window, and we can talk together while you do.' Ann tried to keep her voice unobtrusive and mindlessly pleasant, like she wasn't going to ask again where Ladie had been, like she didn't care.

Ladie's nose wrinkled and Ann felt a sudden panic that Ladie could smell the sour sweat of her menstrual blood.

But Ladie only blinked, and said in a falsely fair-weather way, 'Oh, I think I may be too tired to talk. Perhaps you wouldn't mind leaving me to breakfast, only so I might sleep a little afterwards . . .'

Ann dipped into a curtsy and left Ladie's room. In that moment, she hated her.

29

LADIE'S SECRET HAD wormed its way between them; Ann felt it in the quiet spaces that once had brought them closer and that now gaped horribly wide. It was as if they had shared so much and been unified so tightly that there was nothing left to do but to spring away from each other with insurmountable force, ripping wide a gaping chasm.

Every other second, Ladie was waking up for Ann to deliver her breakfast tray, and in each of those seconds Ann observed her cold skin, her flushed cheeks, her bed sheets falsely slept in, that damp smell of a place outside.

That Ladie might be keeping something from Ann, keeping a secret deliberately shaded, stung an inconceivable amount. The injustice of it all. Ann wanted to force apart Ladie's lips, to dive down her gullet so that she could dissolve inside of her. So she could sit in the smooth curve of Ladie's eye socket and see all that she saw, so she could lace herself between the beating part of Ladie's heart and the wisp of soul attached to it and feel everything Ladie felt, too.

They dutifully went about their routines with one another, following the grooves in the stage without a conscious thought, playing the same play again and again, though now each silence had a new meaning, each morning an exercise in anticipation.

Some days she was not there at all; Ann would find the room empty and lifeless and she would sit in it until Ladie returned with some flimsy excuse, find her breakfast cold and send Ann to fetch a new tray. Some days Ladie was there, laid in her bed sleeping in the most unconvincing pretence, and Ann would pretend she didn't notice that the bed sheets were perfectly tucked and not at all slept in, or that Ladie's cheeks were flushed and ruddy and emanated a cold chill at odds with the warmth crackled into her room by the fire. While Ladie was having luncheon, Ann would check under her bed, at the bottom of the wardrobe, behind the divider, until she found her outside boots, the soles coated in clods of fresh mud, still cold and wet.

Ladie was only ever in one of the reading rooms, or on an early morning walk about the house, or only just looking to find Ann with her breakfast tray because she was so terribly hungry; that's what she told Ann to account for her absence, and Ann would know then, with a vehement triumph, that Ladie hated her. That all these secrets and lies were because she suddenly found Ann deplorable, or because she thought it would be wiser to request the company of another servant, one not so loathsome, not so rotten (impossible). Which was *their* plan from the start, of course.

Downstairs, Ann eyed them warily while she was condemned to eat soup at their table.

For their part, they had perfected the art of ignoring her. Ann would have been thankful for this once, being completely safe in the shell of their ignorance, but she resented it now. She wanted them to notice her, she wanted Cook to scowl, for Old Crone to unfurl vulgarities on her black tongue; wanted Matchstick to cackle and goad until she turned an ungodly red. That way she would have reason to fight back, scream that she knew what they were doing, knew that they were all contriving to ruin her, to drive her mad. But their eyes simply slid past her, as if she weren't there at all.

She pushed her spoon into the muddy liquid with a bitter listlessness, watching it flow like rapids over the metal.

Ann imagined that Ladie had been kidnapped by the groundsman, bewitched by him. She pictured them together. The room would be dark and nocturnal, a deep green, an undergrowth green, and all shrouded in a kind of smoke or fog. The type of place where two lovers – Ann shuddered – might meet. Ladie would be wearing that lilac nightgown; its colour usually saccharine and naive, but in the room it would blend in so well with the smoke it would look a part of it, as if one breeze would dust away the smoke and the dress together. Her hair would be back in a twist, with the two strands either side of her face brushing the points of her cheeks and tickling shadows onto her eyes. The man would look like he didn't belong.

Suppose they spoke; or, worse, suppose they didn't need to. There were things more potent than language in a conversation; Ann had seen that silent conversation they had already held in the woods. Suppose he looked at her like that again; with that demanding closeness that turned the terrible dark in his eyes into an abyss that compelled Ladie to jump. Suppose she noticed all the sharp snags of his hands, how they felt like bark against her skin.

Ann's mind taunted her, it showed them stepping closer and closer while she watched, unable to stop it, unable to help Ladie as he reached towards her, reached for—

In the hollow of her spoon, momentarily, a chunk of carrot bobbed up onto the surface. Ann dropped her spoon in surprise and the orange chunk disappeared once more beneath the scummy liquid. She looked up and saw Rachel watching her from across the kitchen; her brown eyes blinked and smiled.

Soup was only ever a liquid broth; every morsel of meat, every chunk of vegetable, was reserved strictly for upstairs. Yet here was a carrot, orange and glistening, given to her by Rachel.

Rachel smiled kindly, the warmth of it melting her eyes.

Ann stood up sharply, seized her bowl and threw it to the floor so that its contents splattered and skidded along the entire kitchen. Finally, *finally*, they looked at her. Their eyes were big and wide and staring right at her, hardly daring to believe what they were seeing, hardly able to conceal their glee.

The moment was tacky in Ann's throat and she fought to swallow it. She looked directly into Rachel's wobbling brown eyes, drawn and downturned, stupid with the promise of tears. She did not want pity from the likes of her.

'Clean it,' she spat at those watery bovine things. She clicked her fingers and, like they had been waiting for a signal, the others leapt on Rachel like starving mutts.

30

FROM THEN ON, Ropner punished her with strange dreams, many of which featured the half-rotten corpse, perhaps watching her while she washed viscous clots from her rag, slavering after the smell of blood, hankering to have the tarry substance once more in its veins. Or she would be forced to lie for hours beside it in an earthen coffin of black soil, the melancholy sweetness of mud not quite covering the harrowing odour of rot, of mouldering flesh, of rancid pustules bursting from red-raw stinging knots of muscle. Or she would wake up in a cold sweat after another dream had concluded with the corpse unhinging its awful jaw and swallowing her whole.

There were dreams without the corpse, too, usually with Ladie in its place, and those were, in fact, worse.

It would start with Ladie lying, sleeping on her bed, her hair fanned out as if by water, peaceful and glorious like a painting. Ann could do nothing but watch: her skin was marble and her eyes were hollowed out and frozen, so all they could do was stare.

She was doomed to it. Doomed to watch as the house rolled its floorboards and shivered every stone. As its bricks, stiff and unyielding with age, ground mortar between their teeth and slowly contorted and contracted their walls. The house squeezed and shifted Ladie like it was forcing her down the tract of its throat. Ladie was awake by this point, her eyes nothing but those screaming circles of white, a mad, white animal fear that lashed out of her throat again and again and again as Ropner kneaded her through each room, whipped her with its banisters, beat her with each door until it was able to deposit her directly into the steely river, where the waters held her under.

The river garrotted her with tiny mean currents, flooding her eyes, her ears, forcing open her mouth and the dark folds of flesh between her legs. Flowing into every orifice of her body unheralded. Bloating her body and peeling skin from bone until the river had sucked each and every bone raw.

Ann unsheathed herself from her stony skin and picked up each and every bone that floated on the river's surface and buried them where they belonged. In the deep dark black black forever black mud.

When she woke up she heaved into her chamber pot, scrabbling at her throat with fingernails slick with soil. The splatters were iridescent like broken wet opals.

Ann hated each and every speck. They smelt sour and repugnant, and, using the second key, she deposited them onto the patch of grass she used for Petra's sick all those million miles and years ago.

Dawn had not yet broken and a thick slither of the peeling moon was suspended against the hazy sky. It offered little light, a pallid blue-grey that cast everything as a ghostly imitation of itself. The absence of the sun suppressed the grounds to near-silence; only the wind creaked and lone early birds let out plaintive coos, eerie in their solidarity.

It was because of this silence that the laugh rang clearer. Ann recognised its golden-wood echo as immediately as if it had come from her own mouth.

Ladie.

Her heart beat faster.

Ladieladieladie.

This was the secret that had born those silent mornings, that gaping chasm that was ruining Ann entirely. Somewhere, Ladie was here. Ann would find her, and Ladie would share her secret, and everything would be right and good and clean and perfect again. The fading laugh echoed mockingly round the muddy globe of Ropner, distorting its origins.

Blindly, Ann ran towards the summer gardens. The grass was slippery and the mud oily with dew, but Ann's feet refused to falter. The hedges that marked the borders of the summer gardens were impassive with the weight of shadows. With only one moment of hesitation, Ann entered.

'Ladie?' She whispered.

Ladieladieladie?

The rustling of leaves chorused. Their trees looked different in the hour before dawn, their looming authority, comforting and safe in light, disappeared. They stood solemn and naked, shivering as Ann passed.

The entire heavenly garden seemed to be damned to a shade of purgatory until the moon turned its face away and made room for day. At the turn of every corner, Ann imagined the sudden screaming presence of a corpse, of a night spectre, of two entwined lovers. But at each turn she was greeted with nothing but the cadaverous faces of trees and statues.

She had known all along, deep down, Ladie would not be here. She would not be in the winter garden with the fairy-spell flowers, either, or the meadow they had picnicked on. She remembered Ladie's countenance when she spoke of the woods, the way she begged to go.

Ann turned west and Ropner rewarded her by letting Ladie's laugh dance towards her on a breeze. *Here lies buried treasure*, the woods said.

The woods were almost entirely dark. Ann made her way through them as quiet as a mouse, sure that if she stirred even a single leaf, the wet black mud would give way and a great rotten mouth would swallow her whole, just like she dreamed.

'Ladie?' she whispered, in a voice so tiny it could only have been meant for Ladie's soul to feel.

Ladieladieladie.

The faintest of whispers slipped back towards her. 'Charlotte?'

Ann turned.

His waistcoat was undone and the hems of his slacks were stuffed unceremoniously into his boots. He did not hold his gun like a gentleman, swinging it from the crook of his elbow. Instead the snout of his gun rested on his shoulder, nestling towards his neck, and the butt was cradled in his palm.

Even so, the way he had stalked through the trees, and how he let a match trail from his lips like a fag, were as if he were the man of the manor. The groundsman had been hunting, no doubt: there was a glaze of wild elation about his eyes. His clothes were rumpled and slightly muddied, flies half undone, too, as if he had been seized in the middle of sleep by some mad desire to kill. There was a sheen of sweat on his brow, like sap.

In the silence he let hang, Ann tried to calm the rush in her head, to speak like Ladie had spoken to him, without fear. To pick a quip or even just a greeting from the currents. She knew they were there because, guaranteed, as soon as he would leave and the tide in her brain receded, everything she could have said would be washed up, glinting mockingly like seashells. But he spoke before she could.

'You look like her, y'know.'

Ann blinked.

'The Ladie upstairs.'

She dipped her chin a fraction; a meek imitation of acknowledgement that she hated herself for. Head bent, she felt him step closer; the air stirred and brought with it the smell of sweat. It was not unpleasant, it was a thick musk that made Ann think of woven wicker dark with rain, and of mud, and cuts of oozing meat. It was the smell she noticed from the walk and her whole body yearned for it. She had a wild, untamable urge to breathe in the smell so deeply that it coated the lining of her whole body; slicking to her throat, under her nails, under her eyelids, in the curve of her ears, deep into the dark hole between her legs, all around her lungs and her stomach and her heart.

He stepped closer still. This would be how she died. She knew it. (Would it really be so bad?) As the distance between them halved, his rough eyes made quick darts.

'Take away the clothes an the performin' an you'd have no way of tellin' one from the other.'

Nothing seemed to exist but the space between them. In that space alone, Ann could hear the tiniest rustling leaves and the wash of the river, and feel the infinity of the gaping sky above and the never-ending depths of the wet black soil beneath. As if all the world and everything in it had been squashed unceremoniously into existing only in the space between the groundsman and herself.

She stepped back, away from the enormity of the moment, and the space stretched with her, snapping the world back into order. He laughed and let his gun swing down, pushing the barrel into the earth as he lent on it like a cane.

'Run along, rabbit, and I won't say you've been out of your burrow.' He clocked her gaze on his gun. 'I won't shoot you, neither. One snare for the night is enough.'

It was as she lay in bed, raggedly breathing and deafened by the pounding of her heart that had carried her, running from the woods, that she realised he was holding no kill.

Fuck him. Ann scowled. *I hate him. Look what he has done, made me feel foul and soiled, carving out some aching hollow fucking horrid feeling at the bottom of my belly.* (That's all the rot coming true.) That gaping feeling cried out for the heavy thrum of brown, brown brown brown locked-in eyes, for hands knotted and rough; the sickening presence of hair on them, thick and dark, advertised the vulnerability and uncleanliness of the flesh beneath. Ann's lip, without her realising, had snarled to a curl right under her nose. She forced herself to shut her eyes, and the house moved all around her. It moved slowly, surreptitiously, like a crouching predator; you would hardly know it was there.

But even a fox slinking soundlessly through the darkness still secretes its scent, so that the hare it hunts is frozen by the impending doom it can't quite source. The fox doesn't care; prey tastes nicer when it dies afraid.

Floorboards clicked together like loose teeth, and groans of draughts rose through the throats of its stairwells; they harmonised in one low growl of hunger. The thought of being hunted was an impossible notion to quell. He was going to come for her, break the boundaries of the house, break his word, and hunt her like a rabbit, hunt her at her weakest. (*Stop* with that groaning ache.)

Away from Ladie, she was alone and vulnerable. She didn't have any of Ladie's magic, her bravery, her goodness and purity, to protect her. She was alone with stained sheets and badness rotting and festering inside her, and sluggish blood clots spurred on by her too loud heart.

Something was coming for her, something was sniffing her out. It moved in the darkness. There was some*one* shifting the darkness. They had opened the door and sat on her bed and pushed their hand over her mouth and moved so very close that their lips were flush to Ann's ear.

I am going to die, she realised. *Let me die without pain*, she begged. *Letmedieletmedieletmedie*.

It was the bovine smell of hair and warm milk that stopped Ann from reacting. The voice Ann had never heard before said three things in her ear. Three sentences, then it left, and it was like it never happened. Ann wished it hadn't because she knew, no matter how much she scrubbed, the whispered words would not leave her mind.

'It's trying to get you. It's trying to take you too. Please don't let it.'

31

THE THREAT OF their final morning had loomed for days and weeks, and within the hour it had arrived. Ann brought in the breakfast tray, the same as forever, but Ladie was not in her bed to receive it.

Up and dressed, she was darting around the room like a wild thing. Everywhere ornaments had been turned away from the room, their painted eyes stared blankly at the walls. Each picture had been slammed face down onto the dresser and Ladie's embroidery hoop of the two rabbits lay on her bed, miniature Xs heavily sewn over each little rabbit eye.

'Good morning, Ladie.' Ann's voice came out hushed and cracked. She cursed herself for it. It was a show of weakness, exposing evidence that she was unworthy of Ladie's presence. Ladie's voice would never crack like that.

Ladie, who had been reaching out to unhook a portrait from the wall, jumped suddenly and turned wide-eyed towards Ann, her chest heaving, gloved hands curled into claws. Once she saw it was Ann, she seemed to give a small cry of relief. Her hands dropped to her sides, and for a moment she swayed confusedly before apparently remembering her task. She turned back to the painting, gently lifted it from its hooks and placed it face down to the floor. She stared at the milky back of the frame.

Ann still held the breakfast tray in her hands. She felt stupid to have even brought it, to even be in Ladie's room at all. She wanted to put it on the bed and leave, but she couldn't move.

Perhaps this was what happened on one of Ladie's bad days. Perhaps, privileged to see this, the very worst side of Ladie, all this separation, this secrecy, could end, and they would finally have minds as one again. Ann said a silent prayer for Mrs Hardy to stay far away, to not tear her away from such a sacred moment.

'I didn't want to be overheard,' said Ladie, in a voice no more than a whisper. Her eyes did not move from the back of the frame, they refused to look at Ann, but gloved fingers gestured listlessly at the shunned ornaments and paintings. They shook, ever so slightly.

Ann set the tray on Ladie's bed.

'Ladie,' she said, gently stepping towards her, hardly able to conceal her smile. (This was the moment, this was when that horrid gaping space that had opened between them would close forever.)

'I'm leaving, Ann.'

Ladie's voice was dry and low and level and showed Ann's mind the memory of those hollow marble eyes, the whites of fear and madness. Ann stopped moving. Something sticky and awful had begun to sluice up the sides of her stomach.

'Leaving?' she asked.

But she knew what it meant. (*I should like a walk through the woods*, she had said that day. You knew from then, didn't you?)

Ladie did not even blink. 'Leaving.' (In the woods. In the wooooods. Them fucking like the dirty horrid animals they are.)

'Today?' Ann tried for joviality; she tried to make it sound like a joke, to catch Ladie in the silly little game she was no doubt playing.

Ladie ignored her. (The groundsman with the dead hares and the half-mast smile and the snares and the rough tongue that spoke of Ladie.)

Ann's mouth had become so dry. 'Forever?' she asked. It came out violently pathetic. Soon that tiny voice was going to break free again, tell Ladie that she couldn't, she *couldn't*. That nothing existed outside Ropner Hall, that Ladie would become nothing, and Ann would be alone. That she couldn't leave Ann because they were witch sisters bound in blood, so if Ladie left and became nothing, Ann would become nothing, too. (*Charlotte*, he had called her in the woods. A name you are not privy to.)

Finally, Ladie looked up from the painting. Her eyes darted frantically; they found Ann. The grey in them was cold and hard, and Ladie's voice, this new low hollow sound, rasped out harsh and gritty.

'Forever!' this foreign Ladie spat. 'What is forever in this infernal place when time has no beginning or end or middle anyway!' She began to pace feverishly.

Ann felt suddenly like she might be dissolving. Like she was disintegrating into nothing, and with that, each fibre connecting her to Ladie was slowly disappearing. She pressed her hands into her face, into her mouth, feeling the sharp solid bones, clutching at them like they might stop her from the rhythmic rocking that had seized her. Her body was swinging to and fro erratically and it was making her seasick. A soft moan issued in her effort to hold down the vomit that threatened.

This wasn't happening. This couldn't be happening.

But Ladie had conjured a small trunk, the travelling kind, and was stripping dresses from the wardrobe, bundling them chaotically, forcing them into the trunk's belly.

Ann swayed towards the door. Would Mrs Hardy come like she did before? In a nightmare of the marble room? Come to take Ladie, to soothe her, to talk her out of this?

Ladie seized Ann roughly by the shoulders, spun her round and held her tight, so they were face to face, their noses almost touching.

'Do not even think about telling *her*.'

Ladie's eyes were so wide Ann could see the earnestness in the whites, see her own face reflected in them. She was serious and the world was ending.

'I'm leaving, I'm going with Marcus, we're both running and we're never coming back to this intolerable, evil place.' She turned away from Ann and began to pace about her room, babbling and wringing her gloved hands. 'He is the only person who understands. Ever since I met him everything just . . .'

Ann was going to scream until her throat fell out of her mouth, she was going to turn over all the brown brown brown furniture, rip down all the wallpaper and tear off the bed sheets. She was going to wrap herself up in it, suffocate in it, wind herself through a mangle again and again and again until she was flattened into nothing. She saw it all so clearly, all the delicious rage and destruction, and her whole body vibrated with the impulse to do it. (Do it.)

'. . . and he is so strong, the way he looks at me, I feel safe and steady, I can feel my feet right on the ground and there is nothing that tricks and distorts, no more fear of strange faces and . . .'

But listening to Ladie's mutterings, the frustration ran away from her. It blubbered moltenly over the borders of anger, it heated her insides so much they collapsed in and on and over each other and there was nothing left to do but to cry. So she did. And it was ugly, it was dirty and streaming and heavy and racking, her snot trailed on her lips and dangled pendulously from her chin. Salty tears dripped into her mouth and ears, and stung her cheeks. She was a banshee, silently wailing, her mouth a gaping hole, dribbling and drooling and dreading the sound of stunted scraping foot-steps, of black black nights of crying and bloody pulsing aches and twisting burns beneath all those fucking awful folds of flesh. (Sew it up.) Sew them all up with a strong knot and mark them forbidden, and die before you think you might be anything but untarnished and not rotten and perfect.

But here she was, spilling out every inch. She felt wobbling globs of grot blurt out from her body below, piss or shit or blood or all three. Ladie stopped speaking quickly and stared long and hard, looking at Ann as if she had suddenly turned into something slimy and rancid, impossible to bear hold-ing. Her lip curled in disgust.

Ann could feel cracks fissuring all down her face, right by her eyes, so that all the liquid goo was beginning to drool out; underneath her hands her rusty mouth was prising open, tacky with stalactites of spit. She was a thing under a rock Ladie had just turned over, blotchy and half rotten, red raw and sticky. Her knees gave way and she fell forward and clutched at Ladie's skirts, pressing the fabric against her howling face, frantically searching for the hard anchors of her legs behind all the fabric, for something, anything, to hold on to, a raft in this ocean of horror.

Ladie stumbled back away from her grasp. 'Get off me,' she gasped.

Ann slumped entirely to the floor; she had no strength to even cry aloud anymore; tears streamed in silence. She had been refused by her own soul. Shunned by her entire meaning of life. All she wanted, all she ever wanted, was for Ladie to like her, that was all; for Ladie to like her more than anyone else. But she had been denied even that. All thanks to that man. He had come and sprouted between them like an ill-willed weed, separating and splitting them as he splayed his horrid leaves.

'Get out, Ann,' her soul said coldly. 'I am not in the mood to breakfast.'

32

ANN WAS GOING to kill him. She was going to fucking kill him, to murder him, to watch as that thing that made him alive and evil and gave his eyes that brown brown brown heartbeat detach itself from the unromantic mechanisms of his organs and slip out between the dead whites of his eyes.

She sat on the servants' stairwell, on the lip of the door. She slammed the breakfast tray beside her, wrenched open the death mask of hardened tears that had formed on her face, and ate every single stone-cold morsel. She tore strips of bread and fruit meat from her fingers, rusting jam oozed from the corners of her mouth and slicked right under her nails. She ate like an animal, savaging off great mouthfuls that she swallowed, barely chewed.

So caught up was she in this feral feeling, this alien urge, that now had control over every part of her body, that she did not hear the stairwell door behind her click open and shut, did not hear the rustling of black fabric as footsteps descended to stop beside her. They were always silent anyway, those footsteps, you didn't hear them as much as feel them; moving that cold, hollowing presence closer to you, closer and closer until it was too late.

It took a warm hand, pressing on her shoulder, for Ann to become aware that Mrs Hardy was standing over her.

Ann's mouth dropped open involuntarily and, with it, half-masticated food drooled down her chin, landing back onto her tray with a soft splat that would have been comical were the moment not so awfully dangerous.

The housekeeper's face was as impassive as ever. She watched Ann from above, her black eyes boring intensely into Ann's own, not even blinking as she lowered herself slowly, to be level with Ann.

Mrs Hardy brought her face closer, so close that Ann braced herself to feel her hot breath on her skin, but the sensation did not come; it was almost as though the house-keeper weren't breathing at all.

'You ought to be more observant, Ann. Here's one you missed.'

Ann heard the dull clunk of a plate being placed down, felt the small change in weight of the tray balanced on her knees. She did not look. She did not dare break the intense gaze the housekeeper had her locked in.

'Eat, Ann,' Mrs Hardy said.

Ann blinked at her. This was a trick, surely. A test, or some kind of torment, before she was justly punished for such a gross abuse of her position.

But Mrs Hardy was staring at her still, inclining her head slightly, expectantly.

Slower than she had ever moved before, Ann pulled her eyes away, lowered her chin to look at the plate Mrs Hardy had presented her with. It was a little side plate; one she had indeed missed. On it were eggs, scrambled, now tepid and rubbery, but still that jammy colour of orange that was so rich with flavour.

Despite everything Ann's stomach gave an audible growl.

Close to Ann's ear came a quiet, unnaturally high giggle. It was sharp and delicate and glass-like, and Ann's whole body flooded cold. She did not move, she could not.

'Eat,' came the command, and without warning that alien urge took over once more. Her fingers were digging into the sticky mounds of orange, she was slurping at her hands, swallowing without chewing, even scooping up the half-masticated globs that had escaped her moments before. In the frenzy she heard – no, it was impossible with those silent footsteps – she *felt* the housekeeper stand, move, vanish. (*She's made of the same stuff as the house*, remember; she had told you, warned you, *how bad it's going to get*.)

It was too awful to think, too overwhelming to try to understand, so she let the feral feeling consume her once more. She liked it. She sucked the stains from her fingers, and licked each plate and bowl and silver spoon clean. Then came the good part, the part made so much easier by the horror of that encounter: she sunk her fingers deep into the familiar ridge at the back of her mouth and coaxed it out. She counted every rib that pushed yearningly under her skin, she sharpened each finger on her hip bones. She was light and clean and pure and she was ready for her divine mission. She would not let this happen. She would not fail Mrs Hardy, fail Ropner. And most of all, she would not let him do this to her, to Ladie.

Ladie *needed* Ann, to protect her from the groundsman; she was too good, too pure and too sweet to know what they could be like. (She was stupider than a bairn, vainer than a rose, let him kill her, she's asking for it.) How men could burn and pillage and kill and mutilate your insides until they fell out completely and you were just an empty shell, curved and pink and blank and ready to be broken as soon as the tide turned too hard. Ann would be followed round by half-rotten corpses until she died but it would be worth it. For her, for Ladie. She was going to kill the groundsman the way she had killed Scarecrowfootman.

A wave of fresh nausea surged and that night came to her with startling clarity.

Death had hung about her from the trees that night. Skulls sprouted from branches, hard and mean like unripe fruit. She had seized at the mud with her hands like claws, she tore thick black clods, wet and yielding. Her body was damp and cold with sweat from the exertion, her face was sticky with brine and redness, there was redness dripping into her mouth, redness clotting between her legs. The earth was so soft that night, so malleable, so wanting, that it was almost swallowing the corpse, covering pale limbs without effort, gulping at long fingers and licking at the bloody skull, with its crusting of bone-white ceramic. It was almost as if it were helping her. Almost as if it were hungry for it.

It would eat the groundsman, too, she knew it. It would swallow him whole and would be glad to do it.

She was sick once more to rid herself of the memory. And then once again for luck.

33

ROPNER WAS PLAYING night-time once she reached the woods. It sighed and smirked underneath the brooding purple sky. She would take the long route to his hut, through the woods and alongside the river. It was safer that way; Mrs Hardy, the house, whatever might be watching, wouldn't see her.

Ann's feet felt alien in her shoes, felt alien on her body. So did her hands and her legs, her temples and her armpits and her knees. It was almost like her body wasn't her own, or she had somehow been apart from it long enough to forget its nuances. The woods pressed heavily all around her, the air thick with moisture and the absence of sound.

She walked very slowly to the hut. If she ran, it would spur the house and its half-rotting friends to come for her. It was a painful walk and the fear was like a bolt that went through her spine right into the meat of her kidney. (Swallow that surge of vomit, dammit, one moment of stopping and you'll be eaten whole.)

The evil-smelling shed looked like an ugly inverted piece of coal by night; its husk was ragged and black, even in the moonlight, and instead of embers gnawing at its skin, a bronze light, a slow honey orange, sweated out from its cracks and gaps and bubbled brightly in its innards. It smelt of sex and the oozing lamb heart Ann had once watched Rachel butcher.

They were in there, together, Ann knew it. Their presence made his lump-of-coal lair seem to pulse like an organ. The bolt that pierced all the way to her kidney twisted. Perhaps he would be on her like an animal, perhaps he had already killed her. No matter, Ann would tear him off. Ann would kill him like she knew she could. Twist all the strings in his neck until her fingers interlocked and palms met and all the fleshy red pulp between was only water and wet and sticky lumpy fluid and no gush of air could ever, never ever, get through. She could smash through the skull and pop out each vertebrae like a slimy necklace. Pick up all the stained ceramic pieces and use them to saw through his ribs right down to that drooling cavity so she could show Ladie: *See! There is no heart, only mud, black mud like the black, black mud he belongs to.* They would leave him dead and broken and all hollowed out, and Ann would kick his body on the way out for good measure. (Ha.)

The door to the lump-of-coal-organ lair creaked when she pushed it open. The orange fire was burning merrily and jolly, completely oblivious to the part it was meant to play. Ignorant to all the shadows it was meant to cast to befit this place of hell, this naughty den of sin. This horribly empty, glaringly empty, heart-droppingly empty, desolate evil-smelling hut.

They had gone.

She had gone.

Ann stumbled from the doorway, lurching away from the inside of the hut that had suddenly grown enormously wide and stretched out as an eternal empty plane that mocked her aloneness. Everything around her oscillated between being a million miles away and so close she could feel it brushing her skin. Right there, close to the jelly of her eye, she could see Ladie's window, see the screen that hid her room. The Paris green was like an iris, and she saw Ladie as its pupil, slowly undressing, winking thick flashes of skin down to the very hut Ann clutched at. She held the door frame fiercely as the ground beneath her had catapulted away. The trees and the wind bent close and battered her skull. The sky was far enough from her to be nothing but a pinprick.

She sensed a feeling so viciously red, like a wound. Her skin was so heavy she wanted to peel it off and let everything, all that redness, out. She would cut the little strings that held her heart in place, too, for good measure, and then seize that beating brute and throw it so very hard it would fall off the end of the earth. But there in that little hollow she scooped it from, would there still be feeling? Like that little white light in Pandora's box? She could not stand it if that were so; all this feeling would surely be the death of her.

There was nothing left for her now, only this empty, ripped-out feeling of grief. She was alone with her injury and the vulnerability of her loneliness, which the corpse would sniff out like a hound.

Ann turned on her heels and ran.

All the woods flashed past her. Snarling branches, grey dead leaves, Ladie. Silk gloves, rotten hedges, bloody flowers, skull shards, black, Ladie, bark. Bark with clumps of ripped flesh, branches dripping brain, hollow holes, rattling mouths, thorns, grabbing hands, trees, Ladie. That big mouth, that roaring black stretching mouth, gushing and waving, and letting her fall into it just like her nightmares – she was wet and cold but she didn't feel a thing, not when she was being swallowed into the most final finality.

The cold was bliss. The nothing was bliss. An oily slick flowed round her like a current.

Odd. Not water.

Not just yet, Ann, it oozed. *We need you.*

34

A NN WAS BORN into a world that was brown and warm and light. Chestnut bodies twisted above her; a tableau of strangled heads and reaching hands. Sunlight wafted in, spilling between curtains in thick slices. In its rays, she recalled the juice of a nectarine running down Ladie's chin at the picnic, a stream of molten metal that dripped sweetly from her teeth while her mouth opened to laugh.

Ladie.

Ann sat upright and Ladie's sheets plumed all around her. The confusion was dread and the dread was white cold.

She should not be here, in Ladie's bed. (Ladie was gone.) In Ladie's bed, between Ladie's sheets. (Ladie was gone and she was alone.) In Ladie's room, hearing it purr all around her.

Ladie Ladie Ladie.

She clutched her face and felt her own familiar bones underneath, sharp and ugly. (Ladie was gone.)

Mockingly, everything in the room was exactly the same as she had left it. Her little ornaments lined the mantelpiece solemnly, porcelain heads bowed away towards the walls. The fanned mirror on the dressing table hunched protectively over the jewels beneath it like a nursing bitch ready to snarl and bite should Ann come any nearer. Nothing had even a speck of dust to brush from its shoulder. Which was impossible: surely the whole room should be shrouded in sheets of grey, and cobwebs should hang so heavy from the chandeliers that they start weaving into the carpet. It should smell musty and dead, because how could it be alive when the life inside it was gone?

Ann sniffed a dry threat to cry. She wanted to wail and scream at everything in the room; the impassive walls, the unflinching drawers, the reams of curtains and their nonchalant folds. Everything should be lined with grief, doubled over with grief, contorted and screwed and chewed with grief.

Ladie's door creaked open, and Mrs Hardy entered as silently and darkly as night.

Ann was struck with the need to bolt from the bed, to stand straight to attention, to implore that she didn't know how she came to be there but she knew it was wrong and she was sorry, deeply truly sorry, and that Ladie was gone and Ann couldn't save her. It was all her fault – no, all the groundsman's fault. But Mrs Hardy had scooped out all her insides. And it was near impossible to move, hollowed out like that.

The housekeeper stood at the foot of Ann's bed – *Ladie's* bed – and stared right into Ann's empty innards. 'Luncheon begins in an hour. We must use this time to bathe and change you.'

Ann blinked stupidly. Was she still in the river, half drowned and dreaming so near death? Or had she died already, and her mind had not yet caught up with her body?

Mrs Hardy pulled her lips into the shape of a smile. 'You have slept for quite some time. Almost half the day has passed.'

The pleasant tone in her voice jarred against the tension in the air. Visions pulsed and pounded out a nausea in her. Half-dreams swam in her head still: Ann saw her body from very far away, laid out, cold in death. She saw Ladie and the groundsman intertwined so that they were one beating beast.

'Are you feeling quite well, Lady Charlotte?'

Ann said nothing. It was impossible, surely; a dream, a hallucination, that the housekeeper was standing before her, addressing her as Ladie.

Mrs Hardy sighed in a pretence of patient kindness and slowed her voice as if she were trying to explain one of life's most excruciatingly obvious principles to a child. 'Lady Charlotte, you must tell me if you feel under the weather again.'

The housekeeper walked briskly to her side and pressed the back of her hand to Ann's forehead. Ann recoiled into the soft plumes of pillows below her head.

Everything was moving around her so fast it was ringing. Ann's breath had doubled in pace without her even realising; she was struggling to catch it, struggling to catch any of the million trains of thought slipping rapidly through her fingers. Her body prickled cold but the swell of her cheeks burned.

'You feel quite normal, my lady,' said Mrs Hardy, drawing back her hand.

Ann could feel the phantom of its cold weight still pressed against her head.

How could this be happening? Was it a test? Some kind of measure of Ann's devotion to the house? A barometer to discover how well Ann knew her place? It was obscene, the whole thing; her being in Ladie's room, in her bed, Mrs Hardy staring at her like *that*.

The housekeeper's teeth sharpened. 'In your own time, Lady Charlotte.' She bowed her head.

It was a terrible mistake, an inconceivable one. Pretend to be Ladie? It was barbaric, ludicrous. How could she defile an entire system and hierarchy that held up her world? She was penned below, she was penned to work, she was penned to serve, and that penmanship had wrought her very bones, and its ink had deliquesced her very blood. (Blood that was like Ladie's, too.) To destabilise that would be to disintegrate, to deteriorate, to die.

But what could be worse than the being of doom she had become, the abandoned, the cursed, the cunt that Ladie would never think of again? Not death, that was for sure. Nor wedding-cake rooms, or delicate colours, rich colours, or delicate plates and overflowing glasses, or the food. Oh God, the food: no rot, no badness leaking from pores, no proximity to sin and slobber and corpses. The raw edges of her injury were softening; the wound Ladie had ripped diluted its redness ever so slightly at the thought of what she could have.

Perhaps pretending would be like having her back, even just for a moment. Being together with her; like they hadn't parted at all, but had become fused, become one.

Maybe then, too, she would be less afraid.

After all, she was a servant to this house, she was charged to do its bidding.

Ann took a breath, pulled her shoulders back and her chin high. 'Yes, Mrs Hardy, I feel quite well.'

35

WHILE LADIE HAD borne her nakedness like a fairy queen, Ann was wretched in hers. Mrs Hardy had her stand in the bath while she scrubbed her. The water sloshing at her puckered calves was as warm as the myth of summer. She was nothing more than a stupid reed, vulnerable to the will of the weather, watching as the water grew dark like treacle.

Mrs Hardy scrubbed and Ann felt the memories of clutching, tearing hands, of foreign skin touching uncharted places. The walls of her throat met and twisted themselves together, and something heavy pressed on her chest.

Mrs Hardy's hands were relentlessly everywhere, and Ann's own twitched round the handles of phantom jugs. She curled them into fists so the housekeeper could not see how dry and cracked they were. All her insides were going to fall out of that terrible hole that was screaming out against invasion.

She squeezed her eyes shut and tried desperately to take her mind to decadent rooms. To languid hours of stitching little rabbits (dead and twitching under coals), to wearing those shivering gowns (ghosts of Ladie, gonegonegone). The housekeeper scrubbed suds over her legs and Ann's rabbit-heart beat faster. (Think of white marble before the terror; lying in Ladie's arms and dying in Ladie's arms.) She could have died that day, in the marble room, what bliss that would have been, to die and spare this agony. It was too late now, Ladie was gone and the pain was raw and eternal.

Ladie was gone but how could she exist outside of Ropner Hall? The river must lead somewhere: a long silver straw being commandeered by a distant sucking sea.

Were they there, perhaps, Ladie and the groundsman? They might have followed the curves and bends of the river, walked until undergrowth and ferns turned to shingles and sharp sand, with stinging salt and screaming gulls. Perhaps they had built a house of shells with scalloped edges and organ-pink walls to protect them from being licked and spat at by the grimy tide, and there they would stay forever and all memories of Ann would be washed away until Ladie's brain was smooth and slick and unblemished by the finger-prints of Ropner, and her heart was so ossified with salt that the idea of home was frozen and lost, and she would never be able to work that internal compass to find Ropner again.

Ladie was gone and dead, and she had taken the soul they shared with her. Ann was nothing but an empty husk, a hollowed-out death mask.

The gown Mrs Hardy put her in was ivory, embroidered with blues and greys and deep pinks that wove into fairytale-like branches, cold and wintery but stoical with their stub-born fruit. Ann recognised it, of course, from the wardrobe, from holding its jacket against her chest. The square neck was bordered with tightly frilled linen that tickled the skin of her breasts, and its sleeves belched out swathes of a thin muslin that matched the apron pinned over her skirt.

She thumbed the stitching on the skirt carefully. If she dropped dead right now would they bury her in this dress? The thought was dark and thrilling. Ann turned to look at herself in the mirror.

Suddenly, she did not want to die anymore. She could not want to die when Ladie was still alive, looking back at her from the glass.

There was Ladie's face; though more sunken than usual, it still held the promise of inner irradiation. There was the delicate twist of her hair, scooped into neat and beautiful braids. There was the secret swell of her hips somewhere under her skirts. And when Ann stood straight, she saw the proud curve of Ladie's shoulders and the arrow of her back.

'If you're ready, Lady Charlotte.' Mrs Hardy's voice came from the shadowy place beyond the mirror. 'Time for luncheon.'

'Of course,' the Ladie in the mirror said, puppeteering Ann's mouth.

Ofcourseofcourseofcourse. Her jaw clacked obediently on its hinges and her feet followed the housekeeper dutifully. Ladie's soft navy shoes played peek-a-boo beneath the hem of the ivory dress. Her own feet in Ladie's shoes!

'This way, my lady,' Mrs Hardy redirected her gently when she automatically made towards the servants' stairwell.

Mrs Hardy took her instead down the main stairs, the billowing arc that swept down into the saloon behind the marble hall. Each step was smoothed and evenly spaced, its corners sharp and precise, at perfect right angles with the banister that shone and flowed like water down into a whirlpool volute at the foot of the staircase.

The housekeeper stopped at the door adjacent to the marble hall, directly opposite where the stairs had spun them out.

The dining room.

It was one of the rooms Ann had never been allowed to clean. She felt the familiar thrill of being privy to another part of Ladie's life, the excitement at an opportunity to become even closer to her. But, of course, what did that matter now? Ladie was gone. Ladie had left. The skin on her arms grew numb and prickled. Some part of her where her heart might have once been gaped and ached.

Distantly, Ann was aware of a voice leaking through the dining-room door. A woman's voice. A woman chuntering to herself in a way that was almost lyrical. Ann could barely make out the words.

'Frosting and lavender . . . and fig biscuits . . .'

Mrs Hardy turned to her in her slow, sinister way. 'I almost forgot, Lady Charlotte. Your gloves. I know how much you hate to show your hands.' In her outstretched hands were a perfectly starched pair of powder-blue gloves. Ladie's gloves.

Ann took them from her slowly and slipped them on. She stretched her fingers into the silk and shivered as it snagged on the dry cracks on her skin.

'You know, you know,' the faint voice waxed, 'I hate this part, I find it so hard to not grow attached to th—'

In a sharp movement Mrs Hardy rapped once on the door, silencing the voice, before she opened it and held it wide for Ann to walk through.

'Oh? Oh! Splendid timing, she is such a *charmante*.' The voice came louder this time without the obstruction of its wooden barricade. 'Do let her in.'

Ann's eye twitched and gave a wink. She did not move from the saloon. The magnitude of what she had done suddenly seemed incomprehensible. This was too much; surely she should want to run away and throw up, run away and curl into the hollow of that tree in the woods, stay perfectly still and never speak or move again until she fossilised entirely.

But, strangely, she did not. The bizarreness of this pretence was staggering, but somehow it did not feel wrong. (Because you are one, that's why. Your soul is hers and hers is yours. Bound by blood, remember?)

She glanced hesitantly at Mrs Hardy, and the blackness of her eyes gave a terrible gleam that made Ann jerk forward and enter the dining room.

The room was such an assault to the eye she could barely recognise it as a room at all; it was as if she had stepped into the swollen belly of some gorging beast, jumbled in with the rest of his feast. But slowly things began to fall into place, the familiar first: four walls that were splashed with a sickly, almost garish shade of pink, and echoed in overly fussy drapes; the ceiling holding them in place – a swirling cream piped with gold. Gold darted about the entire room, it seemed, twisting into frames for countless paintings and oddly shaped mirrors that reflected the room into a never-ending shapeless mass. It licked up the table legs and spun in tassels on the chairs; it dripped off chandeliers swinging from mindless punctures in the ceiling, and echoed itself in the candlesticks twisting up below. It danced out of a fireplace whose mouth was agape in a grotesque belch and whose marble gums looked nicotine-stained against the ugly pink wallpaper. Golden pools glowed from lamps that were bony ballerinas stopped in mid-spin around the room, their skirts still swirling.

The smell was almost as overwhelming as the sight. A thousand different odours assaulted Ann at once, enveloped her in an ocean fraught with currents of fragrance; waves of heavy fabrics, velvet and heady, ripples of potted plants and flowers, swells and broils and foaming churns of the food and its gloating steam – for the gold-licked legged table, as vast as the ocean, was heavily laden with islands of heaving plates and brimming bowls.

All the temptation from the past was laid out in a banquet before her. Piles of pillow-soft pastries plastered with butter and sugar, hills of chickpea curries, their sticky ova coated in screaming, lumpy reds, ponds of still-simmering sauces; one thick with meat, one fawn-brown and luxuriously bubbling, another bright-white with coconut, broken only by flashes of spices and slithered vegetables, a final one milky with butter-yellow chunks of haddock bobbing happily like they were once again in the sea. Jars cloistered round a smooth wooden board bricked over with bread; jars that caught the light like stained-glass windows. Golden honey, purple plum jam, crystalline marmalade with sugared twists of peel that promised to make your teeth fizz. Mounds of strawberries, scrupulously dipped in chocolate, shone with the promise of a satisfying crunch between teeth.

Countless pairs of eyes lined the perimeter of the table and stared greedily at the feast: the guests for whom all these daily luncheons were tirelessly crafted for. Ann blinked at them stupidly.

Dolls.

All of them, dolls.

Sewn, porcelain, wooden, wax. One looked made from sticks and another from tightly wound hair. The most intricate had reams of black curls and glass eyes with real lashes and veins painted onto her skin; the crudest was nothing but a small sack, choked with thread at the neck and darned with two wonky crosses for eyes. At the far end of the table, a voice introduced itself as the only other living thing in the room.

'Darling Lottie!'

The first thing that struck Ann about the Aunt was that she was fat. Fat in a way Ann had never before seen encompassed in a person. Her vastness seemed to extend beyond Ann's vision; a never-ending cascade of rolls and lumps. To only emphasise her careening largeness, the Aunt was dressed in a frothy lilac tulle that ballooned and billowed at all angles imaginable. She looked, in short, like a giant purple meringue. One adorned with glittering sugars and sweets: glinting jewels winked cloyingly from every shiny pink finger they strangled, a waterfall of garish gems and pearls seeped from one of the rolls in her neck; looking for all the world like sugared blood dripping from a slit throat.

Her hair, or rather the stuffed and netted beehive sponge that whatever wisps and strands remained were wrapped around, was studded with various ornamentations: butterflies, and bees, and fruit, each more garish than the last. The effect was quite overwhelming, so that it took a moment for Ann to realise it was the great bulbous, bathetic mass before her that had spoken.

'*Darling* Lottie!' the mass repeated. She had a rather silly voice and her eyes blinked rapidly when she spoke. They were a funny yellow-white all over, as if webs had been spun over them. 'So lovely to see you, my darling, darling niece, flesh of my flesh, blood of my blood. Your face as radiant and youthful as ever, you must lend me your youth some day, just a drop would be so very amiable. Hee! Hee! Sorry, Mrs Hardy, I should not joke about such things. You must tell me, my sweet, tell me, darling buttercup, what do you think of my ensemble for luncheon?'

The Aunt spoke very fast, in a breathless garble that was so affected in its cadence it made her chins wobble fervently. All the colour Ann possessed threw itself with great vigour onto her cheeks.

Was she to speak to this woman? To the Duchess? Was she to speak as Ladie? How could she when she was incapable and wretched as soon as words were required? When everything came out haltingly, and in that reed-thin voice foreign to her, that went up too high at the end, like a question, like an uncertainty, like a beg? It made her mouth fill with spit and her eyes water and all her insides dry up from the hate she felt for them. But she was Ladie now, Ladie who spoke with ease, with lightness, with smirks that twisted cheekily.

She tried to breathe Ladie in, let her commandeer her soul.

'Well,' Ladie said out of Ann's bones. 'You look utterly overwhelming, Auntie dear.'

'Overwhelming, my sweetness?' came the squeak. 'Over . . .' A chin wobbled dangerously. 'My, my, I . . .' Two more joined the jellied dance, and then the crying began. She bawled as stupidly and lawlessly as a bairn.

The Ladie that had spoken from Ann's bones smiled, and Ann smiled too. *What fun!* Ladie said to her.

Mrs Hardy, who had since been tucked surreptitiously in the corner, emerged, in her way, and glided to the Aunt's side, where she tended to her in the most disconcerting manner; it was almost . . . lovingly.

'There, there, Duchess, it will not do well to ruin a visage as lovely as yours with tears, no matter how delicate and maidenly they are. What Lady Charlotte means to say – that is, means by saying *overwhelming* – is that such a dazzling ensemble, *and* its wearer of course, are so awe-inspiringly breathtaking that one is simply overwhelmed with beauty and can muster no words to quite do it justice.'

'Oh!' The Aunt hiccupped. She looked at Mrs Hardy raptly, her milky eyes widened, and she turned her arse-red face back to Ann. '*Ohh*! How-how . . . perfectly *charming* of you, my dear darling Lottie. You do always so enjoy your cheeky tease, wicked girl! Come here and give your auntie a kiss.'

She held on to the sibilant of kiss so long it sounded like she was deflating. But her mass remained the same, and as Ann edged nearer, encouraged by a whip-sharp glance from Mrs Hardy, she was once again awestruck by Aunt's vastness. Surely she would not be able to reach over the froth and fat to kiss her cheek? She sunk into an awkward curtsy before she brushed her dry lips against the air in the vicinity of Aunt's cheek. Strangely, Aunt was very cold; though Ann had not touched her, she could feel it emanating from her. She smelt of absolutely nothing.

'How sweet,' Mrs Hardy said drily. 'If you are ready, Duchess, Lady Charlotte may sit down and the luncheon can begin.'

'Of course! Do sit, Lottie.' Her piggy smile nodded to the only free chair standing, at the end of the table directly opposite.

Ann sat. Either side of her, tiny doll faces watched impassively. Propped up to her left sat a clay doll with currant eyes and a crudely scored mouth. A haughty china doll took the place on her right, entirely stiff, with lacquered hair and a painted face, slightly lopsided.

Ann sat as Ladie would, prim and erect, with the bones of her décolletage arranged daintily. The plate nearest was a swollen stack of pancakes that sweated honey profusely and blubbered, still hot, under drools of cream and turgid spades of strawberries. *Ladie would eat that*, some distant voice inside Ann said, a part of her brain that hadn't been entirely stupefied by the grotesque vaudeville. Ann pulled it towards herself and cut a slice.

It was with the first bite that Ann realised she had been starving. Just one bite was so imbued with flavour it made her head spin and stomach roar. The sweetness swelled her tongue to something fat and pulsating. She was a mindless entity, an invertebrate mass conscious only of her hunger, existing only for taste. She churned hunks of the fluffy, oozing confection round again and again in her mouth until it became a gooey sludge that she mangled between her molars. Only once she had squeezed out every last drop of sweetness did she swallow and dive for the next bite. Even if she was no longer hungry, even if she became so full she might burst, she would keep chewing, keep eating. She would eat each and every thing on the vast table, indulge in the fireworks they set blazing on her tongue. To think of all those times, all those years and days and endless seconds she had abstained, withheld from herself for love of Ladie. She had no idea she had endured such deprivation.

'Now remember, my sweet Lottie,' a voice chimed some distance from Ann's reverie.

Oblivious, Ann seized the next nearest item, a plate of omelettes, their pregnant bellies lumpy with chunks of spiced meat. She sunk herself into the sulphur of the eggs. Meat tasted as red as a scream. Its blood and fat were spiced, and it burned in the best way.

'This is the perfect way to practise and prepare for the next Harvestfeast. I hope you will dazzle our guests with riveting conversation.'

Immediately Aunt turned to the hastily carved wooden doll on her left. 'Master Hinton, I heard about your boules green. Now, I bring it up because as you well know I am somewhat of an agoraphobe – Ha! Ha!'

Ann forgot the omelette, forgot the comforting mannerisms of Ladie, and felt her mouth hang open as she watched.

'But I do so like the thought of having our own little one here at Ropner. There's something so satisfying about the thought of grass trimmed to be so short it looks like velvet. How becoming it would look, I do think the house would like it . . .'

Aunt conducted an unfaltering stream of dialogue directly to the dolls as if they were real people. She asked questions but never paused for answers. Instead, she regaled her own anecdotes and opinions, tittering at her follies and barely pausing for breath, or to even chew.

She was mad. That was the only explanation. Everything they had said about the fat old Duchess was true. She garbled and laughed like a thing possessed. No wonder Ladie had so despised the luncheons.

Ann turned to the doll on her right. It stared at her raptly, its eternal smile eerie. She felt the memory of the same expression on her own face, at the picnic, in the marble hall, on Ladie's bed, in Ladie's arms. It was like looking at her own body from a distance, and in doing so realising she was no longer alive. The fragrances in the room had doubled in thickness and warmth. They pressed onto Ann's nostrils and every pore like wet clay.

'Lottie? My poor dear, you look quite ill.' Everything she had eaten churned in her belly and fought to push through and escape. 'My dear, you're as green-grey as sea glass.'

Ann moved slowly, taking pains not to disturb her insides. She was a master of nausea, she knew when she was about to vomit.

'Mrs Hardy, you must escort her back to her room and see that she is tended to, perhaps some smelling salts and early bed. Oh, my poor dear!'

'If I may, Lady Charlotte.' Mrs Hardy's voice hovered dangerously over her shoulder and those spider hands hooked on to one of her elbows and steered her steadily to the door.

'Mrs Hardy will look after you, sweet,' Aunt chuntered from the bottom of a well a million miles away. 'Mrs Hardy understands this house and its silly little people like no one else! She, with great skill, understands exactly what it needs, who it needs, when it needs . . .'

36

I N LADIE'S ROOM, Ann was sick, once, twice, a hundred times; she filled two intricately patterned chamber pots with every morsel of luncheon.

Colours blended and congealed stickily; some bites were perfectly intact, the marks of her teeth fossilised into their softened skin. Iridescent bile waved and swayed, and the corners of everything were blurry with tears. Her nose ran and the reward of sharpness that usually came after she had thrown up was absent. Instead, her head felt funny and far away. Dull and numb, and in that space between the shell of her skull and the soft of her brain was warm cotton wool that made only sleep possible.

Mrs Hardy laid her on the bed tenderly, so tenderly that if not for the cotton wool and her heavy, heavy eyes, Ann would have screamed.

'All that rich food,' Mrs Hardy sighed, like she was whispering a lullaby. 'Your body will get used to it again, Lady Charlotte.'

Ladie; she was Ladie.

Ladieladieladie.

With that, Ann fell asleep.

*   *   *

When Ann woke, she did not open her eyes immediately. She kept them squeezed shut, and soaked in everything around her. It was so soft – the bed sheets, the air, the sounds. Even her muscles had begun to melt, aching as they did so, thawing in the absence of hours of toil. It was not an unpleasant feeling. If Ann twisted each of her limbs, explored and flexed each muscle, the ache was delicious and deep and so close to pain it was pleasurable. This was what the start of freedom felt like, surely. Would this be how Ladie felt each morning? Once all the ache had worn off, would she feel as light and supple and free as Ladie? No longer as mean and taut as an arrow, but as smooth and smiling and flexing as its bow.

She squeezed her lids to cement the darkness further and willed all the parts of Ann away. In her mind's eye, she was twisting herself like a sponge, with each flex of a muscle she was wringing out every meagre particle of self, draining all sin, all badness, expunging any hint of rot.

She opened her eyes softly, like the wings of a landing butterfly, like Ladie. She breathed in, she sighed out, like Ladie; she stretched slowly (she had the time now), she contemplated the bed's ceiling absent-mindedly, like Ladie. She felt her stomach gurgle and thought of Ladie's food and, yawning luxuriously, she rang the bell by her bed. When she opened the door she did so like Ladie, and she fought to hold down a bubble of Ladie's laughter at the girl standing with the breakfast tray.

The girl was like an ugly scab, hatched and festering. Such ugliness amused Ladie greatly, Ann knew it. Wasn't it funny that no one could compare to her beauty. The girl blinked her ugly eyes wide at Ann's face and Ann felt Ladie's smile falter.

Petra.

Petra looking at her with her too-close-together eyes, with her offensive troll-like face.

Petra back like she had never left, same black clothes, same pinafore. (Pinned wonkily, the slob.) Petra was going to seize her by the shoulders like she did on the stairs, she was going to pull her back down right to the bowels of Ropner, infect her with badness all over again so that she would never escape.

But Petra (not Petra, how could it be Petra?) only blinked.

She was not Petra. It was impossible. Ann was just tired, that was it. She wasn't used to the rich food, just like Mrs Hardy had said (so gently, so tenderly, so lovingly). This servant was just a servant, with the same ruddy face Petra had, the same ruddy face they all had. With their generic scraped hair and starched pinafores. It was a wonder she had ever been able to tell them apart.

She imagined them all down there in the cellars and the kitchen and the underpasses. An entity of uniform arms and legs and aprons, and hundreds of heads with gaunt cheeks and bulging eyes, stinking of rot. Damn this girl for reminding her of that, for reminding her of Petra, for reminding her of Scarecrowfootman. (No no no, he is dead and buried, you made sure of it, and all the sin and badness he put inside you is dead and buried with him.) Ann wanted to throw her from the room, to tell her to never come again, to scold her for ruining her game as Ladie, for smearing it with her rot and badness. She wanted to be locked in this room as Ladie, leave only to go to luncheon as Ladie, to never have to think about downstairs again.

Instead Ladie, in her high, clear voice, said, 'Bring teacakes next time, too.'

The girl left backwards, squatting like a toad; bowing her head and pulling the door with her. The lock clicked with a heavy finality whose echo lumbered through the corridor and bounced round Ladie's room. (*Your* room now.) The echo defied dimensions and clunked though the day that stretched ahead. *Look*, it said. *All this time, all this space, unspooling ahead of you right now, it's going for miles and miles and miles.* Its voice grew smaller until it disappeared, and all that was left was her, staring at the unblemished road of the day. Ann felt victorious. An infinite day where all she had to do was be Ladie. Did it sting to think of her? (No. Fuck her.) She probed her mind with the name over again.

Ladieladieladie.

Yes, it did sting, in little flashes; wasp stings that made her want to tear her own skin off over her head. But it inspired something warm, too, in the cavity of her torso. Hunger.

She would eat her fill. She would chew on fine clothes and swallow jewellery in great gulps, she would bite into languorous rambles into the woods, swig at embroidery and sip silly little poems, pick laughter from between her teeth and consume that, too. She would become so glutinously full with Ladie that her being would have no choice but to cram itself entirely into the nooks and crannies of Ann's own head, so that Ann's own mind would be silenced and her head would be as empty and light and blithe as Ladie's. So that Ann would be no more and all that would be left was Ladie, Ladie, Ladie.

*   *   *

Time had always teased Ann; the hands of its clock would slip forward inaudibly and irregularly, sometimes by inches and other times by miles. It had always been fragmented by chores, warped by waiting for Ladie, undulated endlessly by prayers for the night to end. And yet now, for the first time, it was shining and long and unbroken.

Of course, it had to accommodate luncheons; little hills on an otherwise perfectly flat landscape. But either side of those benign hills was a wide-open space that Ann could fill with whatever Ladie (whatever *she*) took a fancy to; ambles in the summer gardens, meditative rests in the winter garden's glasshouse, stitch after stitch of embroidery (that little rabbit scene Ladie had started was almost finished now), tracing the titles of books in the library with her gloved fingers. (Those sweet silk gloves were a necessity to hide those horrid calloused hands, that terrible evidence of another life.)

One of her favourite ways to fill time was to walk through the house, trying to discover all the rooms that she had never been tasked with cleaning. All the rooms that would never dream of revealing their innards to a lowly meagre servant. Ann discovered a second drawing room with green arched alcoves and matching gold-trimmed chairs; there was a yellow antechamber with wallpaper so intricate it seemed to pulse; a sitting room with an impossibly enormous chandelier, drooping under the weight of its own crystals like a skeletal leaf drowning in dewdrops.

In a reading room, she found panels covered with tapestry so detailed Ann had stood and stared at it for hours; it wove tales the proportions of Greek tragedies in muted tones of blue and red and grey and cream. Threaded figures danced and dressed in extravagant gowns, they waltzed through orchards of bone-like trees, and curtsied towards plates piled high with food, before falling into one another in a frenzied dance, teeth bared, biting down at each other, softly sewn blood drops crying at their apparent cannibalism.

Each time she found a new door to open, she enjoyed the delicious thrill that Rachel might be in there cleaning. How poetic would it be, how like justice would it be to walk in wearing one of Ladie's fine gowns (*your* fine gown), while Rachel was crawling on her hands and knees scrubbing and mending and toiling beneath her. (Ha.)

Though Ann was delighted with her new discoveries, many of Ropner's rooms remained locked, their polished gold handles refusing to budge. Even to Ladie, Ropner would not reveal all of its secrets.

She had found a door in the long corridor, the corridor with the big painting, and was trying to tease it open, her silk gloves slipping on the handle, when Mrs Hardy had materialised silently beside her.

'My lady?' the housekeeper said.

Ann let go of the handle as though it had suddenly become molten and burning. She stood to attention and threw her hands behind her back, grasping them together as if hiding two culprits.

Mrs Hardy raised a querying eyebrow and her black, unfathomable eyes surveyed Ann carefully. With a quiet horror, Ann watched them flick to the portrait of Ladie hung and observing at the far end of the corridor, before flicking back to Ann's face. 'Are you lost, Lady Charlotte?'

There was an almost mocking tone to her voice. Ann felt the floor beneath her feet slowly open, felt how all her organs, all her liquid insides, slowly dripped down the length of her, leaking out of the soles of Ladie's boots (*your* boots) to trickle down the hole in the floor.

She had been found out, surely. She had committed some glaringly obvious stupidity, revealed she was a fraud, a cuckoo's egg, and made Mrs Hardy finally realise she was not Ladie. (But you are Ladie. You and her are one and the same. You *are* Ladie. You have to be.)

'I quite forgot,' she said, in Ladie's most aloof, dismissive voice, 'that this door is locked. I – that is to say . . .' She saw, again, the tiniest flicker of those coal-black eyes. She cleared her throat with a ladylike 'Hem'. 'If you will excuse me, Mrs Hardy, I will retire to my room before luncheon.'

Mrs Hardy bowed her head and curtsied. Ann turned on her heels and began walking up the corridor before the housekeeper could straighten her head again and show those endless black eyes.

She watched the painting as she walked towards it. The Ladie in it refused to look at her; her eyes were detached and distant, gazing intently at something far beyond Ann. Ann looked at her poreless skin, at the soft full mounds and curves of her body covered and not covered by that lilac fabric. She chewed the slippery gum of her own gaunt cheek, thoughtfully. This was who she was now. Ann was an entity long dead and forgotten; only Ladie existed, just as Ladie was the only thing to exist from the moment Ann encountered her on the servants' stairs. She rolled her shoulders as she walked, felt the crunch of gristle between their bones;

she thought about how loose even the tightest of stays were on her. Eating more was imperative if she were to really look like Ladie. She thought of the mouth-watering luncheon banquets and smiled.

This was a chore that would not be arduous.

37

A NN FILLED HERSELF up on food, day in and day out. The food, the food, the food! She could stomach it now without spewing it back out. It didn't taste like badness as it had downstairs, it never sat heavy in her tummy or made her feel dirty and too large. It seduced her and woke her up, it filled her with fizzing and gave her rich nourishment that she could feel all the way down to her marrow.

Over time, butter plastered over her cracks, wedges of cake and icing packed the breaks in her brittle bones, richwine ran her blood into molten gold, and meat spun thickness and shine into her hair. She had fat now, like half-baked dough: above knees and at the top of her thighs and in the pockets of her cheeks. It convexed all her corners and filled her into Ladie's shape.

'Lady Charlotte, you look perfectly enchanting,' the doll to her right would say to her.

'Yes, my hair is quite delightful today, isn't it,' she would reply.

She enjoyed speaking to the odd little dolls now. She had watched the Duchess closely and tried to emulate her conversations, to remember and recreate each pleasantry and affectation. (Little finger always extended when holding a dessert spoon, hand must be brought to cover teeth when laughing, don't forget to ask their thoughts on the bouquet of the wine.)

It was embarrassing at first; it felt wooden, and forced, to talk to the frozen, impassive faces either side of her. But after time it grew as natural as talking to Aunt herself, and – if she were being honest – far more enjoyable. And the way their little fake eyes followed her every move – so clever!

There was something so satisfying, so gratifying, about talking while their ugly little faces stared back with unaltered adoration, always listening so intently and soaking up every one of her words like a sponge. No wonder Ladie had been able to talk with such ease to her, no wonder she had been able to talk and talk and talk without ever once asking Ann about herself. A small marble of something hard and bitter rolled over in Ann's stomach.

'Lady Charlotte, you look so wonderful,' the doll to her left would tell her in its creaking wooden voice.

'Do you notice my little lavender pin?' she would say. 'I found it the other day and knew I just had to wear it. I'm even embroidering a little lavender sample at the moment; I found that half finished from goodness knows when, and became quite inspired to finish it after we spoke of the lavender jam last month . . . Yes, of course I will bring it to show to you, how sweet of you to ask . . . No, thank you, I can't say I enjoy hearing what other people are embroidering, I prefer to think of my own work only. Otherwise I find I become drastically uninspired. Nothing against you personally, of course . . . By the way, have you noticed my skin? Perfectly glowing, do you not think?'

It was easy to speak as Ladie now to herself, to the dolls, to Aunt, even to Mrs Hardy. Easy when even to her own eyes she saw herself as Ladie. She looked in the mirror when she dressed. Truly looked. She admired for an age all of Ladie's smooth, supple lines. The way she could fill each gown the way they were meant to be filled, her chest spilling over necklines that curved to show the slope of shoulders and bring eyes to the twist and stretch of a neck primed for biting. The swell of her hips teasing and boasting under thick bodies of liquid skirts. Her skin had colour, and her hair was starting to grow lighter from crisp afternoons in the winter garden, from sitting on the window seat in the music room and letting the sun sear her scalp.

Even looking beyond the superficial, she could see Ladie. Ladie came from inside her so strongly, it altered her entire countenance. Just one quick smirk and she was Ladie, vain and carefree and effervescent and sweet and cheeky. Her eyes saw everything Ladie ever saw, so when she looked into them, Ladie peered out. She took a deep breath. No, that wasn't right. Ladie wouldn't do it like that. She pulled back her shoulders and felt her ribs widen, she took a sharp breath in through her nose, so sharply the air felt cold and jumped into her lungs like a hiccup. It made her lips smart into a half-smile. *That* was how Ladie did it. Light from all this fresh air, all this freedom.

She was free in every sense of the word. From pain and toil, from downstairs, from the rot, from blood and blisters and black mud. (Shh.) Even the corpse did not enter her mind, nor did the house haunt her at night.

In fact, the language in which Ropner spoke to her now was entirely different to before. It was kinder, gentler. It purred softly at night and lulled her to sleep, it lavished her with luxuries, and it ordered her days to wind and meander in a warm ocean that rocked her gently as a bairn. All the darkness she was scared of in Ropner seemed to have melted away, washed out by the river. It was only a little harmless doll's house, after all; she could push it gently and it would collapse in on itself. Everything was a game to play and Ropner only existed for her pleasure. Its sugar-spun grounds were her own personal kingdom. She lorded over every one of her botanic subjects under the dome of the winter garden, she held processions and parades for the flowers in the summer gardens, smug as they bent their meek little heads in submission, and she demanded the stone nymphs unfreeze and whisper all their secrets.

Today she stood at the gate of the meadow, breathing out in synchronisation with the wind, pretending that it was her own breath making the long grass sway and buffet.

She was king.

She surveyed her kingdom with her hands on her hips. Maybe it was fancy, but Ann liked to think she could see the grounds thawing. The monochrome of winter was slowly blushing with colours she had long forgotten. She tried to remember if she had ever actually seen spring at Ropner. Did the meadow brighten with wildflowers? Flowers with skirt-like petals whose heads extended to call for the kiss of fat fumbling bees, flowers fluted like champagne glasses filled to the brim with varying shades of pastel? Did the sandy skin of Ropner lose some of its weathered birthmarks and bleach in the sun? Did the leaf-littered undergrowth of the woods become spiked with green shoots that promised snowdrops?

Ann looked over to the dark scythe of the woods. Would she find proof of spring if she dared to go in?

If she dared. Ha! That was a funny thought to her now. What didn't she dare do now that she was Ladie? What fear did she have, now everything was so entirely hers? What worry did she have of a distant evil-smelling hut or the terrible black mud behind it?

None.

The whisper of spring was in the woods. The excitement of its promise drenched the grass and tattooed trees with burgeoning buds of leaves. The sky was flung wide open, and underneath, green and grey met and merged. With bones of bark and a rushing pulsing jugular, it was a landscape alive.

Underneath Ann's feet, the ground seemed to crackle as it thawed. She could already spy sharp green nubs pushing through the black. Each promised to be an atonement from Ropner for all the time she had spent locked in purgatory. She would forgive it, she thought. While she was here, encased in a warm hollow, brimming with birdsong, it was easy to be forgiving.

Thousands of chirps and calls, as diverse and as many as grains of sand, as sharp and clear as tiny shards of clear glass, rang on and on and bathed her in their sharp sweetness. One tree had grown a cushion of moss by its feet. Ann sat on it. So what if her skirts got dirty? *They* would clean it. That's what they were here for, after all. Not for spitting and fucking and cursing and rotting, but for good, clean, honest work, and she would see they had plenty to do.

Wasn't it funny to think of them scuttling around furiously downstairs, just for her. The work eroding their bones, buckling their backs, coaxing welts and calluses out on their fingers (perhaps she ought to start lathering hand cream on underneath her gloves to soften her own), keeping them awake so long that the bleary whites of their eyes were more commonly pink. *Ha! Let them suffer, they deserve it, it's their penance for all the rot; for trying to infect me with it.*

Ann shut her eyes and breathed in time with the pleasant breeze. She let the sweet sounds of the wood wash over her, and she dreamed of spring in full bloom at Ropner: bright golden light and the sweetness of fresh flowers. She dreamed of spring gowns in shiny new colours and of wearing them to a spring ball, thrown especially in her honour, that all the servants would be forced to watch. Forced to watch as she floated down the curved staircase in the entrance hall, forced to watch on their hands and knees, flung out in worship and adoration, forced to watch as their Ladie glided so elegantly from the staircase and into the dining room to eat scrumptious, sumptuous food while they beetled away back downstairs to get back to their burning and rotting.

Ann was soothed into deep sleep right there in the woods by the cruel imaginings of their torture.

38

IT WAS BEGINNING to rain when she woke up. A drop landed on her scalp and ran infuriatingly down the centre of her forehead, like a bead of blood from a neatly cleft skull. With a quiet horror, so long not felt it was almost foreign to her, Ann realised that the blackest part of night was already beginning to bloom.

This is your kingdom now, she reminded herself. *You have nothing to be scared of. You are Ropner's Ladie.*

Ladieladieladie.

She whispered her new name to herself like a spell. She remembered the cool marble of Hermia's skin, and the edges of her mind prickled with bone-white eyes, bone-white shards, bone-white on black mud. (Stay back.) *Breathe in the air, feel it on your skin, Ladie's skin.*

The air had been refreshing when she dozed off, but now the dark had begun to whip it into a wind; the promise of spring was forgotten, obliterated by the sharp sting of winter. She smoothed her hair and got to her feet. It was fine. She was fine. The path back to Ropner was short, the path back home was . . .

If she could just remember the . . .

Sleep had disoriented her, and in the deepening dark all the grey black trees looked the same, none stood out as a distinct signpost for the way back. She tried to focus on the sound of the river, to place it behind her, to use that as her compass. She listened hard and heard the deep bass of the ground, it wasn't crackling with the thawing of spring like it had earlier, it was bubbling with all the bones in its belly. They were reanimating, shifting and clicking and reforming their skeletons, resealing the remainder of their rotting flesh, reaching up and up and up.

Coming for her.

She sifted through tree trunks, trying to see between their masses, to catch one of Ropner's ever-winking eyes. A clawed hand reached from above and dived for her face. She swallowed a scream and tumbled against a tree. Her body tensed to stone and her heart beat inside her ears.

The hand was nothing more than a grey branch, flung out to reach her by the wind.

She smoothed her hair again and set off on a brisk walk, not caring if it was the right way, she just wanted to move, to not stay like a sitting duck. She would find the path soon enough if she was not yet already on it.

God, it was threatening to have her again, that fear. It was sluicing up the insides of her throat, forcing her to take great tacky drawls in through her mouth. Her teeth chattered.

No, she was Ladie, Ladie was not afraid.

She straightened her spine; she had been walking hunched, her shoulders curled in like the leathery wings of a harpy; she had been walking like Ann. But she was Ladie, and Ladie was not afraid. Ann was, but she was not Ann. Ann was afraid of stupid things, of black mud and ivory shards (shut up) and rattling breaths and groping hands. Of dark, dark nights and rattling breaths and whispers scuttling over roots

and under leaves, coming up from that terrible black—
(Stop, God dammit!)

'Ann?'

The voice was tiny. Soft and hopeful. Her real name fastened around her neck once more like a dog collar, and with it all of her humours, all of her fears, all of her rot. Ann turned towards the voice, as obedient as a bitch, a common, wretched little mutt.

Ladie was less than a yard away, yet scarcely recognisable. Her hair was pulled back, but loose strands fell bedraggled round her face, matted and unwashed. Her skin was an-aemic, covered in dirt. Scraps of fabric swung from her scrawny frame. She was like a ghost from the past, a memory from the mirror of time long ago.

'Ann,' she said again, shakily. 'Don't say you can't recognise me! Goodness, how *you* have changed.' Her eyes, still grey, still bright, trailed over Ann's appearance; she drank in the plumper figure, the skin so delicate, the silken hair, the gloved hands that clutched tightly at thick skirts. 'Is that my dress?'

Ann's jaw creaked at its hinges but no sound came out.

Ladie gave a hollow little laugh that wasn't a laugh at all. It ran coldly up the back of Ann's neck.

'What have you done, Ann?' (Just when you thought that name was dead and buried.) Silence stretched between them. 'Ann?' (Here it is like a bad penny, a curse.)

'You left,' Ann managed to croak.

Ladie drew back her chin sharply as if she were swallow-ing a surge of nausea. The wind had stilled, straining to listen.

'I made a mistake, Ann.' (Why won't she stop using that God-awful name?) 'I made a mistake, Marcus is not what

I . . . It is not at all what I . . . We walked for days, Ann –'
(that ugly fucking name) – 'walked for days and days and
days, and nothing seemed to change. I could swear I – Ha!
It sounds so foolish, but I could swear I never even left the
grounds of Ropner.'

Ann thought quite suddenly of a time a million years ago,
when she herself had walked and walked by the river, only to
end amongst the stinging nettles, right where she had
started.

Ladie was shaking now, quite violently, and she began to
wring her cracked palms together. 'It's a cruel and horrible
game that I should have felt all these things so deeply that
I knew them to be true, only to have it all spat back at me
like a venomed *Ha!* and find I had only imagined it all.
Oh, but how could I have? I think if you had listened to
my heartbeat you would have heard his name over and
over.'

Ann's stomach bubbled and she felt the wild urge to grab
Ladie by her shaking shoulders and vomit onto her face.
She was disgusted by her. The once beautiful face was
unkempt and sallow, covered in gouges of sunken shadows
and thin scabs. Her body had been whittled down to just its
frame, stripped bare and naked in bony ugliness: a spindly
sundial shadow of its former glory. (*You* are more Ladie
than her.)

'You left,' Ann blurted again.

It sounded stronger this time. A statement.

'Yes . . . Yes, I left. But the house, it kept . . . *calling* me
back.'

This ghost, this ghastly wretch, couldn't come back, not
when she wasn't Ladie, not when *she* was Ladie now. (They'll

send you back underground. Back with the beetles and the rot and the bones and putrid bodies.)

'You can't come back,' Ann said.

Ladie's eyes were so round, all of the whites were visible and cracking and leaking onto her skin. (She's breaking again. You have to break her.)

'Ann . . .' she said quickly. 'Ann, what is this?' (They'll send you back to a life of fear and evil, with eyes and hands everywhere until they rot you into nothing.)

'Don't call me that.'

'Is this some cruel game, some kind of waking nightmare? I've always found it hard to tell what was real, I think, but now more than ever . . . I'm dreaming, I think.' Ladie began to rock back and forth with tiny steps. 'Yes . . . I'm dreaming that you're in my clothes. Ann, you're dressed all fine and holding yourself like a lady—'

'Stop with that name.'

'And speaking to me. Not being spoken to. Such a funny dream. I think it's making cracks in my brain. You don't know what it's like to see yourself, Ann—'

'Don't!'

'For your reflection to step out of a mirror and start moving. For a portrait to extract itself from its oils and start talking. Oh, Ann!'

'I told you, *stop*!'

A funny thing was happening as Ladie spoke. Her eyes were growing wider and her mouth growing slack and tears were falling very steadily and heavily down her cheeks. It was horrifying.

'Have you walked out of your frame?' she said, tears running steadily into the black hole of her mouth. 'Have you walked out of the mirror like before? Ann?'

'I said STOP!' Ann gave a shriek like a warning siren and lunged towards her old mistress, driving her down towards all the terrible black mud.

The fight was not pleasant.

Skin ripped and frayed. Hair was knotted round fingers and snapped and torn and pulled to make eyes pop. Fingers scrabbled and strangled and nails tore. A tooth chipped and swung from the gum, planting itself into the fleshy mud. A hand, cracked and desperate, scrabbled through the undergrowth, found a loose rock, a pomegranate-sized stone.

It seized it. It brandished it. It beat it down, down, down, to meet a scalp. It beat it down, down, down, to reveal a whiter than white skull. It beat it down, down, down, until the skull split like a fruit, spilled out its ripe flesh and juice.

The blood was more than she had ever seen before. How awful that a person has all that gushing about inside them, so viscous and sticky, like a horrible sap. How was there so much of it? So much darkness? From all the thrashing, the blood and the mud had scored fleshy arcs over the leaves like huge wings.

She dropped the pomegranate rock and looked down at the body below, ready to see the great secret of death revealed, discover the fabled beauty of it. But beneath the blood and the butchered skull, the face (which had looked so uncannily like hers) was nothing exceptional or awe-inspiring or enlightening, it imparted no great secret.

In death, Ann just looked dead.

Spring

1

THE BLUSH OF spring's sun was warm, and its breeze, ticklish and refreshing, made her fan pleasantly redundant. Charlotte watched the summer gardens from her little white chair. The gardens were pubescent with the raptures of an awakening world; bright pastel heads of flowers pierced pin-cushion bushes, water from the flutes of nymphs bubbled happily in the fountains, tanging the air with a clean metallic smell; a thrumming of bees seemed to vibrate in the cavity of her chest.

She bit into the cold flesh of fruit that was sliced into cubes and heaped into a delicate bowl on the table beside her. The juices bled through her gloves onto her fingertips, but the serenity of her surroundings meant that even stains and stickiness did not bother her. Chimes chinked faint and thin from the trees.

It was a good little life, she decided.

She had been told to take each day slowly since the accident, not move too quickly or think too deeply. And that suited her just fine. She could scarcely remember the accident at all, it was all a blurry mystery made none the clearer by Mrs Hardy or Aunt.

'A funny turn,' Mrs Hardy had deemed it, with a smile that Charlotte supposed was meant to be comforting.

'Happens to the best of us, dear Lottie,' was all Aunt had contributed.

She could recall the coppery smell of blood, nauseating, something bone-white; a flash of light perhaps, and black-ness, total and complete drowning blackness. It was better not to think about it, she had been told. And she heeded that with blind faith; it was easier.

Life before the accident had also grown distant and vague. Thinking of it was like viewing some grand abandoned build-ing through a gauzy veil; she could make out the bones of its structure; timber awnings and walls, familiar-shadowed shapes of chairs and tables. But nothing was clear, it wasn't easy to see what each room had been before it had succumbed to rot and suffocated under dust and cobwebs.

It was easier to think only in the now; find starbursts of joy in the little things, indulge in spoils and demands with-out thinking of consequences, without thinking of what had come before.

Beyond the summer gardens, rippling in and out of view from behind the perimeter hedges, the grounds of Ropner spun saccharine green right to the horizon of woods. Although the meadow and the gardens were brimming with the sweetly prim colours of a hundred different flowers, the trees were not quite healed from the bruising of winter. Looking at them, Charlotte felt the chill of the foregone season, although the thought of cold, of frost, seemed impossible to her now in the sun's dribbling warmth. A life-time ago. Only spring, only the present, seemed a possibil-ity, a truth.

In the distance, a hare ran over the grounds, its gravelled fur stretching and springing over its elongated body. It paused suddenly, poised and calm, revealing its pointed cotton tail, the shock of white naked and unabashed. Hare? Or was it a rabbit? Charlotte couldn't tell. She shook her head and fanned herself. What did it matter? How different could they be, really? She wondered if they could tell themselves apart.

Charlotte was aware of Mrs Hardy approaching before she saw her. The breeze seemed to stagnate and the light to grow duller. A childish fancy, she knew, but something about the housekeeper being near made her want to behave like a child, a petulant one who stuck out their lower lip and stamped their foot. Mrs Hardy was always disturbing her peace, ruining her fun with something or other.

'The Duchess would love to see another of your embroideries, Lady Charlotte. I think now would be a good time for you to start . . . My lady, I would ask for you not to go in that room, one of the maids is just due to clean it . . . You are looking a fraction tired, my lady, let me escort you back to your rooms. It will not do you well to be wandering around the corridors in such a manner . . .'

'Luncheon is in an hour, Lady Charlotte,' she said now, 'if you would care to change.'

Charlotte rolled her eyes and laid her fan on the little white table.

2

THE DISTURBING THING about the change of season was that, with it, Aunt seemed to be becoming (dare she be so generous as to say it?) beautiful. What a humiliating thought.

Charlotte was the niece, the younger; it was her place, her duty, to be radiant and beautiful. It was her way to feel some semblance of power, retain some sense of pride, while she had to endure the idiotic, degrading luncheons with those garish dolls. But here was Aunt, occupying the other end of the table with more grace than Charlotte had ever observed before. With the heat of the season her vastness seemed to have translated to a healthy buoyancy; it had solidified from sagging insular blubber to become the smooth marble of Grecian curves. Her hair had thickened and developed a resolute shine that very nearly suited the bouffant style it was pinned into. The shine reflected onto the glittered pins that adorned it so that they seemed to move; pearly butterflies slowly stretching their wings and sighing. Monstrously, it was a pleasant effect. She was not unlike Titania, awakened from her nap by the effects of a love potion that had turned her cheeks rosy and lips full and eyes deep and bright. Her teeth were very white, too, like a skull.

'My sweet!' Aunt squeezed through a smile.

Charlotte sent back a smile of her own, though it felt funny, like it had been sewn on with pins and needles.

She ought to be more careful with herself, really; imagine if, one day, Aunt grew more beautiful than even her! She shuddered and sipped delicately at her rose tea, careful not to purse her lips as she did. She would refuse wrinkles even the slightest encouragement.

'Mrs Hardy was going to read out the guest list while we feast,' Aunt said. 'How exciting that preparation for Harvestfeast is beginning already!' She puffed up her chest proudly, and glanced round at each of the dolls silently lining the table, as though she were expecting them to clamber to their little feet and applaud her. Some of their fake little eyes flickered between Aunt and Charlotte.

Charlotte pulled a little scalloped plate of *macarons* towards her and pretended not to notice.

'Thank you, my lady.' Mrs Hardy's voice oozed from beside the table. 'Of course, the Baudelires will be attending . . .'

Charlotte kept her eyes on the clam mouths of the confections in front of her. Looking at Mrs Hardy, acknowledging her presence in any way, made her irritable; irritable because she was uncomfortable; uncomfortable because of the something like shame that twinged and twisted in the bottom of her belly. The housekeeper knew her in an intimate way that no one else did. She bathed and dressed her, she soaped every inch of her skin with hands warm and smooth, though Charlotte always expected them to be cold, clammy or slimy. It was worse that they were not, because the warmth made it almost pleasant, and Charlotte had never wanted to enjoy

anything less. Mrs Hardy wrapped and trapped and tightened her into gowns, hid her ugly, cracked hands in gloves,
all different shades of pastel silk. In each second of those
moments, Charlotte could feel herself silent and shrinking,
any notion of power, of hierarchy, disrupted and mocked. It
was appalling. She resented it, resented herself, resented that
horrid sickly feeling it inspired, that made everything drop
away and hollowed out her head to a yawning black emptiness atop a cold neck.

'Mr Marley, Mrs Oliver Cuelle.' She had such an insipid
voice.

'Oh, Mr Marley! Perfect, make sure he is seated right
beside Lottie. You do remember him, don't you, darling?'

The pistachio *macaron* she had bitten into was sticky and
gritty and it coated her teeth like wet sand. She could feel it
lumpy under her lips. She would not give Aunt the chance
to see the green chunks barnacling her teeth as if she were
some sort of ogre. It was one thing for her to think Aunt
might become pretty enough to threaten her own beauty; it
was another type of mortification for Aunt herself to realise
it. She nodded passively instead. In reality, she hadn't the
faintest idea of a Mr Marley.

'. . . Lady Mortimer . . .'

As a matter of fact, none of the names Mrs Hardy droned
inspired any particular response – though surely this lauded
dinner carried some meaning for her. She had to have some
memory of it.

'And of course we will be welcoming Mrs Varda at the
Harvestfeast with much celebration, given her recent
success.'

Harvestfeast.

'Oh, naturally, Mrs Hardy, we will be sure to congratulate her efforts!' Aunt giggled. 'This year promises a Harvestfeast to remember, I think.' She winked coquettishly at Charlotte and giggled again.

Harvestfeast, Charlotte thought. The word was poignant somehow, loaded.

'Harvestfeast,' she sounded under her breath.

'What was that, sweet, sweet Lottie?' Aunt waggled her fingers towards Mrs Hardy, who slid immediately to her side and began to slice the chicken breast on Aunt's plate into brassy slithers. Aunt watched on serenely, drooling only slightly.

Charlotte licked the sweet grit from her teeth and swallowed. 'I was musing over Harvestfeast, Aunt. There is something so familiar about that word to me . . .'

Aunt had speared a shining slice with her fork and paused its journey to the gallows of her mouth midway to give herself the opportunity to let out one of her little titters. 'Of course, dear Lottie, we have Harvestfeast every year.' The slither of meat wobbled out its final steamy breaths before she sucked it towards the inevitable experience with her molars.

'But it has only just turned to spring?'

'Lottie!' Aunt had not swallowed before she began to speak, and chewed flesh rolled about with her words. Charlotte felt her own lips twist and purse. 'Try not to mumble and run your words together, it's so uncouth, you must be mindful of it in front of our guests.' Her empty fork signalled to the impassive doll faces.

'I said, dear Aunt –' she tried not to bristle too overtly, tried not to speak through gritted teeth – 'talk of a

Harvestfeast is surely premature when it is only just spring.' In the window behind Aunt, slats of white sun were stoical and unmoved by the light breeze that played through the trees.

Aunt gave another irritating titter, 'Of course! But some years you are – sorry, *things* are ready a fraction sooner. Time is a fickle thing at Ropner. And besides, it's easier to organise Harvestfeast in spring,' Aunt continued to blather, 'while we all feel that little more alive, more youthful!'

'I just, I can hardly recall . . .' Charlotte said softly. There were hazy memories, so distant they may have been imagined; lords and ladies with flutes filled with bubbling amber, throwing their heads back and laughing, their jewels and beads reflecting lightnings of gold from the candles and gas lamps. Parades of food that would make a glutton queasy, kaleidoscopic colours, music leaking underneath doors.

'Oh, don't dwell on it too much, Lottie dear! I find whenever things flummox me, it's easier not to think of them at all! Ha-ha!'

Charlotte mimicked Aunt's silly laugh with little sincerity. All of her memories were fickle and fleeting as of late. Perhaps it was the new heat, the change in season. She plucked a pink *macaron* from the plate, its jam oozing stickily onto her glove.

Charlotte let her mind float away, into that space where time didn't exist and everything went her way. Luncheon droned on around her. Her day droned on around her, too lazy from the warming of the season to form a rhythm. Every day lolled about for eternity without pattern or structure, just the fluidity of nothingness. And Charlotte let it gladly wash over her, like a tide.

This was all her life had ever been, this endless ocean of spring; perhaps it was all it would ever be.

Then so be it.

She had things to pass the time; she could laze in the different rooms of the house, searching for the coolest spot like a lizard; she could sit in the summer gardens and squint at the horizon and wonder if it was a porous seam or a tight seal.

3

AFTER LUNCHEON, SHE lay on her bed and thought of Harvestfeast again. There would be people there, other people. People to see, people to see her. A little thrill electrified her body. There was a place beyond Ropner, then. Its roads and river stretched to destinations abroad. Unfamiliar towns and people and names, exotic to her. How could she have forgotten? How had she not been fascinated enough by guests the previous years to pump them for information? To retain every morsel of detail and compose a plan of escape? Perhaps she had been too scared. No. Not scared, never scared. Perhaps she had decided she was too comfortable at Ropner to forgo its luxuries for the unknown. Perhaps the guests had been as dull as the dolls that modelled them, bad advertisements for a life away.

She invented a swashbuckling type for this year's feast, striding into the dining room in a cloak of foreign material, thick and dark and smelling of skin. He would have an eagle-like nose cutting ahead of him, brown eyes, and strong arms. Warmth sluiced up the sides of her stomach and she sunk deeper onto her bed. What was he to think of her? she wondered.

Beautiful, of course. Why would he not? She raised herself to her elbows to look at the big painting hung on the far left wall. It was of her and Aunt, monstrously large and out of place in her room. She supposed it had always been there, and the accident had caused a lapse that made its presence feel foreign, but it almost seemed like an intrusion, to have her own likeness so close to her. A cuckoo's egg in her own nest. As she assessed the portrait from her bed, a feeling crept upon her, an unfamiliar one.

Disappointment. Disappointment in a highly unusual context. She had never seen her face in a looking glass and felt unsatisfied. Why now should an old portrait make her feel so?

Perhaps because it was not a portrait alone; perhaps the distaste came from having Aunt forcing herself upon her even in that painted space. Or perhaps – and here something little and cold twisted behind her navel – it was that third figure she had missed at first glance. The third figure standing off-centre, removed from the focus of the piece, standing so in the shadows that the black fabric of her dress seemed to blend into the wall behind her. If the idea of having a servant in a painting, let alone one of two ladies, wasn't so inconceivable, it would be easy to presume that's who the third figure was. It would be easy to presume that those painted black eyes, so dark, so endless, belonged to . . . No, it was ridiculous really. A complete impossibility. Surely it was more likely some distant relative, one the accident had marred all memory of. She sat up straighter. Really, it was a pointless thing to dwell on anyway. She was the subject, after all. The way the light hit her, the way Aunt leaned over, drawing any observer's eye to her. The issue was – and surely *this* was the true source of her disappointment – the portrait did not look anything like her. Her painted self did not wear her hair down as she always did, like a child, with simple little twists and ringlets or a headband to stave strands from the fat little diamond of her face. Instead, the oil paint slicked itself into plaits, snaking and looping in painstaking intricacies. They coiled into a crown she could never dream of mastering on herself. Had her hair been like that when she posed, or was it the artist's imagination? She could barely remember posing for the painting at all. She conjured a chair that grew increasingly uncomfortable, stifling hours that dripped like an old faucet, an old, wonky man who smelt of sea salt and sour milk, whose face was concealed by a canvas.

Had she sat underneath another's hands before the sitting? Head bowed while they ploughed her scalp with plaits? There was an intimacy about that image, something tender and meditative and almost animalistic; a ritual that was so fundamental, so instinctive. Her loose hair shushed against the collar of her dress with each tiny move of her head. Suddenly the unimpeded tresses had transformed to a hallmark of loneliness.

The rest of her portrait was unflattering. She knew she was much more beautiful in real life. Her forehead in reality was higher, prouder, her mouth and cheeks softer, her eyes not so horribly vacant and staring. The eyes of the painting refused to look at her; they stared past intensely, as if seeing something just over her shoulder. Instinctively Charlotte turned to look. There was nothing but the same tired old room.

But when she turned back, something niggled at her eye. A minuscule movement. So tiny. As if her painted self had only the second before settled back into position. As if it had moved while she turned. As if, had she been facing away a moment longer, it would have succeeded in lunging from its frame and seizing her.

A horrid little thought. *Take it out of your mind immediately, Charlotte,* she scolded herself. Because with the thought of a moving likeness she had grown hot at the back of her neck and all her hair on her arms had stood on end, like her skin had become charged with something. A static warning before a storm.

Silly nonsense. She huffed herself from the bed and stomped along to the library. She would sit and read on the windowsill and watch the woods until the sun turned her sleepy, blissful.

4

CHARLOTTE WAS NOT hungry. The food around her was beautiful, but it could not have been less appealing. Near her elbow a plate was dressed with garlicked vegetables, turgid and bright, that curled round a marshmallow of steak. A fillet whose insides were searing pink leaked purple liquid like a glutinous spring. Nudging to be next in her affections was a platter bricked with slabs of sugary stodge; their caramelised tops glistened and set her teeth on edge. Peeled lychees bobbed in a bowl of punch like eyeballs.

She had always enjoyed her food, had she not? Yet today each offering was quickly transforming from the delectable to the detestable. The centrepiece, some sort of towering jelly, wobbled sickeningly each time Aunt turned between dolls to converse. It was red, with flabby lady's fingers stood to attention around its base. The idea of scooping out lashings and slapping them onto her plate churned her stomach.

In her peripheral vision she saw Mrs Hardy step closer to Aunt; lean over her and gently tuck a napkin under her chin. Great fat Aunt, who was alarmingly not so fat anymore, looked at the housekeeper with a wet and unadulterated adoration in her eyes. Charlotte felt sick to her stomach. She knew their dirty little secret. They thought she didn't, but she knew.

She had taken to wandering the corridors in the endless hours bookending luncheon. Bored of trying to probe her memories of a time before the accident (running, amongst trees, a wide aching hollow), embarrassed by the pinpricks of fear she felt every time she looked at the portrait in her room. (Silly really to be afraid of your own likeness, but it was so insistent on trying to trick her into thinking it had moved.) She had never known where Aunt's chambers were, yet that day she found one, quite by chance.

In a corridor on the western side where she had not often wandered, voices had leaked out softly from a room, like gas. There came that silly titter that she had heard so often at luncheon.

Aunt.

She followed the hiss and hum of faint whispers to a door at the end of the corridor. Its handle was round and gold, like they all were, but underneath gaped an empty keyhole.

Charlotte, without hesitation, crouched and pressed her eye to it.

She had always imagined Aunt's chambers to be an echo of the dining room; pink and fussy and entirely ghastly. But the room through the keyhole was almost sepulchral in its bareness. The walls were a pale grey, like dead skin, and one corner was so covered with what looked like cobwebs that they had congealed together into a sort of sac.

Right in the centre of the room, the only furniture Charlotte could see was a high-backed chair, and in it sat the housekeeper. She sat like she was posing for a portrait; as straight and as still as a poker.

But there, lying with her torso across Mrs Hardy's lap, was Aunt's tulle-bedecked form. Her face was turned away from the door that Charlotte crouched at, and was pressed close to Mrs Hardy's chest, and she was . . . No, it was impossible, surely, but for all the world it looked as if Aunt were *suckling* at Mrs Hardy's . . . No. It was surely a trick of her eye, of the angle. But almost as if to prove its reality there was a great sucking sound as Aunt . . . unlatched, and a maid Charlotte had not seen at first hurried into view, a large linen napkin in her hand to dab at Aunt's wet mouth.

The maid turned and stepped back when she had finished her duty, away from the two women while they righted themselves nonplussed, as if this were something they had done a million times before.

The maid had impossibly large brown eyes, like cattle, and they were staring right at her. Right through the keyhole, right into Charlotte's own grey ones.

She stepped back from her crouching place quickly. As silently as she could, Charlotte ran. She raced to the devilish speed of her pounding heart, she ran and ran until she reached her own room, where she hid behind her Paris green divider, blinking again and again and again, trying to blink out the image of the tableau she had just witnessed like it was a stuck lash.

'You're so quiet today, Lottie, I do wish you would try with our guests,' Aunt said, snapping Charlotte back to the luncheon table. The napkin was tucked securely under her chin (chin, singular, though she had so many before), and Mrs Hardy had retreated back to her corner. Aunt gestured to the dolls. 'It *is* important to practise.'

'Sorry, Aunt,' Charlotte said unfeelingly. 'I was quite distracted.'

'Oh?'

In the window behind Aunt, the dark colours of the trees had healed to green. Apple-green, glass-green, fresh, sharp, herb-smelling green. Charlotte fancied that when the wind parted leaves and branches, she could see the steel blade of the river cutting through.

'I was thinking it might be nice to have a walk in the woods one day,' she said. If she held her eyelids closed a fraction longer than a blink, a fluorescent green stain bleached over the dark red. 'I suppose it would be quite safe now it is spring. The light would lend much more of a friendliness to the path.'

Aunt's lips puckered and made little wet pops as she opened and closed them. Finally, the wet pops gave way to speech. 'I'm not sure it is wise to venture there on your own, not so soon after your accident.' Her words were sticky and loaded, and Aunt seemed to be working hard to peel them from the roof of her mouth. Her cheeks were pink with the exertion of it. 'Woods are . . . are dangerous places. What do you say, Mrs Hardy?'

Mrs Hardy stepped forward from her recess against the wall and spoke altogether more smoothly. Charlotte always had the distinct impression that whenever she posed a question, the housekeeper had already anticipated it well in advance and practised her answer so often that the words slipped slickly and fluently from her mouth.

'I would be happy to accompany Lady Charlotte should she care for a trip into the woods.' She caught Charlotte's eye, and in it was a glint of something like greed.

'It's quite all right,' Charlotte said hurriedly. The voice from her was little, embarrassingly small. 'I wouldn't want to be too much trouble.'

Mrs Hardy nodded impassively and melted back into the dining-room wall.

5

I T WAS DRAMATIC, it was pitifully woebegone and lamentable, to compare the lines of her beloved summer gardens to a cage. But it was so satisfying to wander the linear paths and imagine herself as a little linnet bird fluttering against ensnaring bars again and again, weak with frustration and dwindling hope. How tragic she was. How horrid that she had to suffer the indignity of not having everything fall perfectly her way.

They had not forbidden her from the woods, she had not been *explicitly* denied a want. But the conditions she would have had to endure were too much of an insult. Supervised like a child. Accompanied by none other than Mrs Hardy herself.

She did not like being left alone with her. There came memories of invading hands and hungry black eyes, knowing black eyes. It made her shiver, even now in the warmth of the spring sun.

Let them be damned if they thought they could control her. She would slip between the bars and fly as she pleased. She wanted to walk in the woods, and so she would, God dammit. She wanted its coolness, its wildness, perhaps she might even find it familiar, might find a piece of herself the accident had eclipsed.

There was another reason the woods had grown appealing, of course. They were so far from Ropner that, shielded from its view, Charlotte might breathe a little there, feel her sensibilities return to her. Because ever since the accident, ever since she could have sworn she saw her own portrait move, she kept experiencing the uncanny feeling of being watched. She was not someone to be cowed, not her; not Lady Charlotte, niece to the house; and yet she had begun to hesitate a fraction before opening the doors of empty rooms, she had begun to avert her eyes from dark corners, she had begun to jump at ticks and clicks and untraceable creaks as if she had been doused in cold water. It was ridiculous, deplorable.

Still, she had ordered Mrs Hardy to remove the big painting from her room. It was hung in one of the corridors now, which seemed a more natural home for it anyway, almost as if she had seen it there many times before. Not that she looked at it often; she avoided that corridor when she could. It wasn't that she was scared – she wasn't, not her: Lady Charlotte, niece to the Hall. It was just disconcerting to have to view your own likeness, an unflattering one at that, every day, that was all. It wasn't anything to do with the fear of what her portrait was looking at, what it might be seeing behind her, nothing to do with the morbid fascination, the horror, that one day her likeness would look right at her instead.

She would not even think about it in the woods; she would forget to torment herself with such foolishness somewhere so hidden from those oily eyes. She would feel free and cooled and rested from the sun that seemed to be growing more fierce and spiteful every day. Could it be that it was nearly summer already? The sun seemed to declare it so.

The meadow that bordered the summer gardens had sea-like grass that waved and dipped to bank into the river. If she walked along the low part of the meadow, right by the river, she would be largely concealed from Ropner.

Charlotte glanced over the neatly trimmed hedges towards the house; its sandy hide was smooth and becoming in the light of the sun, and its many eyes stared benevolently up at the sky, echoing the strange wispy clouds. She laid her little fan on the white table and made her way serenely out of the summer gardens to the meadow.

By the time she reached the bank, she was running as much as her skirts would allow. The grass was bright and springy underfoot, its obnoxious green wafted up a thick warm smell that made the air vibrate. Her fingertips tingled under her gloves, and she swallowed the wind in great gulps as she ran. She felt as free as the wind. If she swallowed enough she might become light enough to leap up and join it, whipping and flying and soaring and free.

Laughter bubbled and burst. Oh, how sweet the feeling of mischief!

'*Mischief.*'

Charlotte giggled to herself. The word tasted coy and naughty, the way it bounced and buoyed from her tongue, hissing a final escape through her teeth, as she herself slipped through canines of trees into the woods.

If Charlotte had dived into the river, had let the current carry her out, and then swum down and down to the depths of the sea, she supposed she would feel the exact same way she did now, standing in the woods. There would be the same shutting out of sound, the same pressure and weight of blue-green bodies, the same darkness between shafts of light. She could taste the faint tang of moisture around her; rich rancid soil and rain.

It was if she had entered some enchanted world, suspended away from earthly place and time. It turned her movements gluey and dreamlike, and she let them be so; to make any kind of sound in this place would be a kind of blasphemy, would ruin the hush of the fairytale. The ground was foaming with moss that had barnacled itself to the tree roots, turning their spines spongy and soft. The contrast of the black soil bleeding through was deliciously eerie.

Charlotte pressed on. There was no path of any kind to her eye, but she kept the river to her right; a rushing trail of breadcrumbs she could always follow back if needs be. In dappled clearings, wildflowers poked through the rusted ground; licks of red and orange like embers, white and purples and tiny uncanny blue flowers, so bright they seemed artificial. Speckled boughs of beech interwove with moss draped oak, and slender aspen, and larch, and alder.

She could be imagining it, of course, wishfully, but there was something familiar about this clearing. Her heart was beating hard with recognition, as if it were guiding her in a game of hide-and-seek; warmer, warmer, warmer. The pressure of the trees, the latent warmth of the hidden sun, the fragrant smell of the wood's wares seemed to turn everything psychedelic. Even the magpies in their usual tedious monochrome flashed by in oily blues and iridescent purples.

The woods seemed to pulsate in rhythm with her heart: *This is the spot!*

What spot she didn't know, and it was getting tiresome to try to remember. Thick pockets of sweat were pooling on her back and neck.

Mrs Hardy had told her that since the accident her mind would be prone to bouts of delicacy. She had chosen to ignore the housekeeper; she, Charlotte, would not be so weak, so imperfect. But perhaps Mrs Hardy had been right. Charlotte was feeling the woods around her growing thin and fragile; her mind was fluttering sleepily, like a nectar-drunk butterfly. It flitted from thought to thought, image to gauzy image, quite erratically. It noticed, with infinitesimal detail, the fat beads of sweat dripping further down her back and under her skirts, then it flighted and swung kaleido-scopically to the cool belly of her room, where she had sat mornings ago with her embroidery and thrown it in a rage after dropping stupid little stitches of ivory and blue she was training to mimic a petal's veins. It zipped away again and zoomed onto the cracked terrain of tree bark lining a person-sized hollow, back away to a glob of pudding like phlegm on her plate, now to thread from her gloves caught on rough skin of one of her calluses, then to the ceramic jug on the dinner table at luncheon, then suddenly to the memory of a sharp-edged figure.

A man.

A man in these woods. *The* man, standing as solid and as steadfast as any one of the trees around her.

And in remembering the man she remembered her heart; that red fist-sized clot. She remembered how she had felt it, truly felt it, for the first time ever, because God, it had burned. It had ignited, set itself alight with want and some-thing like love but perhaps not as pure. Because she supposed it wasn't pure to want to watch his eyes so carefully as they watched her, roved over her, it wasn't pure to want to see his lips so closely that his breath was hot and wet on her own, to want to know how all the thousand browns in this world were able to fit neatly into two round irises, to want to feel the broadness of his dry hands on hers, on her hips, on her neck, on her breast, in between her ribs, over her organs, squeezing at that red fist-sized clot.

God, she had wanted so badly, how could she have ever forgotten?

She had wanted to follow him wherever he went. And she had, hadn't she? Hadn't she followed him in these very woods? Watched him with his pack and his plumes of blue smoke? Hadn't there been moments when there was nothing but him and her and the brown grey black of all the trees? Yes, and those moments were so terrifying in their wonderfulness because her want was so wide. Perhaps it had scared her then, but it did not now. Where had he gone, this man? She wanted him back, wanted him here, now.

Charlotte's eyes flicked frantically over the trees, trying to spy which one would shake off its bark and reveal its skin underneath, which one would twist its branches into his sinewy limbs, and harden its sap into those brown brown brown eyes. Her heart was pulsing hard in time. He had something to do with her accident, whatever it was. *Here* had something to do with it. Right here; the undergrowth beneath her feet, spattered with thick and horrible blood.

No, that wasn't right.

Her own blood pounded in her head. There was nothing on the soil but the old mulch of leaves and the persistent heads of little flowers, vivid blue. A cooling colour, quiet, light, and probably cold to touch. Her gloved finger reached out to run its seams against the petals, prise them open and look into the flower's heart. The little flower obeyed, yawning open to reveal its centre. And there, glinting innocently from between the petals, as if it were trying to pass as one of them, was a fat yellow tooth. Charlotte stared for an eternal blink at the smooth curve of ivory, and the trees pressed on her from all sides so that her stomach lurched and she heaved out a hacking arc of bile.

She fainted dead.

Charlotte came round underneath familiar brown twisting bodies, glistening and frozen in a carved immortality. There was a heavy, almost choking smell of lavender smoke that kept rolling in waves.

'A bout of delicacy,' came an oily voice. 'Not to worry.'

Charlotte felt her arms, like wings, tucked in firmly by her sides. She shut her eyes and slept.

6

THE NEW-FOUND, HORRIBLE heat of the season simmered like soup. The air was aromatic and terrible with it ever since she had found the tooth. (Although it wasn't a tooth: why would there be a tooth there? It had been a heat-hazed trick of the eye.)

Charlotte found it harder to breathe outside in the weighted air. She wandered through cool corridors instead, ones not housing the big painting. Or she pressed her skin to the icy marble in the entrance hall. It felt nice to do that, like being kissed. She thought about what it would feel like, when she lay pressed against the marble, to have the white hands of the statues animate, and curl around her neck, pressing their coldness to that hot throbbing artery. Had the man ever done that, before? Or had she only imagined it? (What man? There is no man, there is no before. Only here and now; only Ropner, remember, just like she said.)

The window seat in the library became another little oasis. It faced east, out to the summer gardens, now full in bloom, and the sweating glass dome of the winter garden. It was shaded and chilled in the hours after luncheon. She pressed her forehead to the window, diminishing blood from a plot of skin with the meeting of bone and glass. The curtains drawn to close her into this private little space. There were no oil eyes watching, nothing to be spiteful to her senses or make her see teeth and other things that weren't really there. Nothing to disturb or alarm or confuse or frighten. Just the soft green light from outside, and a papery moth, like a little flake of old skin, fluttering again and again against the windowpane.

Charlotte was safe and entirely alone. She ran gloved fingers through the loose waves of her hair. Perhaps she would ask for a servant, a lady's maid, to braid her hair. Someone her age, someone who maybe would understand pulsing clots and wide-open wants; a friend.

Friend. The word, the notion, was distant and funny, and made her stomach flutter as if she had swallowed the little paper moth without knowing. She was a lady. Ladies did not have friends. They could not, not truly. They could have people to admire them, to shower with affection, to listen to each qualm and anecdote, but they could never reveal their most intimate selves, never truly trust. To do so would be a sign of weakness, of mortality. People, servants especially, were there to be used and discarded once their purpose had been served.

A friend was a dangerous thing. But it seemed a chance of solace from whatever this was.

She stopped stroking her hair, and with a gloved finger she reached for the little moth and squashed it to dust. At least it was away from its misery now.

7

ALL THE NEW heat made luncheons more unbearable than ever.

Air blew in listlessly from the open windows, making little effort to abate the stagnant warmth. The woods waved mockingly at her from behind Aunt's head: *You'll have to try harder if you want to know our secrets, coward.* Their leaves were becoming full with colour, reaching a bursting point from which the way forward was only to wither and die. Some of the more hopeless ones had already begun to. She bowed her head to her plate. Even the food was insufferable; too sickly, too heavy for the season. She was being fed as if she were a great bear about to go into hibernation, or a prize pig to be fattened up for a banquet. Did they not know how to make anything else? All those teeming underlings to Mrs Hardy. She pictured them as she stirred a spoon through coagular mince and islands of dumplings, scurrying through dark, rotting tunnels beneath her feet, like moles or beetles.

Of all the servants they supposedly had, she had only ever seen Mrs Hardy surface from the bowels of Ropner. Mrs Hardy and the maid who had been there to wipe Aunt's mouth after she had— (But you're not to think of that.) Perhaps they were doomed to the underworld of the grounds, never to know that spring and summer reigned above them, and so they made food fit for the season they experienced: warming soups and thick cakes, chutneys and stews and pies and hash.

The soulless eyes of the dolls stared all around her; she pretended that she couldn't see their eyes moving, couldn't see them watching. She watched Aunt talk animatedly to one about cloud shapes, and felt a sticky sense of dread. Is this what she was doomed to? Would these bouts of delicacy make little fissures in her brain until it cracked entirely and she too sat like an over-sugared meringue, half blind and raving?

The doll to Charlotte's left had crosses for eyes gouged into its clay face.

Do you ever get lonely? she wanted to ask.

She dreamed for the first time since her accident. Of Ropner at dusk, burning and blackened by the sun's setting. The woods had defied the borders of the grounds and ravaged the landscape, bursting through the acres of grass and uprooting the order of the summer and winter gardens. Panes of glass were shattered by unburdened branches, fountains toppled by the unfurling tendrils of roots, prim and trimmed bushes cowered under the shadows of their wild cousins.

Charlotte knew, with that uncanny omnipotence dreams bestow, that her portrait from the big painting had made it so.

It coaxed the woods to ferality, had manipulated them into growing round where Charlotte sat, in her once beautiful garden, on her once white iron chair, so that she would be easier to hunt. Charlotte felt her own likeness all around; the vacant eyes stared from the knolls in trees, slickly oiled hands extended from branches, reaching for her. She began to run and found she couldn't. Her skirts were weighted with lead, and though her legs moved furiously she could only crash through trees and shrubs cumbersomely.

Come now, Charlotte, she admonished herself. She seized at her skirts with calloused, gloveless hands to take some weight from her legs. She moved faster by a fraction. The woods rippled all around her; snarling branches, leaves whose colours were no more than a deathly grey in the darkness, black bark, thorns, hands reaching, grabbing, seizing at tendrils of loose hair that were flying out behind her.

No! Charlotte screamed.

The presence of her own likeness behind her was white-hot. The malevolent shadow closed its oily hands around her hair and pulled. Charlotte felt the slow peeling of skin from skull, viciously red. Her likeness moved around to face her and those horrid vacant eyes stared directly into her own before swallowing her whole.

8

'Your hair, my lady?'

'Yes, my hair. I would like to wear it in a braided fashion. I suppose you would be able to find someone capable.'

Mrs Hardy had poured her into swathes of champagne fabric for luncheon; skirts that hissed against one another like they were fizzing.

'I think it's a fashion that would be quite fitting. A sign of true womanhood to forgo girlish tastes.'

'I would be quite happy to do this for you.'

Charlotte hesitated. 'I had rather hoped . . . I thought it might be pleasant to have a girl, perhaps of my own age, to do it for me. I would hate to burden you.'

'A wonderful suggestion. But let me attend to your hair until we find a girl suitable.'

It was a statement.

'We?'

'Myself and Ropner, naturally.'

Charlotte felt small and stupid, and could not find any words to say. Mrs Hardy nodded to the cushioned stool at the dressing table and Charlotte sat. She could think of nothing else to do.

The moment was sticky and florid. Charlotte was horribly aware of the softness of her own skin, of her breakability.

Mrs Hardy advanced, and her stomach churned, it cramped, and somewhere, maybe at the bottom of her skull, pointless tears began to prickle and well. Her throat seemed to swell, pushing on all the vessels in her neck. All she could do was breathe.

The housekeeper began to braid.

The movement of each hair sent a shiver across Charlotte's scalp. She became worried that each follicle would serve as a little peephole for Mrs Hardy to peer into her mind. Charlotte imagined her thoughts unspooling from her head instead of hair; private tendrils and unfinished threads that Mrs Hardy was running through her fingers, plaiting into ploughed lines and curls. It was grotesquely intimate.

The housekeeper pulled firm and tight, weaving under and over. Charlotte watched her triplet of reflections in the mirror, trying to focus solely on the fat diamond of her face slowly revealing itself, and ignore the shadow of Mrs Hardy. The heads swayed obediently with each precise tug and twist. Her hair was being woven into a crown, and as she rocked with the movement of its creation she caught a flash of her portrait on the wall, watching her through the glass.

But no, she remembered with a shock, the portrait wasn't there. It couldn't be. That portrait was in the big painting hung in the corridor. It should not be here, reflected in the mirror. It should not be here, its vacant eyes looking right at her.

She tried to twist her head to check the wall behind, but Mrs Hardy's hands righted her firmly. Charlotte searched the mirror instead, looking for the lie in the reflection. The wall where the painting had once been was bare.

Charlotte shut her eyes. It was a hallucination, a delicacy. She swallowed. She would not let this get the of her, she would control it.

Mrs Hardy stuck in a final pin. Charlotte, for the fir time, did not want to check her reflection. She followed the housekeeper dutifully to luncheon, like a little lamb.

Despite the warm weather Charlotte observed sitting at the windowsill of her room, she had no desire to venture outside. Not after the incident in the woods. Every time she thought of it, she swept the point of her tongue along the ridges of her teeth, counting silently.

It was only a strange after-effect of her accident, she told herself churlishly. That was all the incident had been. But until she was sure it wouldn't happen again, she took to wandering the corridors of Ropner whenever she needed to stretch her legs and escape the thought of that infernal painting. Experimenting with which golden handles would yield to her touch; the same sitting room, the jaundiced antechamber, the various reading nooks, again and again and again. She walked listlessly from room to room, corridor to corridor. Wandering along the lengths of carpets, half-heartedly watching the landscapes changing from frame to frame; arid deserts, ruddy streets, sleepy lakes.

She twisted her head to look at them, and hairs pulled at the nape of her neck. That stupid girl had plaited her hair too tight again.

Mrs Hardy had found her a maid, as promised. A squat girl with oafish hands and eyes too close together, which was grossly unflattering, almost offensive to look at. Though it was nice, Charlotte supposed, to feel beautiful against something so ugly.

Not that Charlotte looked at her reflection to confirm the fact. She avoided looking into that three-sided mirror just in case she saw . . . well, saw something she didn't want to see.

Her gloved hands skimmed at the golden door handles, skipping over their stubborn immovability, slipping as one turned.

She stopped in her tracks. Here was a door that she did not recognise, and as the silk glove of her hand glanced at its handle, it turned and clicked and creaked.

With a childish eagerness, she seized the golden sphere and thrust the door open.

All the air in the new room was charged. The light from the corridor caught on the tiny atoms of dust slowly floating through the space. It was a dark and gloomy room. The walls were a strange grey brown, as though they had once been black, but the pigment had been worn and smoothed away by time. Soft breezes of warm air blew as Charlotte walked further in, like the room was breathing. Gilded frames glinted from the trickle of corridor light which wasn't strong enough to show their occupants.

Just as she thought of fetching a candle, Charlotte spied the hulking shadow of a desk. She reached it through the dark and fumbled at its surface. Her fingers skittered over sheafs of paper, cool pebbles of paperweights and thick bodies of books before they found the tiny rattling body of a matchbox laid by the tall curves of a lamp. She fumbled with the bell jar globe, flared a match to life and set the lamp to its purpose.

The small puddle of light spread across a corner of the desk and the darkness around it seemed to sharpen.

The wooden surface was littered with black notebooks and pages on pages of thick cream paper, curling under the weight of black scribbles. Charlotte picked up the nearest, tilted it towards the lamp. The orange glow stained along the page, throwing the thick black lines and muted grey shading into sharp focus.

It was a face. A sketch, hastily done, of a woman's face. Cheeks plump, hair elegantly braided around the crown, eyes wide and round and staring sadly at something over Charlotte's shoulder. She felt a horrible dark whisper of recognition rush through her body. She picked up the lamp and thrust it high in the air, flooding the puddle into a lake that washed over the whole desk and illuminated each page. Every single one bore the same strokes, the same shading, the same vacant, staring eyes, the same woman.

The same her.

The gold frames caught the glint of the orange lamp light spilling up the wall and called for Charlotte's attention. She spun around on the spot, the light wobbling and flaring, and caught frame after frame lining the room, image after image after image of her: sketches, sepia underpaintings, blocky oil drafts, and fully detailed miniatures of her likeness from the big painting. The one she swore had moved, just like these were now. Their eyes, their little whispers were following her. No, impossible, it was the sickening sway of the light distorting her vision. She stopped dead and the light stopped with her, but the paintings did not. With sounds of rustling paper, of sticky, oily squelches, her heads, all hundreds of them, were turning towards her, were blinking their vacant eyes trying to find her real ones, widened in a silent horror; they were all trying, with difficulty, to loosen their jaws, open their mouths.

'No,' Charlotte rasped with her real mouth barely working. 'Nonononono . . .'

She half dropped, half threw the lamp back on the desk and did not wait to see what happened; if it smashed, or extinguished, or belched out flames that began to tear at the pages. Let them burn. Let it all burn. Let flames ravish every single portrait, let them catch alight the whole room, the whole house, let them engulf her, too. She would rather the agony of perishing in fire than hear any one of her likenesses speak, than have any one of her mirror images reach their hands out of their frames to seize her.

She stumbled from the room sweating and panting and sobbing. She slammed the door shut and pressed against it with all her weight, slumping nearly to the carpeted ground.

'Stay in there,' she hissed. Tears fell in heavy drops and shuddering gasps. 'Stay. In. There.'

9

'**D**EAR LOTTIE, YOU are so quiet.'

Luncheon was never-ending. With the punctuation of every other minute, Charlotte was there, sat in the hard-backed chair looking at a brown clot of chocolate cake that wobbled from the expulsion of its own steam and let out dying blubbers from the caramel sauce that drowned it.

'And you look so tired,' Aunt said. 'I do hope you have not been suffering too greatly since your accident.' She made a great pantomime of whispering 'accident'; hiding the word behind her hand and looking dramatically at Mrs Hardy, as if the housekeeper might admonish her for uttering the word.

Charlotte had not slept. Her own face was everywhere. Her brain had invented the cruel idea that her portrait had gained animation, was alive in some way, that it could peel from its frame and follow her. She could feel its dead, vacant eyes on her, staring too keenly, knowing too much. She had begun to check for it everywhere; under the bed, behind the dresser door, in the fold of each curtain, in the reflection of the bathwater. At night she would sit up in bed, watching her multitude of faces looking out from the dressing-table mirror, waiting for the false one to reveal itself. The waiting was sometimes worse than finding it.

'Do remember to eat up, Lottie. We need to fatten you up for the Harvestfeast! There's nothing so becoming as a healthy young woman.'

From the corner, the housekeeper cleared her throat. 'That reminds me, Your Grace. If I may?'

'Of course, Mrs Hardy.'

'The time has almost come to procure a new maid.'

'Just like last time?' asked Aunt eagerly.

'Yes.' She smiled like a proud mother. 'Just like last time.'

They both looked at Charlotte and smiled. She busied herself with the hare meat on her plate and pretended not to notice.

Luncheons steadily transformed into Harvestfeast rehearsals, which Charlotte liked to think of as lessons for a most complex dance. There were the numerous formalities to contend with before the dance could even begin; her posture, her entrance ('Navigate your stride so that you appear to glide rather than float, Lady Charlotte'), her curtsies to the guests who were so kind to have graced her with their presence, yes, thank you all dearly for attending ('Make sure to address Mr Marley especially'), it's simply *wonderful* to see you, sir.

Then there was the choreography of the chair; the neat step away from the table (feet under skirts in third position) as Mrs Hardy pulled it out to make space for her to sit. And, of course, the delicate waltz timing of doing just that, with skirt two-three, bend two-three, sit two-three, breathe two-three, tuck *in* two-three.

The quicker steps of conversation were easier, more manageable, as long as she remembered to elegantly navigate the moves of etiquette. (Polite nods, smiles without teeth, never reaching, never slouching, eating only after food has been sliced to bites so small they almost disappear on the plate.)

After only the first few rehearsals, Charlotte found the rhythm of conversation and stuck to it like second nature. She could laugh (mouth covered) and quip pleasantries, and nod her head to each doll with a well-timed beat. Charlotte surveyed each of their faces politely (How delighted I am to see you, please do make sure you try the pickled pears), welcoming them all with a gracious smile (Such a lovely gown, the colour is positively heavenly against your complexion), and raising her fluted glass in a delicate, ladylike toast when prompted. (Cheers to *you*, with your odd little painted face that suddenly looks so horribly familiar.)

The trick was, she had learned, to not look for too long at the faces of the dolls lining the table. For if she looked too long she saw how uncannily their sewn or moulded or painted faces shifted to echo the vacant, staring, horrible faces in the paintings, the ones that had stared so terribly, reached so longingly, resembled so sickeningly her very own.

'You are coming along quite splendidly, dear Lottie,' cried Aunt. Charlotte started at the sudden exclamation and mechanically tried to manoeuvre her oily, painted mouth into a smile. 'Mrs Hardy and I think it is high time to choose a gown!'

Trying on gowns for Harvestfeast was a task of momentous proportion. Early in the morning, Charlotte was led to the dressing room. The room was fairly large, typically ornate, with mirrors rushing around all four walls of the room, breaking only to leap over the doorway from the corridor and the doorway to the antechamber. Each gown was escorted to the antechamber, unseen, by a maid, before Mrs Hardy would lead it into the main room where Charlotte was waiting, awkward in only her linen chemise.

The housekeeper held the gowns with the tenderness of a lover, mid-waltz, and when she helped Charlotte slip the sheaths of material over her head, tighten the bones of stays and arrange swathes of skirts, her hands caressed Charlotte's skin with the same affection; a tenderness that was excessive. Each stroke seemed to be marking her territory. *This flesh is mine*, her fingers seemed to trace in cursive. Charlotte shivered at each touch, though her head felt hot, inflated with sounds that were coming through her ears too loudly.

The housekeeper had plaited Charlotte's hair for the occasion; perhaps she had realised how undeserving of the position that ugly-eyed maid had been. Charlotte felt sick to her stomach the entire time. She would take that oafish girl any day over Mrs Hardy's sickly touch, over her roving, greedy eyes.

She thought of what she had seen through the keyhole and grew hotter still.

The late summer heat was terrible. It made her body swollen and awkward; each garment struggled over shoulder blades, caught rolls of stomach between its teeth, gagged and choked limbs, and snaggled around her neck. The mirrors surrounded her with whirlpools of synchronised eyes and arms and waists and nipples. She felt like a throbbing blood clot, albeit a beautiful one, because each gown was indeed beautiful – each like paintings, in their own way. The first had tight, precise brushstrokes of scarlet, a splash of wine in the accompanying bead-stippled shawl; another was in watercolour pinks and blues, a barely there sash leaking down the bodice; one was composed of a dozen shades of cream and white; a ruffled jacket blended and feathered into an extravagant, sweeping skirt. The complementing shoes for each were lined up obediently on a low table, neat empty shells, agape and inviting. They looked pretty like that, but the deceitful little beasts would chew her feet to blood puddings as soon as her soles met their throats.

Charlotte had struggled into a blue gown, a liquid blue that slicked over her body in an iridescent current that foamed and frothed at her feet. It was beautiful; she could tell without even looking at her reflection. She looked down at the beat of her belly's breath underneath the steely stomach and watched the fluid ebb and flow of the fabric.

Mrs Hardy stepped away to admire her, and Charlotte felt a little shiver, like a beetle crawling up her spine.

'The matching gloves!' the housekeeper said, clasping her hands underneath her chin.

The dressing room was made never-ending by the mirrors, and when Mrs Hardy slipped into the antechamber to fetch the gloves, the mirrors stretched it to infinity, with no light at the end of the tunnel.

So many millions of her faces moved in such sync; it was sickening. Charlotte forced herself to move slowly and stared at them all. Within seconds, she found what she was looking for, and all the blood dried up in her body. One reflection stood out, different from the rest. Behind her – no, it was to the side – no, behind that one, on the left. She spun around, and all of her selves spun with her, blurring the imposter, hiding its true spot.

But Charlotte knew it was there, her portrait from the big painting. It had followed her from the corridor. She spun desperately and lunged for the mirror closest to her. It was cold and bloodless under her fingers. She searched its surface and the millions of surfaces echoed within. Where was she? Where was the damned fake, the silent imposter? Her breathing was so heavy it fogged the mirror. She swiped at it with her glove, and there, underneath the fog, was the painting's face, right where her own face was meant to be. Its oily skin ripped open like the flesh of rotting fruit and screaming erupted into the dressing room. Charlotte backed away before her own painted hands could reach out from the reflection and throttle her. But the scream kept ringing and pulling on every white nerve that stringed through her body.

She screamed with it, from the terror, the pain. She seized a shoe from the table – one, ivory-white, whose heel was sharp and thick – and she kept screaming as she threw it with all her might against the mirror. Right in that bitch's face.

When Mrs Hardy came in with the gloves, Charlotte was standing in the centre of the room surrounded by fragments of mirror, some crushed to powder. She had the shoe clutched in her hand still, its white heel broken, held on only by a scrap of sole so it was dangling as if from a handle.

'Yes,' said Mrs Hardy. 'I think that dress is quite perfect, Lady Charlotte.'

The wallpaper where all the mirrors had been was black and peeling, like dying skin.

10

T EN WAKING MOMENTS and ten thousand nightmares later, she had been clamped into that steely bodice and had her knee joints bent underneath the watery skirts like a doll, so she could be placed squarely into the hard-backed chair in the dining room.

It was Harvestfeast.

Charlotte did not know if she was awake or sleeping, alive or dead.

The dining room was the same as it was during luncheons. Charlotte anchored one end of the table while Aunt, positively glowing with the excitement of it all, stoppered the other. She looked like some kind of idol furnished from molten gold. Oh, how such a nice sentiment could taste so sour!

Charlotte hated her; she hated how she had great grey shadows under her eyes while Aunt had none; she hated how she was glad Aunt was sat so far away lest her own ugliness be more apparent next to Aunt's radiance; she hated how Aunt had become a sun, while she a great ugly moon, infernally round with great chunks missing that her hatchet-like nightmares had hacked away.

She was a great stupid ugly moon, crammed into this infernal room that she was doomed to return to like a bad penny. This infernal room that was so full, it was screaming. In the place of the dolls, people – real people – were crammed in from every angle, surrounding the table, bearing in from every edge of her periphery, and music leaked in through the seams of the room.

It made her senses fumble and the edges of her nerves sting and itch. There was so much colour everywhere, so many flares and flashes from the chandelier's twisting glass, that she thought everything might explode. Perhaps her mind had already, because the food looked fragmented before her on the table, like a stained-glass window. Panes of slimy mushrooms and swollen pods of seaweed adjacent to a shard of soup so dark red and glutinously rich, it looked horrible enough to chew. On one fragment there were rabbit feet, hair and all; another showed bloated rolls of bread sweating with yeast and thin heron legs with cracked black skin that protruded comically from their plate. And there were flies. Flies swarmed above it all, their horrible blue-black bodies with all the diseases festering on them. She could see them up close, all their putrid hair and horrid bulging eyes and corrosive vomit that dribbled over their mouths. She wrinkled her nose at them.

'There are flies,' she said. Her voice was swallowed by the cacophony of the room. How embarrassing, to be ignored. To be ignored at the ball at which you were meant to be the belle. How mortifying to feel so out of place and time.

'There are flies,' she insisted, louder, demanding. But no one seemed to notice, or hear her.

'Say, do try the sugared lavender.'

A man sat beside her. He was very old, with an unshapely head and a napkin tied around his neck which was failing most drastically to catch the drool that tracked down his chin. It kept scrunching in on itself and cringing from his spittle. He smelt like sour milk.

'It's better than that stuff, at any rate,' he said, or seemed to say at least. At this point his mouth was so stuffed with half-masticated food that his words were all slurred together, unshaped and hardly recognisable. He pointed to the flowers of lettuce blooming on a plate between them. It was so green Charlotte could hear its crunch.

'Rabbit food,' he garbled, and hacked a rumbling mucus cough from his throat. His face was so covered with crooked lines he looked like a crumpled piece of paper rather than a man.

She turned away, nauseated by his entirety, and concentrated hard to take in the other faces from the chaos around her (at all those wretched people who ignored her, damn them), without going completely insane. Perhaps she had accidentally eaten one of the flies, and in doing so had adopted its bulbous eyes and their view; because everything was split and scattered into a million tiny hexagons that made it hard to focus on anything.

Or, perhaps, this was what dying was like, all things getting scrambled and faded just before everything vanished completely.

She squinted hard and her vision found a young woman at the top of the table, not too far from her silly, once fat sunshine Aunt. She was sitting with a fan that she wafted lazily to keep her from going red, and used it to hide her titters with the woman next to her, who was as red as a beet-root and may as well have been the same person.

Behind her, footmen lined the walls of the dining room. All young and clean with slick skin the texture of alabaster, like they had been painted with one stroke so their poreless faces smoothed all the way to their collarbones without the interference of contours and shadows. It gave them the curious look of being half formed, like larvae.

Her vision swung and slurred, interrupted by the parenthesis of the nauseating dishes, and found another woman, sat straighter but shyer. She sipped her drink meekly, big bovine eyes downcast, and Charlotte wanted to scream. There was something teeth-gratingly frustrating about them all. Like she knew something important about them but couldn't quite remember.

(There was something: she *knew* she knew.)

To her left sat an older woman, whose age was not betrayed by her skin but rather the primness of her clothes and the greys softening her black woollen hair. Her skin was almost without a wrinkle; it was radiant, in fact. She smiled as Charlotte turned to her, displaying perfect pearly teeth.

'A positively wonderful feast this evening,' she said. Her accent was heavier than the others Charlotte heard, her vowels weighted and flat. But she spoke in a clipped manner that was highly refined.

The centrepiece of the table was a huge brazen beast; a kind of roasted animal Charlotte did not recognise. It was huddled foetally on the vast plate, its long limbs folded underneath its body.

'Quite,' Charlotte replied with a tight-lipped smile. 'How is it you arrived at Ropner today? I hope your journey was quite pleasant?'

The old woman gave another smile, and Charlotte observed the even gaps between each tooth. The little black spaces were harsh against the ivory, rudely at odds with the rest of her appearance. It gave her grin a quality that was almost crone-like. 'My dear,' she said kindly. 'We've always been here.'

The others sitting around the table must have overheard, because they all turned their heads to look at Charlotte and echoed the woman's tittering laugh.

Something cold and uncomfortable shuddered inside her. She tried to catch sight of their faces before they turned away again, tried desperately to identify what it was she recognised about them. It made her so mad, her fingernails could fall out.

She tried to listen to their conversation to decipher clues as to what it might be that she knew she knew, but their talk was so odious and over the top that her brain kept slipping away from it like jelly. She clamped every muscle in her leg tight, as if that would undo the knot of frustration in her belly. (Who *are* you, God dammit?) She wanted to scream or cry or let something evil out of her chest, holding it in made her head spin.

She ran her hot tongue over the cool wet teeth in her mouth, subconsciously counted. She missed a number and tried to count again.

'The toast!' came a cry.

Her teeth had all fallen out by now and she clamped her mouth shut in the fight to focus her eyes. (If only everything would stop spinning.)

Aunt stood; she held aloft a teeny-tiny thimble glass with an incredibly long stem, and her tulle billowed all around her like a lazy breeze. What a vision she looked.

(Damnherdamnherdamnher.)

'A toast to Lottie, who I'm sure we can all see is growing so well, and who will be such a credit to the house, and to us!' The others were standing now, too; she could feel them all rise upwards and thicken the air round her face with their stares. The spinning of her vision picked up pace and she held her breath to stop her brain from leaking out of her ears.

'That being said, let us toast to Ropner, too; for all the bountiful goods it has supplied us with.' She gestured to the mounds of food, the browned corpse. 'For all the – ahm – *benefits* we are able to reap. And to spring, and to it allowing all to begin again: *ad vitam aeternam!*'

They raised their silly glasses and the woman with brown eyes and a few of the others bowed their heads like lowing cattle. '*Ad vitam aeternam.*'

It wasn't only her vision that was swinging now, she was sure. The whole room began to spin, slowly at first so she barely noticed it (had it been spinning this whole time then?), but now it was flying past so quickly that it took all her strength to try to ignore it and not dash herself against the walls that were moving so fast they blurred. Specks of white kept popping out bright between them. A bright white speck that wouldn't go away; no matter how she turned her head it kept appearing (*there!*) right in the corner of her eye. A horrible ivory ceramic, like that ugly tooth (that wasn't a tooth, because how could it be a tooth?), or a milk jug. This was ridiculous, it couldn't be real, any of it.

But sure enough, she was there under her skin, so it had to be.

'Mrs Hardy.' She spoke very boldly, and it surprised her, but then again why should it? She was used to getting her own way, after all. 'I'm sure none of the guests desire milk this evening. You may take that jug back downstairs.'

Mrs Hardy swam up from the blurred walls and glanced down at the ceramic jug in her hands, apparently perplexed. 'Forgive me, Miss Charlotte, but this jug holds wine, not milk.'

'And the guests definitely want wine,' piped up a smooth maggot-face.

'Don't you dare take that jug anywhere, Mrs Hardy,' added another.

Strange giggles broke out like tiny rashes; it all itched, and she couldn't help but feel rather that the guests were laughing at her. Only one guest didn't laugh. The woman with the big cow-like eyes, who had bowed her head at the toast. She was looking at Charlotte now, looking at her so intensely it was as if she were looking inside her. Her mouth moved softly, silently, shaping one word for only Charlotte to see: 'Sorry.'

The giggles of the others turned redder and rawer so that the laughter became so loud it bounced off the walls and seemed to spur them into spinning even faster.

(It was going to send *her* again.)

The table was spinning now, too, and all the faces began to spin together in a conglomerate blur, and the flies sprouted shelled backs and began to crawl over it all like beetles.

(*She* was coming.)

Beetles that crawled over white specks of ceramic and teeth and bones and out of the nose of that portrait, whose face was now painted over all the guests.

Every single one of the painted faces turned to her, their eyes blinked slowly, and with rusty scrapings they began to work the hinges of their oily jaws so their mouths slowly widened and widened. They were going to speak. Some flakes of paint peeled onto the floor. She didn't want them to speak. Their mouths were so terribly black inside. She didn't want to hear them. All mottled with tar or treacle. They were going to speak and then they were going to swarm over her and eat her, until there was only gummy skin left to pick from her bones. She had to leave.

(RUN!)

She stood fast, and the room at once righted itself. The guests stood to attention so suddenly it was as if she had burst into a secret they were all trying to cover up. Their faces had been returned to them and the deceitful walls stood firm and stoical like they had never spun once in their lives. Mrs Hardy stood against one, her empty hands clasped under her chin in a prayer.

Charlotte's breathing was so fast it took her half a minute to catch it and force it into words. She stammered an 'Excuse me', and as soon as the door clicked shut behind her, she picked up her skirts and ran.

She was in hell. She had to be, because the air in the corridor was molten. Its heat shimmered and the walls began to wave and flap, presenting door after door, each one with a burning handle whose rattling laughed that they were locked. She had been running for hours and had tried a million doors. She would lie down and die, or if she was already dead, then she would lie down for the rest of eternity and just let herself burn to ashes if it were not for the fact *she* was behind her, and the house would surely send *her* to follow.

This house was once a dream, this house had once been as blithe and as tiresome as a cardboard doll's house. Why wouldn't it remember that, and collapse in on itself and die, so she could stamp her silly little shoes all over it and crumple out all the spite? Now it was so solid and real and made from bricks and mortar and all the badness it was punishing her for.

She ran and rattled door handles and ran and yanked and pulled until she nearly tore her gloves, she ran and shook the handles until one took pity on her and hissed open and she fell into its cool gullet.

The door slammed shut behind her. It was a dusty grey, so dingy she could only just see it was the servants' stairwell. She shouldn't be here. But it was cold and there was no spinning, no strange stained-glass windows; everything was cool and muted and in order. Oh the bliss, the pure bliss of everything being in its proper place and so obviously *real*! She sunk onto the lip of the door and began to pant with sobs.

Far in the back of her mind, under all the folds bleeding brine, a tiny animal voice twitched its whiskers and told her she was not alone.

'Excuse me, my lady.' Sure enough, a voice stammered through the blankety dust. It was a thin voice with no colour to it. Charlotte had been so jarred by feeling like prey herself that for a moment it was quite delicious to encounter something below her on the food chain.

'Oh!' She said. She stayed on her haunches but squinted to make out the figure on the steps below. 'You frightened me.'

'Sorry, my lady, I . . . I—'

'It's all right, I probably gave you a turn sat here all forlorn like this.' She sniffed rather dramatically.

'Yes. I should say, my lady.'

She squinted some more. The voice was really quite pathetic, and Charlotte wanted to see if the face matched. Perhaps it would make her feel a trifle better to look at a face uglier than her own for a while. 'M-Mrs Hardy should not like to find you here.'

'Yes, you're right, I . . .'

The door shook.

'It was the only place I could think to come . . .'

So they were hounding her still; all the beasts and demons, for the beasts seemed to be pressed against it, listening in. Breathing was harder, her eyes started to prickle with tears again.

'To come away from it all.'

But she wasn't away from it. Not truly; Mrs Hardy was out there conducting them all like a Fury. Or in here already, even. Somewhere in the darkness, oily eyes were staring right at her; they ripped out all the hairs on the nape of her neck.

'All the beastly . . .' The tears took over and throttled her.

A girl stepped out of the darkness of the lower steps and pulled a tissue from her wrist, ripped it and extended it, half-mast. Even through her tears and her fear, Charlotte noticed the girl was gristly thin, with a face an uglier mask of her own.

That made Charlotte feel better. She took the tissue delicately between her gloved fingertips. 'Thank you. I'm sorry, I rather hoped no one would find me like this.'

The tissue had likely once been white, but now was dirtied with God knows what – it looked like a rain-soaked map of the grounds. 'Oh.' She scrunched it in her glove. 'I must look in an awful state.'

The girl began to blather a steady stream of compliments, and Charlotte rose to her feet; it didn't feel right to be smaller than something so pitiful. The girl was speaking fast and breathless, her wide eyes bulging with a sickening kind of excitement. Charlotte thought back to the flies at the dinner table, the laughing eyes at the dinner table. So familiar, all of them.

Do I know you? she wanted to ask the girl. A silly question. She stopped herself from uttering it just in time. The words crashed against a dam of tongue and teeth, and receded silently back down her throat. A bout of delicacy, from the accident, from the heat; that was all that had happened to her at the table, that was all that was happening to her now; making her recognise faces in strangers – in servants, no less.

The girl had finished her breathless blather and was looking at her expectantly. That look in her eyes. Charlotte couldn't help but smile; those bulging saucers were so souped with admiration they practically *begged* Charlotte to bathe in it.

'Ah, yes. Well in that case, I daresay you may be able to help with my hair, it must be all falling down by now.'

'Oh no, my lady, only just so.' Her hands were rough and deft, she made short work, and stepped back almost as quickly as she had stepped forwards. Those greedy eyes. Charlotte couldn't help but check the servant girl's hands as she stepped away to make sure no jewels from her hair had been concealed in them. But they were empty. Their skin was rough and worn and calloused; the sight of them made her own skin crawl beneath her silk gloves.

'Thank you.' She felt at her hair; it was smooth and neat once again. 'I shall speak well of you to Mrs Hardy. What is your name?'

The girl blushed furiously and Charlotte suppressed a snicker.

'My name is Ann, my lady.'

The urge to laugh dissipated as quickly as it had come. A cold, sick feeling had reached Charlotte's stomach. She forced a smile. 'That will be all, thank you, Ann.'

The servant girl nodded and made towards the stairs again, and Charlotte herself turned sharply back to the door.

The lady went back through the door, to the heart of the house, while the servant girl ascended.

Outside, the sky was thick with darkness, thick with clouds, thick with the change of yet another season.

Ropner blinked up at it impassively; immobile and immortal, the only constant in all of this never-ending change. Perhaps, if it were a person, it would roll back its shoulders; it would yawn contentedly, a yawn as wide as its grounds, and it would let out a satisfied belch, its belly full once more.

Acknowledgements

Thank you really seems like the smallest phrase when trying to encompass the gratitude I have for all of the people I'm about to write about. But it's the only one that will keep my acknowledgements a reasonable length so unfortunately it will have to do.

Thank you to Katie, Melissa, and Catherine who were the first champions of this book. I still can't fathom that I found people as passionate about it as I am and I'm forever grateful for it.

Thank you to Jade and Zulekhá and to the entire wonderful team at Baskerville for their expertise, encouragement, and enduring of my million and one questions, I truly could not have asked for a better home for Ann and Charlotte. Thank you to everyone involved in turning my manuscript into an actual book, it has been such a fascinating and humbling experience to see just how many incredible people are involved in getting a book onto shelves.

Thank you to Adana who was kind enough to share her invaluable feedback and creative talent.

Thank you to Amal and PICT, and to Anna Davis and Curtis Brown Creatives for their wonderful guidance and support.

Thank you to all my friends who bore with my terribly late replies while I was secretly hunched over my laptop writing.

Thank you to my family, I promise that next time I'll write a book that's more palatable for you to read. An extra thank you to Aunty Mena for always encouraging my love for reading and giving me birthday books that became fast favourites.

And finally to Mum, Dad, and Lucy. Everything I do, I do to make you proud. LYTTMAB.

About the Author

Jessie Elland is an actress and author from the North East of England. An avid bookworm from the moment she could read, Jessie spent most of her childhood dreaming of writing books and scribbling down half-finished stories. *The Ladie Upstairs* is her first novel.